I0665906

DOUBLE LIVES, REINVENTION
&
THOSE WE LEAVE BEHIND

WISING UP ANTHOLOGIES

ILLNESS & GRACE, TERROR & TRANSFORMATION
2007

FAMILIES: THE FRONTLINE OF PLURALISM
2008

LOVE AFTER 70
2008

DOUBLE LIVES, REINVENTION
&
THOSE WE LEAVE BEHIND

HEATHER TOSTESON
CHARLES D. BROCKETT

Editors

Wising Up Press
Decatur, Georgia

Wising Up Press
P.O. Box 2122
Decatur, GA 30031-2122
www.universaltable.org

Copyright © 2009 by Wising Up Press

All rights reserved. No part of this book may be used or reproduced in any manner whatsoever without written permission, except in the case of brief quotations embodied in critical articles or reviews.

Catalogue-in-Publication data is on file with the Library of Congress.
LCCN: 2009931469

Wising Up ISBN-13: 978-0-9796552-6-5

IN MEMORIAM

P.K.E.
a.k.a.
Penelope Kinsley Marias Tosteson Harris Ellis
&
M.K.
&
L.P.
&
D.C.T.

Le 3° Mars, 1958

Chère Soeur Jeanne Yvonne,
à J'ai beaucoup pensé
de vous et j'éspère que vous
me pardonnerez parceque je
n'ai pas pu vous visité
l'été dernier. J'avais
beaucoup de malade d'esprit
et j'ai pu seulement exister.

Maintenant nous sommes
retournés aux États-Unis. Nous
avons une petite maison
très charmante et moderne
en face d'une école
où mes trois enfants ainés
attendent les classes. J'étudie
vant en

TABLE OF CONTENTS

II. SEX, LOVE, DIVORCE & ALL THAT STUFF

III. REINVENTION

IV. INVERSIONS

V. SPIRIT TURNS

HEATHER TOSTESON

FOREWORD

A week after my father's eightieth birthday, which had been celebrated with pomp and circumstance more reminiscent of his retirement a decade earlier than a family gathering, his second wife of thirty-five years, twenty years his junior, over-dosed on pain pills heartsick and enraged by the discovery that for the last twenty-five years he had sustained a long-term liaison with a woman his own age, in other words, the age of my own mother. For reasons that are still not clear to me, she had, knowing this for months, still initiated and orchestrated his elaborate birthday celebration. Perhaps she had hoped by this to recover the man she believed she had married.

In all the *sturm und drang* that followed, it was curious to me that no one expressed any curiosity about the woman, now close to eighty and in failing health, who had earned my father's loyalty for a quarter century. This anthology is inspired in part by my desire to acknowledge the complexity of her experience—as well as my own, having lived through this more than once, for my father, it was now clear to all, had a penchant for double lives. I include in this anthology an essay written and published over twenty years ago when, in my late thirties, in the midst of a tumultuous relationship that challenged my own understanding of myself, I tried to make sense of the formative effect my father's dual lives had had on the daughters raised in those circumstances. I include it, in part, because the woman who wrote it and the resolutions she reached feel both persuasive and mysteriously distinct from the woman who is now writing this introduction.

Twenty years later, in my fifties and happily married, disconcerted at having to revisit these questions I too had understood as specific to only one time, one relationship, I didn't choose to write in brooding solitude but shared these latest revelations about my aged father with friends in tones alternately bemused, wry, ironic, or exasperated and was fascinated by what I learned in return—for a surprising number of them had grown up in similar situations. My favorite story was that of a friend now in his seventies, whose father, a wealthy socialist, had divorced one socialist wife for another, his mother, but continued to have children with both women and to visit and parent both families to the intense discomfort of both women. In their late sixties and seventies, the two sets of siblings, all bright and highly accomplished, began to celebrate joint reunions. He was quite a bit younger than his full siblings, not to mention his half ones, because his mother had taken some years to reconcile herself to the situation. These reunions revived in him a sense of lost opportunity. "We all had wonderfully similar experiences of our father," he said. "It was our mothers who kept us apart."

What delighted me in my friend's story was the transparency, the suggestion that divided affections do not necessarily lead to double lives. It also made more sense of his assumption that his own present and past wives would enjoy joint camping weekends, an assumption they both quickly and thoroughly squished under their separate heels.

What exactly, I wondered, defined a double life? Secrecy was only part of it. Irreconcilability seemed even more core. Irreconcilable, however, to whom—and why? A first wife who cannot acknowledge that the man she knew as an unfaithful husband and haphazard father has become in his sixties the doting husband of a wife younger than his daughter, the assiduous father of twins? Or a second wife who looks at the children of her husband's first marriage with incredulous disdain. "What planet did they come from?" she asks her friends. "What galaxy?" Or a man who, after the death of a father who never chose to see him, meets his half-siblings, who appear blithely indifferent to the significance of that absence? Or those same children who grew up knowing, deep down, that the father who abandoned their half-brother was not so very different, whatever he might say to the contrary, from the one who cared for them now?

The same questions can be posed in a life seemingly free of large ruptures. How often, browsing though photo albums, do we pause and look at a picture of our parents, or our children, or our younger selves, and wonder what became of them? It is these simple, ubiquitous questions that have also inspired this anthology, perhaps more than the dramatic ones I began with. Their influence can be seen in the artwork, for as I began to develop it, I found I wasn't inspired, as I often am, by double exposures, dual narratives, or by my father's sad, compulsive history. The images and history that fascinated me were those of my mother, whose life was both typical of her generation and also, in its stages, often irreconcilable to those around her. I was a strong advocate of its totality, however difficult to integrate, and remember my irritation at her funeral when my siblings tried to reduce her life to just the third of it in which she actively parented us, reducing the rest to myth and detritus. I felt the American Medical Association, which mailed all its letters to her using every name she ever used, had it truer (although I rail at my own alma maters for sending me mail under a name I rejected a quarter century ago).

I was also fascinated by another dimension of double lives—which is the intimate mystery we each pose to one another and to ourselves, a mystery most parents experience as they watch their children grow up. "How did they ever fit inside us?" I remember an old friend, the mother of five, asking me. And how did we, still in development ourselves, ever fit into their pure scheme of things? I remember a poem I wrote at twenty-two for my nine-month-old son, so curious about what was going on in there, a curiosity I retain when I look at him now, a man in his mid-thirties, equally familiar and unknown.

So I have included in this volume images of real people in real time who have, for me, regained the mythic freedom of strangers.

The writing gathered here also, I believe, takes its inspiration from these powerful, often incongruent, drives: our need to find a coherent narrative in order to steer a steady life course with all the narrowing this requires; our need to know ourselves and to feel known by others and, simultaneously, to keep opening ourselves and our relationships to what is essentially unknowable, unpredictable, fertile, and, we can only hope, beneficent.

The contributions to this anthology seemed to fall quite naturally into five themes we've titled *Memory & Family Ties; Sex, Love, Divorce & All That Stuff; Reinvention; Inversions;* and *Spirit Turns.*

The section on memory and family ties opens with Sylvie Terespolksi's "When Mama and Papa Danced," a wonderful evocation of the life of serious, hard-working immigrants in the Bronx during World War II, and this one astonishing moment, in the middle of a blackout, when other more joyous worlds became possible. Joan Fondell's memoir describes growing up in the sixties in California, the tensions between her parents' desire to live an apparently coventional post-war life, and the slow revelation, verging on well-intentioned deceit, of her father's difficult history as a survivor of Auschwitz.

In most of the selections in this section, authors—specially those looking back on their lives from their sixties or seventies like Emilie George, Don Thackrey, Edward Beatty, and Phyllis Langton—ponder the stories they have told themselves about their lives, the selves they once were and the people they knew their parents to be. Now, at a distance, they are able to claim unexpected richnesses, explore unacknowledged pains. Emilie George, the daughter of Albanian immigrants, suggests all immigrants live double lives: "When I went into my house I heard and spoke Albanian; when I went out I heard and spoke English. The quick separation of languages was like shoji screens, the sliding Japanese panels that can open a room or close it off." She describes her later life as a teacher of foreign languages as one of "shoji screens sliding endlessly open!"

Phyllis Langton describes what it was like as an illegitimate child born in the 1930's to be, with her open nature, the unwitting heart of her mother's double life and to be able, after her mother's death, to find blood relatives who, like her, could make a story large enough to hold them both. Alexandrina Sergio's "Baby of My Bones" speaks from the point of view of a grandmother holding her grandchild for a precious hour before the child is given up for adoption, and holds open the prospect of another story in some gracious and unpredictable future.

Others, like Anna Steegmann and Yolande House ponder difficult responses they had in their teens and twenties, revisiting them as adults, allowing some questions into actions that once felt compelled by necessity. House writes of the consequences of choosing in her early teens to leave her abusive mother:

I am still waiting to come into my own, to merge the torn pieces of my self so I can become more than the sum of my parts, so that I finally accept and put forth my best self, free of fear, wrenching off the once comforting confines of a self-imposed invisibility. I no longer need that cloak. Why do I clutch it so?

Lynn Hesse and Shireen Campbell write about the choices through which seemingly irreconcilable realities are actively being woven into a single coherent narrative. In Hesse's story, an older woman decides to show compassion for a young murderer whose secret life is now tragically exposed. In Shirleen Campbell's memoir she comes to understand that the experience of raising a child with congenital heart problems has abruptly and permanently redefined how she understands motherhood, and herself as a mother.

In the second section we hear about love and lust from all different perspectives. David Harris Ebenbach writes of a wife's response to discovering her husband's secret life. Eboni Hogan writes about being a sex-phone worker and how she integrates these fractured parts of other people's lives:

When we empty the contents of your locker,
we return to your family only the things they need to know.
You will always be too dangerous to handle with
open palms
and closed minds;

Frank Salvidio's elegant sonnets explore the intricacies of infidelity and unrequited love. Katharyn Howd Machan and Maria Nazos explore the shifting perspectives on our selves, past or present, that love provides. Nazos captures this well in her poem "First Person":

I've been the man who has fucked four times a day, you said, struggling to get your pants
back on like a better-fitting skin.

And I've been that woman, I wanted to say. Though that woman seems faraway as the I
was from the you, until I'm only sure it's possible to escape

not through your skin, but by shifting focus from the first person to third,
then back to gain perspective, like a camera lens

zooming in and out. Like an eye pupil exposed to dark, then light, then
dark—Rilke said metaphysical. I call it plain goddamned human.

In "My Green Card Marriage," on the other hand, Wendy Brown-Báez describes the unitive power of a marriage that others might find unusual:

When we tell people we are husband and wife, they are startled, disbelieving, but finally,
they like it, they approve. We provide a counter-balance in some indefinable way. I travel
in Mexico as a married woman. I like the sense of security, of identity it gives me. A new

identity. Alejandro's wife. Or a secret identity, my gay husband. We love each other, of that I am sure.

In the third section, *Reinvention*, the focus is on identity and the struggles that we undergo reconciling within ourselves abrupt schisms in our lives, whether those schisms are frequent cultural shifts, kidnapping, and the mutating identifications of adolescence, as in Nicholas Samaras' poems; the existence of an unacknowledged half-brother in Emilio DeGrazia's "The Other Brother"; or the oddities of explained shrapnel in Carlos Reyes' more playful "Fantasy"; the death of a sibling in Stefan Kiesbye's "Water Park"; and Deidra Razzaque's invitations to reinvention both for herself and a troubled young boy.

Both Samaras and DeGrazia explore the experience of psychological twinning. In Samaras' poems, language is absolutely crucial to one's sense of self. One's name is not one's name, your own image is the ghost image of someone who is both you and not you. The underlying story in his poems is mysterious, never completely defined, since that is its definition, a chameleon nature and bedrock sense of loss. These states are true of all of us who move, uproot ourselves or are uprooted by others, and who try to hold ourselves together only in our imagination. We sleep with grace, but no one answers the haunted questions of where we end and love can begin.

DeGrazia plays with both the psychological experience of twinning and the mysteries of biography, the children our parents may have left behind to haunt us. Finally, the experience of seeing our features, subtly modified, in those far off and near, is more powerful and transforming than biological fact—and leads, unlike Samaras' experience, to a sense of profound identification with the world around us.

Stefan Kiesbye's fascinating and difficult story "Water Park" explores a brother's responsibility, and captures the tension between the lives we wish we'd lived, and our need to be faithful, however terrible that fidelity may be, to the only one we have. This tension is captured in the teen-age narrator's discussion of tattoos, which he begins by saying he wouldn't like to be restricted to a single symbol or picture all his life: "I mean, if you don't like the person anymore, it's still there, and you're constantly reminded of them." But he also poignantly imagines being tattooed with an exact image of himself, just a little smaller, "but one hand would be missing, or a calf." When chastised for the image, he responds, "But there would be two people, only one is incomplete."

Deidra Razzaque's poems, urgent, warm, complicit, are quite different in tone from the other work in this section. For her, reinvention is possible, whether for herself or for those around her. It is also not something that is willed, rather something by which we are graciously surprised and into which we are magnanimously drawn. She describes this well in "Today," a poem about writing her father after thirty years, when she is surprised into love:

*You always hear whispers of the transformation—how the garbage of life
sometimes blooms as daisies and pepper plants.
Today I watched this happen to the ground where I was standing.*

The idea of double lives is deeply intriguing to us imaginatively, but the stories we write about it are a little different in quality than the memoirs we write. In our memoirs, there is a powerful undertow as we try to integrate this sense of doubleness within one skin. The stories in the fourth section, *Inversions,* are not as close to the bone. There is more pleasure and bite, more ironic distance, and more humor, in our imaginative understanding of this common phenomena. There are possibilities open to us in fusing identities with others, jumping tracks, that we may offer more freely to our characters than to ourselves.

In "Green," Natalie Haney Tilghman explores dimensions of alienation and belonging that are part of our experiences of adoption and also of identification with someone else. Eloise, the young social worker in the story, finds herself drawn into the life of one of her clients whose story enriches and illuminates her own, and, ultimately up-ends it as well. In Susan O'Doherty's wry and ultimately moving story, "Lizzie Farrell Gets Hers," we watch Lizzie, changed by motherhood, trying to write a new life for herself so that she can write a more promising one for her son.

The main character in Judith Turner-Yamamoto's ghost story, "Far Away," finds that a ghost may be more firmly grounded in life than she is, and that through inhabiting the ghost's home, opening to the identification, she may find a way to inhabit her own life more completely. In Kerry Langan's witty "Live Your Life," a soap opera actor has inhabited a second, imaginary life so fully and gratifyingly over the years that it completely usurps his own. Reversely, in Christopher Willard's "Compensation," a bitter old man, who seems trapped in a life story whose sad steps he obsessively annotates and retraces, tumbles through no conscious act of his own into a new and more resilient story. It is life, rather than his own constricted imagination, that saves him.

In the last section, *Spirit Turns,* we have a young woman in the 1960s and one in the twenty-first century make decisions that they believe will provide an essential unity to their life story. In Mary Kay Rummel's "Enough," which describes the year when she decided to leave the convent which had been her home for all her formative years as a young adult, she comes to understand what holds her inside a story that has come to feel increasingly false to her—and what gives her the courage to break free.

I'd spent eight years hungry for a miracle, waiting for illumination, the bright promise. There had been beauty in that idea, but I never wanted to be that hungry again. I no longer wanted to be a saint. Still more nun than not, I was on my own for the first time in my life. There was no one to watch me, no one I had to please, neither God, nor those who spoke for him and that was enough.

Devon Ward-Thommes describes, from the vantage point of twenty-six, the marvelous integration and immediacy that followed her reading of a Buddhist writer, Pema Chödrön, on a beach in Mexico in her troubled nineteenth year, at war with her body and thus with herself. She is moved by the tenderness in Chödrön's approach, "I thought: of course, yeah, I knew that. But now I could really believe this truth, this truth that spilled out in the quiet relationship between writer and reader." However, the intensity of the insight is best captured by her rapture at the sight of pelicans diving for their supper: "I felt euphoric and exhausted, as if I'd just plummeted right out of that dark sky, eyes wide and black wings spread, and hit the water with a crash." A crash that opened up a new life story she is living her way into now.

We hope as you read these poems, stories and memoirs, which are moving, funny, insightful, sometimes anguished, your own thinking and, more importantly, *feeling* about what makes us hunger for coherence, what requires us to split or twin to stay whole, enlarge as ours have in the process. Lighten—and toughen—too. As I read through the collection yet another time, preparing the manuscript for press, I think of my own father, who recently died, of the women he loved, ineptly, faithlessly, but with all the grace he knew, and what it would have been like if he had known his own nature to be reconcilable—inside himself and with the world around him. I honor the events, intentional and not, that required him, in his last few years, to ponder this question openly, and recognize his halting willingness to do so as his last and best soul work. My mother died of dementia over a decade ago, but I treasure as well the opportunity to open up her own complex life through images, to welcome the multiplicity of mysterious stories, lived and unlived, they evoke. I think, where they are now in their infinite journeys, my mother and father would each enjoy this book and the questions it raises, questions so crucial to their own lives—not to mention to mine and to the lives of the many talented writers gathered here who have, each for fascinating reasons all their own, chosen to explore these same questions openly, thoroughly, and with invigorating variety. We hope it will inspire you to do the same.

I
MEMORY - FAMILY TIES

SYLVIE TERESPOLSKI

WHEN PAPA AND MAMA DANCED

Papa came home on the New York City subway five days a week. Usually, he took the IRT Express and got off at 177th Street. Sometimes he took the Seventh Avenue subway which stopped a little further away from our six story apartment building, but he always walked the wide cobble stoned streets slowly, past the trolley depot on West Farms. He crossed over the Bronx River bridge and you could sometimes hear him murmuring to himself when he entered the apartment, "A bridge. They call that a bridge. It's just a big slab of gray asphalt and concrete connected to other slabs of concrete thirty feet above a river. That's not a bridge." It was hard to convince Papa of the beauty of anything in New York City.

When Mama would say it was special to live near a river even though we couldn't see trees, meadows, or flowers. Papa shrugged and muttered, "It's ugly. Just ugly." The Bronx River flowed with discarded tires. Papa said that people who threw tires into the river didn't have a lot of brains. "Where was the tire going to go? *Danken got az mir habn nit gehat gemen raifen in der haim.* At least in the old country, we didn't have to worry about tires." That was a lot for Papa to say.

A photo of Papa in a cart with a horse leading the way was on the mahogany upright piano in the living room. Another sepia-toned photograph captivated me: my father's four brothers and three sisters standing behind their seated parents with the siblings' hands resting on each other's shoulders to affirm what I thought was unity and family love. I wondered what family love was like. Their father, my unknown grandfather, clearly a patriarch with his upright posture and neatly trimmed beard sat next to my grandmother who rested her hand on her husband's arm. Their dark eyes without a hint of smile looked straight into the camera. When I asked Papa where they were now, he was brief. "Hitler took them. Only Benny and I are here."

By the time the elevator took Papa up to the fifth floor of the apartment building, I knew he was tired. You see, Papa had just finished a long day standing on his feet cutting arms, backs, front, and collars of ladies coats and suits that he could never afford to buy for Mama or my older sister, Golde, or me. I understood, it was the Frostmann Wool that made a coat or suit fancy and expensive. Mama told me that being a cutter meant that he was the elite of the garment center. "Cutters are smarter than sewers or pressers," she said. The designers were not in the union so they didn't count. In the summer, the subways were hot and crowded and Papa's shirt was always wet with perspiration.

When Papa came home, he immediately went to wash up in the one bathroom used by six people. Mama jokingly said that if any more people came, we would need to take numbers. In the second bedroom lived Zundel and Label, young relatives from Papa's town in Russia, who also worked in the garment center and needed a place to stay. Golde, older by five years, and I shared the other bedroom and slept on Salvation Army beds. I fully expected the "army" to come one day and forcefully take the furniture away. Mama and Papa kept their clothing in one of the maple dressers in our room and in the hallway closet but never once did I see Papa undressing. I did occasionally see Mama struggling to get on her pink girdle reinforced by metal stays.

Mama cooked all the meals and kept the house clean which was not easy to do as so many people in a small apartment created a lot of mess. I don't remember what we ate most nights but on Friday night chicken, chicken soup, matzoh balls and tzimmes—a mixture of potatoes, prunes, and apples, magically came to our small kitchen table. On Friday, Mama scrubbed the kitchen floor on her hands and knees; she claimed that was the only way to get a really clean floor. Washing it with just a mop would have been heresy to her. She covered the floor with yesterday's newspapers so the linoleum would remain clean for the Friday night meal. Mama ran the household with very little money and Papa always sat at the head of the table and no one nibbled or picked at food, or starting eating until Papa began. We ate in complete silence. Mama passed the food around with one word, "Eat." Then Papa went to the living room to listen to the radio while Mama washed the dishes and Golde and I did our homework.

Papa would tune in WQXR, the classical radio station in New York and listen to the evening news and symphonic music. If the station played a Wagnerian opera, he immediately shut the radio off. In the summertime, after dinner, he would sit on a stool by the kitchen window and look out from that fifth floor window at the rumbling el, or the pair of enormous dice painted on the building wall across the street, above the post office that screamed "Don't Gamble, Depend on Us." That faded advertisement for a moving company must have been on the wall for forty years.

If Papa wasn't sitting by the window or listening to classical music, he would read the *New York Post*, or *PM*, or the Yiddish newspaper, *The Forward*. He didn't talk about the news. He would put the newspapers down intermittently and stare at the picture of his family.

His brother, Benny, sometimes came by to visit with his black shiny new Hudson from Brooklyn. Benny was a paperhanger who had been quite successful and owned his business. Maybe Papa could afford a car but Mama just didn't think he could learn how to drive in this city. "After all," she said. "All he ever drove was a horse and cart." Papa and Benny would sit and play chess with hardly a word being spoken. I saw two quiet men calculating and moving their chess pieces around. No triumph over a win —no quiet exuberance. Occasionally, I heard, "Checkmate." That's all. Just "Checkmate."

When friends came over to visit, nuts, dried prunes and fresh fruit covered the table. The women would gather in the kitchen talking about bargains in food and clothes and the men would gather in the living room to play rummy or pinochle. I know Mama laughed when she sat with those women in the kitchen. I never saw Mama laugh with Papa. I never saw them planning, deciding, fighting, or embracing one another and I assumed that's the way all Mamas and Papas behaved.

One night the radio announced that there was going to be an emergency air raid drill. Not only were we to draw the shades but we couldn't have a single light on in the apartment. The sirens would sound at 8:00 p.m. and New York City was to be in darkness until the dawn. It sounded as though we were preparing for a German attack and I presumed our little street in the Bronx was going to be a target because of the United States Post Office that stood beneath the "Don't Gamble" sign. We had already eaten dinner; all we could do was wait. I couldn't do homework and conversation wasn't a natural standby so we just sat in the living room on the pull-out sofa. Golde and I read our books with flashlights. Mama folded clothes. She didn't need a lot of light and Mama didn't believe in wasting time.

Papa tuned the radio to WQXR and I recognized that it was playing Smetena's "Moldau" one of his favorite pieces so I thought he was content. In the middle of the piece from someplace in the darkened room he said,

"No." I was startled. My eyes had adjusted somewhat to the dark but it was still difficult to see. "No, we need something lively. Get the Frank Sinatra station."

I was incredulous. "My father knows the Frank Sinatra station? The station that played Frank Sinatra and Make Believe Ballroom?"

Whenever I had access to the one radio in the apartment, I would tune in to Make Believe Ballroom and its top songs and wonder about all those happy people who listened and danced to music. I thought those were the most sophisticated people in the world and for me, they might as well have been from another planet. When Frank sang I'd close the door to my room and pretend that he was singing to me because I was dancing like Ginger Rogers. I became that ballerina when Vaughn Monroe sang, "Dance, Ballerina, Dance."

I would shut the door because my parents told me that the music was frivolous and dancing was even more so. The mantra was study, think, read, play chess, listen to classical music.

My father said, "What are you waiting for?"

I turned the radio dial to Make Believe Ballroom and The Andrew Sisters were singing "Don't Sit Under the Apple Tree." I had stopped reading and I could see Papa slowly getting up from his armchair. He walked to Mama and offered his hand to her. Mama was in the middle of matching socks when she slowly put them down. She reached up, took his hand and obediently stood up. He opened his arms in dance position and she stepped forward to ease into his arms. He held her gently in that position and they did a slow fox trot to "I Don't Know Why I Love You Like I Do." Golde and I grabbed each other as we could see their bodies moving as one. He guided her surely and she followed hesitatingly then easily, then dreamily. I thought I saw a slight smile on her face and my father's thoughts seemed far away although he kept a perfect fox-trot beat.

When the music quickened to "The Atchison, Topeka, and the Santa Fe," they did a quick two step, their version of the jitterbug and it seemed to me that the whole apartment shook with joy. My flashlight fell out of hand as I watched open-mouthed. For a moment they disappeared in the darkness and suddenly I saw my father's arm outstretched toward me. The music was "The Jersey Bounce" and my father was my partner while Mama danced with Golde. In the small space of the living room in darkness, we managed to bump and glide, hop and shake, each couple managing without bumping into one another. When my mother and father became a couple again, my sister and I jitterbugged furiously. I was delirious. I was Ginger Rogers and for a moment my family seemed spontaneously joyous. I detected family love. In the darkness, the dark cloud lifted. We danced until the light of dawn crept between the cracks of the darkened shades and the windows. The next day was Sunday so we could sleep late.

When we awoke, I looked for Papa to tell him how happy I was that we had danced. I wanted to kiss and hug him and see if he would promise to dance with me again. I wanted him to take me and Golde to a Frank Sinatra concert at the Paramount. But when I approached Papa, he was reading the Sunday paper and Mama caught my eye and shook her head at me.

I never told Papa about my happiness and I never saw Mama and Papa dance again, but whenever I hear the "Jersey Bounce," I become delirious with joy—a joy that came in the darkness of a night that portended fear.

JOAN FONDELL

A LUCKY LIFE

Flesh and Blood—Beverly Hills, California 1966

The first time I asked my father about the bluish green tattoo 71088 on his left arm was during a commercial break of Combat, starring Vic Morrow and Rick Jason. I reached for his left arm and touched the spot where his number was branded. It was soft there, the dark hair and skin was just like the skin on the rest of his arm.

"What's this number on your arm?" I asked, as I stroked the five-inch span of space that held the numbers in place.

A silence came over our living room. Everything shifted to slow motion. My father reached for the Magnavox remote sitting atop the gold leaf coffee table, and pressed the volume button down. He took a protracted drag on his Kent cigarette, and then breathed deeply as though preparing his descent underground. He blew the smoke out past his right shoulder and set his cigarette down into the already butt-filled heavy crystal ashtray in front of him. The smoke plume drew upwards toward our white cottage cheese ceiling. He turned his narrow left thigh towards me, squeaking along the plastic cover protecting our white upholstered couch. He crouched down to bring himself closer to my eye level.

"It's an old girlfriend's phone number, sweetheart," he said cupping his right hand under my chin.

I smelled the lingering scent of burnt ashes.

Back then it would never have occurred to me that he and my American-born Mom had conspired to concoct this answer. In fact, it sounded like the kind of response she would have come up with. Dad would have just delved into it—how he and his parents were torn away from their home in Brno, Czechoslovakia, rounded up, taken to Theresienstadt, a ghetto-like concentration camp, where his father died from pneumonia and then how months later when he heard his mother was being transported East, he volunteered to be on that transport, how they traveled on crowded cattle cars to Auschwitz, and how he survived. All of it would have been told to me right then and there in the comfort of our two-bedroom apartment on South Palm Drive in Beverly Hills. Dad would have described everything in meticulous fashion, down to the last detail. He would have infused each story with the historical backdrop to give me the context that even he did not have during the real-time events. He would have explained it to me, answering every question I asked.

But Mom must have cautioned him to go slowly, to tell me the truth in small parcels, a little at a time, so as not to frighten me. So without my knowledge, they created a strategy for how he would share his tragic life's experiences with me, their only child.

At first, his response upset me. I pulled back. My red Danskin pants slid along the plastic. I couldn't look at him. Instead, my eyes focused on my long narrow feet inside my matching red canvas Keds sneakers outstretched above the high-ply stringy rust-colored carpet. I shot a look across our large living room dressed in royal blue and gold leaf toward our dining room window to see the brick building that housed Earl Sheib's Auto-Body Paint shop across the alley.

"You mean it's not Mommy's phone number?" I asked focusing on the broken and uneven creases traversing his forehead.

"No, honey," he smiled and shook his head. "I would never forget Mommy's number."

Relieved, I smiled back at him.

His usual steady hand quivered as he brought his cigarette back up to his grey lips. He looked at me again, analyzing whether I had accepted his version of the facts. His dark sad eyes said more than words could. They held their gaze on me longer than usual and made me feel as though he wanted to tell me more. He tucked a section of my curly dark hair behind my ear and stroked my head.

"Remember, you're my only flesh and blood," he said his dark eyes searing into mine.

I sensed even then, that he knew I would be the one who would want to know everything. It was as if he understood that once he began to tell me his stories, I would be the one most touched by his life's experiences.

I wedged myself back where I had been before, under his left armpit to watch the rest of our favorite show. Snuggled next to him, I breathed in the smell of his sprayed-on Mennen's deodorant mixed with Aqua Velva aftershave.

It felt safe there, even though we turned back to the television, where we were engulfed by black and white images of war, death and destruction.

Another Life—Los Angeles, California (1967)

From the time I began writing my name, I learned how Dad differed from other men I knew. When he arrived at Ellis Island on October 29, 1948, he was still known as Kurt Fischl, an immigrant from Brno, the second largest city in Czechoslovakia. He had $10 in his pocket and although he had no formal higher education, he spoke Czech, German and a little French, but no English. Like many other immigrants who arrived on its shores, he found work in the garment industry in New York and learned English.

Four years later, he and one of his fellow Czech boyhood friends decided to travel to Los Angeles where they heard the weather was warmer and the girls more glamorous. Seduced by the beach, the vast landscape of orange groves and swaying palm trees, Dad couldn't resist. Santa Monica's pier with its breathtaking view of the sea must have made Dad feel a million miles away from where he had come from.

The black and white photographs of Dad's years in New York showed him dressed in a charcoal colored suit jacket with wide lapels and a white handkerchief poking out of his left suit pocket. He wore a white shirt with a tightly knotted diagonally striped tie. His hands were tucked behind his back. His full forehead stretched temple to temple. Considered handsome by most standards, he had little trouble finding women to meet and date. However, without a car and without much money, he told me about his experience with an ugly and inhospitable dating landscape. He'd meet a woman at a local dance hall and ask her for her phone number. In a high-pitched whiny voice, he mocked her, "Do you have a caaar?" emphasizing the word "car" holding the "a" for a few seconds, recognizing the transparency of what she was really asking: "Do you have any money?" In those days, most of the immigrants had little money and traveled by bus or subway.

"Unfortunately, I didn't have the luxury of getting an education," he said. "The Nazis came in just as I was headed off to *Gymnasium*," referring to Europe's place of higher education.

Unlike most survivors who married immediately after the war, Dad didn't marry Mom, a recently divorced woman without children, until 1955. I never asked him why he didn't marry earlier or why he hadn't married another survivor, like most of his friends did. Mom told me Dad dated a lot of women, including a non-Jewish Czech woman, Bubinya, who he met when he returned to his native Brno after the war was over. But his relationship with Bubinya soured when at dinner, her parents made an anti-Semitic remark. Soon afterwards, he left Czechoslovakia and came to the United States.

Soon after Dad began dating Mom, he met her parents Ella and Joseph Hoffman, both European-born Jews, who had arrived in the United States during the mid 1910's. Dad felt more comfortable and at home with them.

At Mom's prompting and before they married in Las Vegas in 1955, Dad Americanized his name. Mom convinced him that no one would be able to spell his last name Fischl—they'd forget the "sch" or they'd spell it with an "el." She also encouraged him to Americanize his first name from Kurt with a "K" to Curt with a "C." The man previously known as Kurt Fischl, who had survived a time in history when Jews were branded, gassed and burned had now transformed himself into a newer version of himself as Curt Fondell. It seems odd to me now that they didn't pick the last name of Fisher or Fishman, which seemed a more logical choice. I wondered if they chose the name Fondell because it was not recognizably Jewish. Its only similarity with Fischl was that it started with an "F" and ended with an "l." The name Fondell had no recognizable ethnicity attached to it and had no connection to Dad's past.

From the outside, Mom wanted their world to be wholly American. But it didn't stop Mom from buying Dad all of the European delicacies he enjoyed. She made special trips to neighborhood markets that stocked his favorite Liederkranz cheese, that I renamed "stinky cheese," because of its pungent odor. I watched him handle the brown three-inch box. One might have thought it was a present from a long lost relative or the last box of cheese he'd ever eat again. As though they were prongs, he placed his thumb on one end and his middle finger on the other end and lifted the top of the box straight up. Then, as though he was performing surgery he unwrapped the foil, unveiling the soft creamy cheese inside. With a butter knife, he smeared a generous portion of it onto fresh rye bread, then sunk his stained yellowed teeth into it and closed his eyes. He savored each bite, as though it was the first piece of bread and cheese he'd eaten since the war ended. Satisfied with his two cheese-smothered slices, he'd fold the foil wrapped cheese back into place, protecting it like a fine gem and placed it back in the side compartment of our avocado colored Fridgidaire refrigerator.

His love of his stinky cheese equally matched his love for rich chocolate mousse desserts that sent Mom to the European-owned Bênes bakery on a weekly basis. She returned with several pink boxes tied with twine and set them off to one side of the kitchen counter.

While Mom's efforts to make my father a nice home were reflective of the traditional 1960's era we were living in, it also underscored her tireless effort to be a perfect wife and avoid another rejection. She wanted me to understand that "making your husband happy" was the key to a successful life.

Every morning, Dad and I arrived at the kitchen table to find that Mom had prepared our place setting. At Dad's usual place at the kitchen table, she placed one vitamin C tablet, one Theragran M pill next to his spoon on top of a white paper napkin. To the side sat a turned over empty orange juice glass, a coffee cup and saucer and a small cereal bowl for his Rice Krispies. The Maxwell House coffee was pre-measured and ready to percolate at his flip of the switch.

On some mornings, Dad and I could see when Mom had dusted off her electric frying pan and set it on the kitchen counter, near the sink. This was her way of letting us know that she was making his favorite breaded *Wiener schnitzel* cutlets sprinkled with paprika.

Mom looked for ways to make him happy and to show me by example how to show our love for him.

"When you hear Dad wiggling his key in the door," she instructed, before Dad arrived home from work, "help him open it up. Greet him with his slippers. Help him off with his shoes. He'll appreciate it."

She lit up another cigarette, blowing out that first deep puff.

"Don't immediately start telling him about your day," she went on. "Let him look at the mail. Let him have some time, before you start in."

A few puffs later, she'd remind me, as if I hadn't heard her tell me countless times before, when it came to telling him anything that would hurt him or bring him pain.

"Don't upset your father. He's been through enough."

Hockey Nights—Los Angeles, California (1967 to mid-1970's)

During ice hockey season, beginning when I was eight-years old, Tuesday and Thursday evenings were my favorite nights of the week. I had Dad to myself. Though Mom joked that she was a "hockey widow" she was pleased that through our love of hockey we developed a close bond. She knew that Saturday nights were reserved for them, as their "date night," so even when the Kings played on Saturday, Dad took her or gave the tickets away to friends.

On weeknight drives to the Inglewood Forum, Dad shared his stories with me. I looked at his long pointed nose in profile, his olive complexion, rose gray lips and the 5 o'clock shadow dark beard peppered with gray whiskers.

He drove the company burgundy Ford station wagon with wood-paneled sides confidently—an outstretched left arm on the wheel and a cigarette dangling from his lips. To anyone else looking at Dad, they saw an ordinary man with a simple gold wedding band and an inexpensive Seiko watch, driving what looked to be the family station wagon. Dad used it in business for his Store Equipment Company to do light shipping and delivering of pegboard, shelves and brackets to some of his local customers. Inside, the worn pressboard that laid flat on top of the back seats made the car smell like kicked-up sawdust. To me, as I watched him precisely flick his Kent cigarette ashes into the dashboard ashtray, I saw a man who had seen the worst in mankind and yet softness marked his touch and demeanor. He wore ordinary clothes—a pair of gray slacks, a striped gray and black Van Heusen shirt covered by a V-neck black cashmere sweater.

While we drove to the Forum to watch *our* lowly Los Angeles Kings play a stronger team, I listened intently. His elegant European accent enunciated the English and German words with emphasis. With one hand on the wheel, his other arm dramatized each scene.

"Each morning in Auschwitz, the Nazis woke us up with 'Raus Raus,'" he shouted imitating how the Nazis yelled at them. "'Wake up. Wake up.' It was early in the morning and very, very cold." He tensed up his body to show how cold it felt. "It didn't matter it was raining or snowing, they barked their orders and we scrambled out of our cramped barracks and went outside. There, we huddled in loose lines. There were hundreds of us, trying to keep warm, shuffling our bare feet against the rocky sometimes muddy ground in our Dutch-shaped shoes." He rocked from left to right.

I imagined Dad in a striped uniform and his long narrow feet trying to fit in the cramped shoes. Now, he blew smoke from his cigarette into the air with the flair of a movie star. His clean clothes and closed black leather shoes seemed more than a lifetime away. I listened closely as he continued.

"One morning, they asked, 'Are there any carpenters here?'" Dad looked over at me.

We both smiled, knowing he wasn't very handy around the house other than hanging a picture straight or putting in a light bulb.

"I knew I wasn't a carpenter, but with winter approaching, I knew that without proper clothing, I'd freeze to death or catch pneumonia. Everyone had the same clothes, scratchy cotton striped pants, flimsy cotton long sleeve shirt and a cotton cap. So I raised my hand, and pretended to be a carpenter."

"Uh, oh," I murmured. If I lied about being able to do something I didn't know how to do, I would get into trouble.

"Well, it was risky, but what was my choice?" He looked over at me, as if he needed me to understand that lying in this instance was permissible.

My eyes widened, my interest never wavered. I didn't think of it then, but did he think I questioned his conduct? I knew he was teaching me how to survive—how to think several steps ahead and anticipate events.

I looked back toward him.

"Then what?" I asked.

"They said that those who raised their hand should come to the front. *'Schnell, schnell'* (Fast, fast), they said. So I ran up there as fast as I could. A *Capo*, a fellow Jewish inmate with authority over the other inmates, joined the group. There were four of us. The *Capo* pointed to another building nearby and directed us to go inside. Just being inside was a good thing, a *mekhaye*."

In Yiddish, it meant "a pleasure." I smiled. I liked hearing my father use that word. He said it with such emotion it resonated pleasure in my heart, as I heard the word come from deep in his smoker's throat. When I heard Yiddish expressions like that spoken by my parents and by my grandmother, it saddened me to imagine the Nazis, who despised Yiddish as a bastardized version of German, beating them to death with their clubs.

He continued.

"The *Capo* gave us hammers and nails and we started on a project. We worked all day, with little to eat, but we were warm. After a day or so at this job, the *Capo* motioned me toward where he was standing."

Dad titled his head to one side to show me how the *Capo* gestured to him with his eyes to get him to meet him at the other side of the room, away from the other inmates.

"He pulled me to the side and said in a lower tone, 'Kurt, you and I both know you're no carpenter. But you speak a good German. There's a new job that opened up in the Nazi Laundry. You'll start tomorrow.'"

Just hearing him call himself by his former name "Kurt" and pronouncing it like "squirt" with a K, made it seem like he was describing a different man's experience.

Dad tossed his head from side to side, showing his relief at the *Capo's* treatment of him.

"At first, I wasn't sure if this was such a good job or not. I'd be in daily face-to-face contact with the German officers and the camp *Kommandant*. Usually, the less you saw of them, the better."

I nodded my understanding.

"Its what I've always told you," he began. "If you have a choice between being smart or lucky, always pick lucky."

In that moment, I understood how fortunate he was to survive. It wasn't dumb luck. He had taken a huge risk pretending to be a carpenter, but it was a calculated risk knowing that if he didn't get out of the treacherous Poland winter climate, he was as good as dead.

"In front of them," referring to the Nazis, "I only spoke German. They hated hearing Yiddish."

When the traffic light turned red, he turned his body toward me and in a voice lower than usual said, "This job saved my life."

He turned to face forward and nodded slightly to himself, as though he was agreeing with his assessment of how things turned out. The car drew forward heading southbound on La Cienega Boulevard. After a few blocks, he continued.

"Remember, Joannie, I was in the Buna laundry for two years, so I got to know some of these guys. They'd give me *cigaretten*, chocolate, and made small talk," he said interspersing German and English. Later, I learned Buna was a sub-camp of Auschwitz, commonly known as Monowitz. It was here where factories built by IG Farben produced Zyklon B used in the gassing exterminations.

Some of the words were so similar to English, I felt I was learning more German from Dad than I was learning Spanish in school.

"I'm surprised they'd give you stuff."

"They knew they were losing the war," he said. "I could tell that from what they said was happening on outside. They knew what the Russians would do to them."

As we drove, I thought about the October day he arrived at Auschwitz as a 21-year-old boy. He had already lost his father and would lose his mother that day. His normal existence turned upside down. Three years later when the war ended, he had no home to return to, no family alive, and no money in his pocket. His 5'10" frame weighed 115 pounds. He had lice in his jet-black hair. His teeth were yellow from poor hygiene and he suffered from jaundice requiring medical treatment from the Red Cross. That was then.

Now, he was the co-owner of C & H Store Equipment Co., and we lived in a nice apartment on Palm Drive, south of Olympic Boulevard in Beverly Hills. Some would have thought it a miracle. But Dad would have told you he had remained resilient and had *mazel* (Yiddish for luck).

"I don't live here for my ego," he acknowledged to anyone who seemed impressed by him now living in Beverly Hills. "Its so the kid can go to the schools. When she graduates from High School, we're out of here," he stated proudly.

When Mom heard this, she'd throw him one of her looks, because she could have lived in Beverly Hills forever. In time, we moved to a more spacious and luxurious apartment on North Palm Drive, north of Burton

Way. It was Dad's intention for us to move somewhere where he could afford
a house, with a pool. Mom always had an eye on a house in Beverly Hills that
was more than Dad could afford.

While he might have been a step behind her desires, he was the first guy
in any social setting to grab for his wallet. His generosity extended to family
and friends. In 1969, he bought Mom a brand new Coupe de Ville Cadillac.
He supported my grandmother Ella when Grandpa Joe's life insurance policy
money ran out. He helped two Fischl families, cousins on his father's side
of the family, to emigrate from Czechoslovakia to Los Angeles. He gave one
of the families Mom's old Pontiac Bonneville. He set each family up in a
fully furnished two-bedroom apartment in adjacent Beverly Hills, near where
we lived. He encouraged his friends to offer them jobs. Mom enrolled their
children in nearby schools.

I'm sure he felt he was living a double life, one borne out of reinvention. He lived a life never thought possible during his days in
Auschwitz.

When we stepped out of Dad's station wagon, I felt the chill in the
November air. I blew my warm breath on my hands as we made our way
across the street to the Sizzler restaurant for dinner.

Though we were safely indoors, I felt the lingering chill in my feet. I
thought about Dad's size 12½ feet crammed into hard shoes without socks. I
imagined how cold it must have been during the roll call for carpenters.

"How cold was it in Auschwitz?" I asked, sliding my cafeteria tray
along the chrome countertop toward the register.

"20 degrees," he said. "Sometimes colder."

In my life experience living in Los Angeles then, that number had
little meaning. The coldest it might have been was in the 50's. Even now
it is difficult to imagine what it truly felt like because when I've been in
below-freezing temperatures, I've been bundled up in thermal underwear, a
cashmere turtleneck and an insulated parka.

Without those comforts, I wonder now how he could have had the
composure and split-second decision-making ability to respond to the call for
carpenters. How then could my father, with overwhelming hunger gnawing
in his belly, with fellow inmates shuffling in line to keep warm hear the call

in German and respond so definitively? If he missed his chance to get inside, the opportunity might never have come again.

We each ate our dinner quietly. I watched him as he chewed each morsel of his baked potato slathered with butter and watched him use his knife and fork as most Europeans do by cutting his teriyaki steak in distinctive cross-section diagonals. I considered the contrast now for him with the abundance of food he had before him compared with the scarcity of food during his years in the camps. He previously told me about the thin broth passed off as soup and the small piece of bread he was given each day. Now I looked at him, 160 pounds, and a normal weight for a man of his height. I had difficulty imagining him as one of those emaciated skeletons I had seen in black and white photographs taken by the liberating armies.

He pushed his nearly empty plate to the side and looked at his watch.

"Okay, sweetheart, you done?" he asked, looking at my nearly finished plate of food, then up at me. He returned his sight to whatever morsel hadn't been consumed. It was his way of letting me know that he expected me to finish everything on my plate. He didn't like good food to go to waste.

"Yeah," I said, sticking my fork into the last cube of pineapple that came with my teriyaki steak and chewed quickly. I knew that Dad liked getting to the game early to watch the Kings in their pre-game skate.

"So what do you think about tonight's game?" he asked as we got up to leave, always wanting me to know my opinion mattered to him. "You think the Kings can win?"

"Not if they take stupid penalties," I said. "Their penalty killing stinks."

He chuckled. He took my hand and we walked across the street through the parking lot to the Forum.

At the time, I didn't consider how easily my father transitioned from memories in his past to seamless shifts into the present. For the next three hours, nearly everything involved hockey. We wrapped our cold hands around a Styrofoam cup of hot chocolate, our pre-game ritual and sat in what felt like cold storage. Our vinyl orange bucket-like seats in Section 29, Row X, seats 3 and 4 were ours for the season. Dad's Kent cigarette butts soon littered the front of and side of his seat.

The air conditioning blew strong and the fresh sheet of ice glistened as the players came onto the ice. The scant crowd stood clapping. The announcer called for the National Anthem and we remained standing.

Chills ran down my spine listening to the velvety deep voice of Frank Mahoney sing the anthem. Dad bent down and whispered into my ear with his warm breath and deep European accented voice, "This is the best country in the world."

I nodded, but then at that age, it was all I ever knew. I imagined that for him this must have been a *mekhaye*.

Soon after the start of the game, one of the orange uniformed concessionaires approached, his arms were shaped like twigs and his veins popped out. His cheekbones showed the skeletal shape of his face. His eyes were deeply set in their sockets. Dad's eyes focused on him and away from the game.

"Peanuts, a buck a bag. Peanuts," he hollered in an east coast accent.

"A *musselmann*," my father murmured under his breath. I understood the term to describe concentration camp inmates that were emaciated and close to death.

He threw a bag to Dad, who caught it and dug into his black leather wallet for a dollar. Dad held his arm out longer, hesitating for a moment, leaving his wallet billfold open implying he wanted to give him more money, as a gesture for his effort, or for what Dad perceived about this man's life.

Watching the concession man walk away, I imagined Dad looking just like him.

"Imagine at his age, doing that job," Dad said to me, shaking his head.

But I sensed that Dad had other thoughts about him. He had lapsed out of the game, for a moment, stunned by what reminded him of the past.

The games shifted Dad out of his work and wartime memories into what was his favorite escape. There were the occasional lapses like the concessioner and our favorite player Butch Goring's last name, resembling Hermann Goering, but I wondered then and even now how much hockey could be an escape for Dad, given that ice hockey had been a large part of his youth in Czechoslovakia. Maybe it was a return to his boyhood passion. I will never know if he had remembrances of his parents coming to his games. Or of his friends who played along side him who had been killed during the war? Or was it one of those emotional breakthroughs for him that enabled him to watch the game as a spectator and not be pained by his remembrances?

Whatever it might have meant for him emotionally, he never let on. And I never asked him.

EMILIE GEORGE

LEARNING AT THEIR KNEES

If I had ever been accused of leading a *double life*, I would have been astounded, hurt and outraged! Duplicity has nasty vibes. Yet, as I tried to interpret the theme *double life* in all possible contexts, I started to consider some surprising possibilities. My father and mother both came from Korçë, a small village in Albania; I was born here, but my first language was Albanian. My parents were immigrants, but I was Albanian-American. I realized that all immigrants lead *double lives* by having two or more languages and two cultural heritages. This can be a source of painful problems, but can also be the basis of a wider ranging sensitivity and appreciation of others. Here then, is a glimpse into part of my *double life saga*.

In the seventies, when I taught high school French in the Wappingers Central Schools near Poughkeepsie, New York, our Foreign Language Department added an ESL Program. ALM, the Audio Lingual Method, was then in vogue. It was purported that by frequent repetition of sentence patterns students learned to speak "as if at their mother's knee." ESL meant teaching English as a Second Language. Well, I learned Albanian at my mother's knee, my father's, aunt's, uncle's, and their friends' knees. English I learned at the knees of society at large. Sometimes they were friendly, sometimes I got kneed! I was puzzled by the S in ESL. My father spoke Albanian, Greek and Spanish first, so for him English was a fourth language. Even my mother, whose education ended with the fifth grade, spoke Greek as well as Albanian—for her, English was a third addition, even though it was a wounded bird she carried around in her speech cage. A more accurate term for such a program would be: EFL—English as a Foreign Language.

When I went into my house I heard and spoke Albanian; when I went out I heard and spoke English. The quick separation of languages was like shoji screens, the sliding Japanese panels that can open a room or close it off. In time, I learned to dart nimbly between panels. During my childhood some of my friends on the block were also ESL-ers. Whenever I went to

Marion and Eddie Eckhart's house, lemon and ginger baking scents wafted from the kitchen, and occasionally, the authoritarian bass voice of the father speaking German was heard. When we moved to another neighborhood, across the street was the Greek Kotsis family with six children, who also skipped effortlessly in and out of the sliding panels.

Albany, New York: When I was four-years old we lived in a flat over a shoe repair shop. An Albanian ran the store, and he and his wife lived in quarters in back of the shop. I loved to visit, fascinated by the whirling lathes, the smell of new leather, glue and shoe polish. At this time, I lived completely in the world of my mother tongue. One day, I decided to go downstairs, then onto the sidewalk to see the outside world. There were some neighborhood children playing hopscotch and milling about. I approached them and spoke in my language, which I thought was everyone's language. I chattered on about the blue dress I was wearing, that was a present from my mother and father. At first, they were dumbfounded, then realized that I spoke real weird! So, they formed a circle around me and asked questions or made comments. Although I didn't understand, I kept replying blithely in Albanian. There was a burst of laughter after each response, and some began to mimic me. By this time my parents discovered that I was missing and came to investigate the commotion. My father ran over, picked me up in his arms and scolded the children for making fun of me. I was amazingly unscathed by it all. I hadn't understood a single word of their insults and jeers. For me, it was like being in the spotlight while I made my stage debut! This feeling stayed with me and surfaced again much later.

Kindergarten—Children's Garden: For me it was more like a patch of thistles! My father took me to Public School No. 21. He left me with the teacher, Mrs. Walsh. He didn't mention that I couldn't speak English, since that's what they were supposed to teach me in school, wasn't it? Mrs. Walsh had a routine, and every afternoon she would say, "Children, fold your arms and lay your heads down on your desks—nap time." For awhile, all heads went down but mine—my eyes were the only periscope above water; all the others were submerged. No matter what she directed, I did not comply. This angered Mrs. Walsh. She thought I was a vindictively rebellious child. Her solution was always the same—punishment. I was sent to stand behind the upright piano angled in the corner. It also served as a storage area for classroom detritus. I spent a lot of time muttering in Albanian to a five foot cardboard Santa Claus carrying a bag of gifts.

Children do learn a new language fairly fast, and I had made some progress, but I was still not fluent when my mother asked me to do an errand. She wanted me to go to the corner grocery store to buy a bar of Palmolive Soap. She said it in her inimitable way. Albanian is a phonetic language, so she pronounced every letter: "palm-o-LEE-vey sohp," with the accent on LEE. I marched to the store, feeling quite intimidated, yet proud to be entrusted with such an important mission. I looked up at the grocer who stared down at me from behind the counter. He didn't understand what I wanted, and I had to repeat "palm-o-lee-vey" a number of times, and may have even forgotten to add "sohp." When he handed me a soft, squishy package wrapped in waxed butcher paper, I panicked. I knew it wasn't soap, but I was too frightened and inarticulate to do anything about it. Mother was aghast when she opened it and saw a pound of liver!

In the second grade they gave us Stanford-Binet Tests which determined whether or not we advanced to the next level. We had worked on addition and subtraction. We were taught to subtract the *subtrahend* from the *minuend* to get the answer. On the exam, some problems were not represented numerically, but were in a story problem format which I had never seen before. Many kept asking for the *difference* between various numbers, for example: 325 and 79. I chuckled and said under my breath, "Boy, are they stupid! 325 is larger than 79!" I had never heard the term *difference* to indicate the result of the calculation! Apparently, I chuckled too many times. On the last day of school, the names of the students who were to go on to the third grade were read aloud in descending order of their test scores. Mine was the last name read.

In the fifth grade, the music teacher came to class once a week and taught us the "every good boy does fine" lines on the treble clef and the "f-a-c-e" spaces. We learned to sing the scale: do, re, mi, fa, sol, la, ti, do, then how to identify the key from sharps or flats. Finally, we sang well known songs in solfège, i.e. by using the scale names for the notes. For example, she would blow the beginning note on her pitch pipe, and for "America," we sang: "do, do, re, ti, do, re, mi, mi, fa, mi, re, do, re, do, ti, do." One day she told us we could take music lessons once a week in school and asked what instrument we would like to play. What a thrill it would be to play a real instrument instead of all this do-si-do pitch pipe singing! The previous year I had gone with my mother to a grocery store owned by an Albanian. While they were chatting, I explored the back storage room where there was an upright piano.

When I opened the dusty cover, the yellowed keys, some of them cracked, looked like the teeth of an aging horse. I cautiously pressed down a few. The piano hadn't been tuned for awhile, so it sounded with a nervous whinny in its voice. Despite all of this, my God! What a marvel! I became bolder and my fingers galloped over keys in different tempos and patterns. I had entered another realm, and I loved how it made me feel. Remembering that experience, I said I wanted to play the piano. Unfortunately, this required that I have one at home for practice. The school loaned all other instruments out to the students. I begged my parents to get one. They didn't have the money for its purchase and delivery. We rented and moved frequently, and besides, a young Albanian girl didn't need to learn anything as useless as music. I had to learn to cook, keep house and sew a dowry for the day they picked an Albanian husband for me. It never occurred to me or the music teacher that I could learn a portable musical instrument, and perhaps the piano later on. Every week on the day for music lessons, I envied the children who walked to school carrying different shaped instrument cases like coffers that contained treasures. I felt some shoji screens closing.

My parents had told me often that I would go to school only until I was sixteen, the legal age to quit. Any further education was in the same category as the piano lessons. They considered school to be a holding tank. I loved the aquarium where new knowledge flashed like exotic neon fish. It was an old three story rectilinear brick building. On the first floor were the Principal's Office, kindergarten, first grade classrooms and a long hallway that led to broad stairways on the right and left. Since the building had no auditorium, for the few assemblies we had during the year, we stood on both sides of the hallway; the stairways held the rest of the grades in sequence, as if on risers. I recall Christmas programs and some Native Americans who performed in Native dress chanting and beating drums.

School was completely different from my world at home and I loved it. My sixth grade teacher Miss Johnson was a brunette, sometimes wore a turban, had dark red lipstick and red nails that she occasionally polished in class while we did our lessons. I thought she was exotic and adored her. She was the magician dispensing the magic we learned.

Before school holidays, we would sometimes end our work early and have a program. Students would recite poems, tap dance or sing songs. Once a tall, lanky boy started singing "Camptown Races" with great gusto. My friend Ellen and I had never heard it before on the radio, and all that was played on our phonographs at home was Albanian or Greek music. When he belted out the refrain, "Doo-dah, Doo-dah," Ellen and I looked at each other and froze. He was exuberantly repeating the Albanian slang term for a woman's private parts! He knew all the verses and sang the dreaded chorus unrelentingly. We started to laugh uncontrollably that doubled in intensity with each refrain. Miss Johnson was not amused. She thought, of course, we were laughing at the boy who was unwittingly fueling our hysteria! "Tell us what's so funny," said Miss Johnson, "so we can all share the joke." We were literally speechless—we only knew that expression in Albanian. Even if we had known it in English, it could not have been uttered! The program ended with threats to inform the principal and our parents about our misbehavior. That was Friday afternoon. I spent the entire weekend in excruciating fear. We had no phone, but I guess I expected Miss Johnson to show up at our house and knock on the door with her red nails. The dread lived in me like a thorn, and diminished only when I realized that no action would be taken.

Across from our school was Swinburne Park that had swings, slides and a pool. I was in the seventh grade at Philip Livingston Junior High when my period started. My parents spoke to me in serious tones, "You are now capable of becoming pregnant, capable of dishonoring the family. From now on, be careful how you sit, close your legs together, don't ever let your thighs show." I had just been running in the park with my friends, I had slid down slides with those thighs, been on see-saws with those thighs, swum in the pool with those same thighs. I wondered what had happened to my thighs all of a sudden! I felt more shoji panels closing. Henceforth I would face more restrictive Albanian codes of conduct.

Detroit, Michigan: I attended Northwestern High School whose student body was an ebullient inter-racial mix. It was a grand old building, and despite its age, it maintained a solid curriculum. I was still chasing the exotic neon fish and took Latin, art, extra literature classes, and as after school activities, fencing, and modern dance. What was prohibited: dating, telephone calls from boys, attending school dances. Looming: the deadline to quit school at sixteen. By this time some acculturation had occurred in the Albanian community, and most teenagers were finishing high school. My parents finally agreed that I could graduate.

Then I took an English class with Kathleen McCurdy Nova. I was very enthusiastic about the American literature we studied and had started to write a little poetry. Mrs. Nova took an interest in me and my work right from the start. Under the guise of helping her with clerical work, I started visiting her after school more and more frequently. With her Irish heritage and her husband's Italian family she was very aware of first generation immigrants' problems. She became my mentor, friend and advisor. In order to fill the gap in my cultural background, she bought me books, took me to plays and out to lunch, and won the acceptance of my parents. She also warned me to resist the temptation to rebel wildly against them and end up on a destructive path. And most important—she convinced me that I owed it to myself to go on to the university, which up to that point, I had thought was totally impossible! She even suggested that I could study to be an English teacher, ensuring a way to earn a living when I graduated. She had some acting experience and had directed high school theater productions, and recommended that I take the Speech Class to gain self-assurance. As a result, I even entered city and state competitions in the category of "Oratory" and "Dramatic Readings." (Remember my "stage debut" on the sidewalk when I was four?)

Well, now I was convinced that I should go to college, but how could I actually accomplish it? I won a scholarship to the University of Michigan in Ann Arbor, which only paid tuition, and the dorm fees were quite high. After I graduated from high school, the only summer job I could find was in Kresge's Basement Snack Bar for minimum wage. Needless to say, I didn't earn enough to pay the dormitory fee. Besides, it would have been a lost cause, as my parents wouldn't have agreed to let me move away from home. However, winning the scholarship did evoke some admiration from the Albanian community, and when I suggested an alternative, they acquiesced. I would live at home and attend Wayne University. I got a job at the Main Branch of the Detroit Public Library which was near the Wayne campus, and I got a loan from their Credit Union for tuition each semester, which I paid back in installments from my salary.

I did get a degree from Wayne University, but not as an English teacher. After a few months in my French 1 class, I decided to switch my major. Albanian contains most of the sounds of the European languages. I was so delighted with the linguistic acrobatics that my tongue could perform, that I was hooked forever on foreign languages. Besides Latin, I studied French, German, Spanish and had introductory classes in Modern Greek and Russian. I heard someone say that when he learned a new language he felt like he was being reborn. For me, it's shoji screens sliding open endlessly!

DON THACKREY

MA'S SECRET HERITAGE

The neighbors were amazed at how our ma
Could heal the sick with ointments, herbs, and prayer.
When Ma's hands pressed, we reckoned God was there.
Friends said it's like she were an Indian squaw.

Their praise pleased all of us, except for Pa,
Who didn't want it known that Ma was heir
And granddaughter of famous Standing Bear.
Pa's secrecy was deep, a lifelong flaw.

We children hoped to honor, glorify
Our heritage but couldn't talk of kin
Or what occurred when Pa and Ma first met.

Ma smiled when, rooster-proud to qualify
As breeds, we boys asked her if it's a sin
To tote a scalping knife—just as a threat.

KNOWING MA

The storm lowers at us with greenish frown,
It roils and thickens as it eats daylight.
Pa herds us to the cave and helps us down
The makeshift steps to darkness worse than night.

The lantern, finally lit, shows eight white faces,
Shelves packed with canned goods, spiders here and there,
But where is Ma? Pa scrambles up and raises
The door, which rips its hinges, takes to air.

The rain and wind roar in. Soon back comes Pa
With tarp in hand. We raise our frightened eyes:
"Won't leave her canning, nope! …you know your ma."
We nod and keep our peace. The baby cries.

The storm easing, we scamper through the rain
To find Ma sealing jars, our meals for winter.
Our worried faces ask her to explain
Why she risks her life, the family center.

She smiles and holds the baby for a while
And tries to speak, but lets her smile say more.
To work! We throw debris onto a pile
For burning. Pa retrieves the split cave door.

Before chore time, we have most things set straight.
Then in to wash our hands and to the table
Where Ma still has her small smile for all eight
That tells us she would answer, were she able.

"You know your ma," he'd told us in the cave.
We knew farm work and how we should behave,

But there's a clause somewhere in natural law:
No child can ever fully know his ma.

PRODIGAL SON

Pa took it hard when young Joe ran away
At harvest time to find a job where he
(So said a note he left behind) would be
Able to send home part of his first pay.

We boys had known that Joe had gone astray
And wondered if our parents couldn't see
Joe's needs, which led him to debauchery
With men, not women. He was what's now called gay.

Months later, Joe came home, drunk, filthy, ill,
No money left of what he stole from Pa.
When I got in from fixing fence, Joe was
Sleeping in my bed, Ma's healing skill
At work, Pa sitting close, his heart rubbed raw.
I knew he'd take Joe back; it's what Pa does.

PA'S SILENCE

Pa said he could not talk about it yet,
It seemed tight lodged in him somewhere deep.
He said he'd tell us—unless he should forget—
Before he lay down for his final sleep.

We dared not ask again. And then Pa died.
Whose life, whose death, what art, what love, what war
Had wrung Pa's heart and left it petrified?
Ma told us: "…finding words…can be…a chore."

I asked her why he hadn't even tried.
She held her peace; I stared at her moist-eyed.
Seeing my hurt, she took me then aside,
Drew two long breaths, looked down, softly replied:

"When one can't fully say what's in his heart,
It's best he should stay silent…and depart."

NOVEMBER MAN

Born in November, he enjoyed late fall
As if he thought he was part polar bear.
He welcomed winter as does a glacial wall
And thrived in circumstances cold and spare.

The neighbors pitied us children and his wife,
Imagining, wrongly, that he *never* spoke,
For when he ventured out to public life,
He gathered silence round him like a cloak.

At home, he earned the family's esteem
As did George Washington, the Father of
His Country. That was near enough to seem
(Just as affairs one has with God) like love.

Our late November pa passed years ago.
He searches there, no doubt, for ice and snow.

on Ferry

EDWARD BEATTY

IRON MAN

From the depths of a red barn restored by reflection
a stern voice calls and once again I am a boy drawn
through sweltering August air, struggle to breathe,
face my father, gather enough courage to respond.

I trudge across a cattle yard, rubber boots crushing
a crust of dried manure and dirt, pass a fallen gate,
tangled barbed wire, bullet-riddled milk pail, hatchet
head stuck in a tree stump stained scarlet and split.

Thistle skeletons leaning against a flaking water tank
seem to stir as I plod past cracked silo, inhaling heat
emitted by its concrete and fumes from a black pool
at its base pressed from decaying silage, its surface

humming with silver-green wings. Legs, arms, lungs
stiffen until I halt paralyzed before a half-open door:
ruptured bales, rotted rafters, hayforks held by frayed
ropes and a pulley, and hanging near the roof's peak

my father. He shouts my name like a curse and I try
to reply, but again my body has become iron. Rust
grips my neck, crawls over lips, nose, eyes, encrusts
my ears. All is still, the only sound air eating metal.

THE BIRTHDAY PARTY

The light that supports the barn's beams and roof is almost yellow.
A rope appears, sweeping back and forth, steady as the pendulum
of a grandfather clock, and a scrawny kid clings to the knot
at the rope's end. He crosses the abyss between the mow's
two sides, his legs pushing away from one, straightening,
then bending to absorb the other, again and again.

On one half of the mow, atop stacked bales, two boys franticly call
his name, on the other two girls, for the collie leaping and barking
below has become a roaring lion and forks clanging on a pulley
at the barn's peak cannibals' blades hacking the vine from
which their friend swings. Today is his eighth birthday
so he is the hero, come to rescue his helpless pals.

In the farmhouse is a kitchen with a fridge containing five cupcakes,
five pints of ice-cream, five cokes, and a counter holding four gifts,
a card attached to each. Here too light is almost yellow, like barn
light, with bits of hay suspended in the air, and all the doors
are shut and locked. In the cellar, for years now, a skinny
boy crawls across the floor, searching for the key.

THE ROAD TAKEN

A solitary child departed at noon, paddling his small sandbox
with plastic soldiers and fort across the farmyard to the drive,
glided over the pasture, waving to grazing cattle he passed.
Decades away, but headed in the direction of a mythical city.

At midnight an old man cast off, rocker, shoulders, and back
creaking as he rowed through Chicago streets to the suburbs,
drawn by a concern for the past to again slip outside of time.
This journey determined by an unexpected, urgent memory.

The two approached twilight and the DeKalb Oasis, rest stop
halfway between the old farmhouse and one room apartment.
In the McDonald's a man peering into a paper cup of coffee
imagined he saw himself swimming circles in a black pond.

He stared; gradually the pond grew wider, deeper. Suddenly
it was an ocean, he out of breath, struggling to stay afloat,
the weight of reality pulling him down. "Should I give up
and go under, return home, or continue on?" he wondered.

The child paddled faster and old man strained as both neared
the golden arches shining above the highway. "I am going to
drown," the man gasped, as did the face staring back at him.
Then out of the corner of their eyes each detected two crafts

rapidly approaching, one from the west, one from the east.
When they entered the head in the cup, met and combined,
the image shattered and there was only a pine box bobbing
on froth. Two hands broke the water, clung to slick wood,

and the man breathed deeply, forehead and cheeks cold, arms
cramped and trembling. He lifted, swirled the cup. Fragments
of boats, his double, and the coffin were nothing but bubbles,
now. He rose, tossed cup into a trash can, walked to his car.

"What can I make of these fantasies?" he mumbled as he took,
without thinking, the off ramp leading to a nondescript town,
menial job, nights at a typewriter. In the east glowed a maze
of lights, in the west fireflies flickered above a black pasture.

THE AUCTION

A lightning-tongued man with straw hat and raised hammer
stood paralyzed in a whirlpool of dust as bargain-hunters fled
to porch, trucks, cars. Then a wail of rain swept parched cornfields,
muddied the bare feedlot, shook brown pines, leafless poplars
and willows, struck barn, cribs, sheds, beat the emptied
farmhouse. The draught had ended, but two years too late.

Out of sight a boy crouched in a shack he had tacked together
between two corn cribs, its floor warped planks on bricks, walls
splintered plywood, roof corrugated tin. A burlap door flapped,
tied half-open by twine. Room enough for a child squatting
like the native in a grass hut who once startled him, staring
back from the glossy pages of a *National Geographic*.

As rain drummed the metal roof a foot above his head the present
receded until his family's failure was a shadow beneath the sea
and he the pilot of an ark carrying mother and father, cows,
chickens, ducks, cats, and his quivering Collie puppy over
blue waves to a land of forests, streams, green pasture.
Rain pounded and soon he was conscious of only

a hammer at his feet, its handle worn and split, head chipped,
claw rusted. He said "hammer," repeated the word, fascinated
as meaning gradually vanished leaving just a shape on a plank
that grew mysterious as he spoke. Suddenly he imagined
it was a chest of gold, then a weapon waiting for a hero's
hand, next a tongue cut from a demon's mouth with

which a witch doctor could transform the past, present, future.
Feeling he was dissolving, he chanted his name to save himself
but the hideout became the hut in the magazine and he the native,
now staring at a camera on a tripod manned by a headless body.
Then the hut was a coffin sinking in the ocean, his lungs fists
beating at the lid until he felt nothing. Mother still calls

from the farmhouse, but he remains hidden where memory left
him. Sun cannot break through and in the yard machinery rusts
a circle around a hayrack stacked with boxes, tools, furniture.
The crowded porch sags, rain pounds like a mallet striking
a wooden block, and the man who speaks lightning, so fast
only grownups might understand, can never shout "sold."

52

PHYLLIS A. LANGTON

CLANDESTINED DAUGHTER CLAIMS CLAN

During the Christmas season in 1988, a woman called me one evening and said, "Come up here and put me in a nursing home. I'm dying."

"What? Who is this?" I asked.

"This is your mother."

I hadn't heard from Margaret (the woman I had called mother until 1952, but more on that later), since she told me to stop calling her six months earlier—a year after my sister Molly died.

Margaret didn't sound like she was dying. Her voice was quick and demanding. I didn't call 911, since she wouldn't let anyone in her house. Also, I knew she had food, heat, and a neighbor who could help her until I got there.

Leaving my family at home, I flew to Boston the next morning, rented a car, driving to Cape Cod in a blizzard, trying to remember how to find her house. I wasn't prepared for what I found. When she finally cracked open the front door enough to peek out, she stood supporting her four-foot-eight frame with a cane—eighty pounds of sagging flesh, wrapped in a soiled, chenille bathrobe. Her matted clumps of hair framed her gaunt drawn face. All the other times that I had seen Margaret in my life, she was dressed to the nines, her hair stylish and colored.

"Hello, Margaret. Sorry I'm late. This is a helluva blizzard. May I come in?"

"Yes," she answered. "It is quite a storm."

When I entered the house, saw the squalid conditions and smelled the putrid air, a mixture of whiskey and incontinence—I nearly choked.

"When was the last time you ate today, or drank any water? I brought some chicken soup for you. I thought it would taste and feel good in this weather."

"Thank you, but I don't want anything."

"You didn't answer my question. Look, you called me to help you. I can't help unless you cooperate with me, at least a little."

"Maybe later."

"It is later already. I'm tired and need to see you are all right before I go to the Bed and Breakfast down the street. Tell me how you feel." I could hear her chest congestion, but her breathing wasn't labored. I knew by her constant cough that she had a slight case of bronchitis.

"You can come back tomorrow," she said.

"No, I'm not leaving until I help you loosen the mucous and drain some of the fluid from your chest. You know I'm a nurse, and I can help you. Otherwise, I will call your doctor."

"He died this year."

"Then you have to deal with me or the Falmouth Hospital. Your choice."

As she lay on her side to drain the fluid from her chest, I was able to loosen her mucus, thumping lightly on her back, forcing her to cough, and later to drink fluids and soup. When her temperature was normal, her pulse steady and her breathing easy, I left. At the magnitude of her decline after my sister's death, I buried my face in my pillow and cried myself to sleep.

After cleaning her and her house, throwing away her dirty clothes, sheets, and towels, I bought new ones, two fans, and prepared meals for two weeks.

At the end of the holidays, with her chest clear and her appetite adequate, she was well enough for me to leave. I asked if she still wanted to go to a nursing home. "I'm not going to any nursing home. I'll fight you in court," she said.

Taken off guard for a moment, I then realized Margaret was up to her old tricks of manipulating people to get what she wanted. In this case, to stay in her home and be sure someone was going to care for her there when she wanted them. Also, she wasn't about to give up her whiskey habit.

"Fine. Stay in your home, but I have to know that someone can get you what you need and check to see if you are okay," I said. "Or you can come live with us. I can't take on this responsibility long distance. What will it be?"

"My neighbor across the street will help me."

"Great," I said. "Please give me her phone number. Do you have any family that I should call?"

"They're all gone. I will call her later."

"No. I'm not leaving until I talk with her on the phone, or in person."

That was the beginning of a nearly eight-year journey with me traveling at least twice a month by car or plane to Cape Cod to tend Margaret. It was a heart-wrenching experience to watch this Catholic woman, who had crucifixes, statues, and rosaries throughout her house, destroy her mind and body. In an attempt to stem the demons that possessed her, she had given up her vanity and dignity to Seagram's VO Canadian Whiskey. Years earlier my sister had mentioned casually that Margaret had been personnel manager of an Air Force base on Cape Cod for years until she retired in 1964.

I wrestled with her drinking behavior, but kept her whiskey available as her pain medication of choice. Early on, I took her car keys. I knew she was in physical pain because of severe arthritis and malnutrition, but she wouldn't talk to me when I was there, and kept her radio blaring. I had watched my sister and now I watched my so-called mother die in front of me. She refused to have a priest or anyone visit. I wondered if she was ashamed of her life, her secrets, her lies—or of me.

She needed to be in a nursing home, but I had no legal authority over her decisions. When I called the local Social Services Counseling Agency and Alcoholics Anonymous for assistance, they told me, "She has to hit bottom. Until then there is nothing you can do except see she is cared for and safe." Not an easy task from 600 miles away.

As she grew older, my need to understand my roots increased. I felt that once Margaret died, I would have no chance to find out whom else I might belong to, or with. I couldn't let it rest, especially now that I no longer had Molly.

Close to my mother's death in July of 1995, I said to her, "I know who you are." I had just received a copy of her birth certificate from the Boston Registry. I had been trying to find a Margaret Atkins for years with no success. She sat up tall in her chair and said, "No, you don't know who I am."

I placed her birth certificate on the table where she could read it. Her face paled, her eyes widened. At the age of eighty-five, her secret life was on the table. The mask was off. It was only a matter of time before I would find her family. Then I would find mine.

"Your maiden name was Margaret Langton, not Margaret Atkins as you reported on my birth certificate. You were named after your mother,

Margaret Fleming, and your father, John Langton, was born in England. My father wasn't George Thomas Langton. You invented him. Who was my father? What was he like? Please tell me about him."

She glared at me, her eyes crunched up into slits, her stone cold face fierce, but her eyes were ringed with fear. "I don't remember." She lowered her chin on her chest, her usual signal that a conversation was over.

I burst into tears, grabbed my purse, and said, "I don't believe you. I'm going home." I waited several minutes. She said nothing. What an atrocious ending for both of us. I knew she would never tell me what I wanted to know. She would go to her grave with her secrets.

She died at home the next day.

After she was cremated and her ashes scattered over Woods Hole on Cape Cod, I prepared to close her house until I could bring in a cleaning crew. As I was leaving, her phone rang. It was a woman named Betty. I told her of Margaret's death and that I was her daughter.

"Margaret had no children. She was never married until she married Colonel Taylor in 1964. Are you sure we're talking about the same person?"

"Yes. I look like her. I know little about her since I never lived with her, but I had a sister who died in 1987."

Betty was unable to speak for several seconds. When she finally spoke, she said, "I was your mother's personal secretary at the Base for more than ten years. I was known as Margaret's girl. She lived a secluded life, going to Mass many times during the week. I still can't believe this."

"Do you know anything about her past life?"

"She said she was engaged to a Protestant man she loved, and still had his diamond ring, but her father wouldn't let her marry him. She said her father was German. She didn't like him."

We agreed to stay in touch. In her last note, she praised Margaret saying, "She always took care of the little people."

To make sense of the phone call, we must return to the beginning— to a strange beginning, return to a child in an orphanage who wasn't an orphan, to a girl in foster homes who sometimes may have glimpsed her real mother.

I was born in Boston in 1933 during the Great Depression. My earliest recollection at age four was bouncing from one foster home to another. My mother visited me occasionally. This wasn't unusual during the depression when people were forced through economic pressures to put their children into care. But it made for a strange sense of connection.

In 1942, I was sent to a Children's Home, or orphanage in those days, until 1946 when I was discharged from the Home, where I was happy. I was told that I was going to California to live with my sister and mother.

Instead, a woman, who claimed to be my mother, took me from the Home to live with my sister in Boston. While happy to see my sister, Molly, I was frightened to be taken by a woman I had no recollection of knowing. I didn't like the way she treated me. She physically pushed me around and cut me off when I asked questions. After telling me to meet with the school counselor the next day to find a job, she left my sister and me to take care of ourselves.

The next day, I set out to find stores to buy food and places to wash our clothes. The first place I went to buy milk was the Elliot Lounge on Massachusetts Avenue near our building. I remember that the man at the counter was shocked when I asked him if I could buy some milk. He asked if I was sick. Not every day does a thirteen-year-old girl shop for milk in a cocktail lounge. After he heard my story, he took me across the street to the delicatessen and asked them to help me.

Molly and I lived in Boston together during our high school years because our mother lived on Cape Cod, about three hours away. There was no pattern to her visits. I gave up trying to get answers about this arrangement from my sister and mother. They wouldn't tell me anything. When I asked Margaret the names of my parents for my high school application, she told me to list her as my mother and to list my father as deceased. I told her I didn't know her name, or what deceased meant. "Look it up in the dictionary," she said.

During my junior year, I worked at the Women's Hospital in Brookline as a dietary assistant—a valuable experience in learning how to prepare meals. Everything we ate came from cans, especially Franco American Spaghetti. Remaining at Women's Hospital, I worked as a laboratory assistant, as a receptionist at the receiving desk, and finally, as a nurse's assistant, which shaped my decision to go to nursing school.

During my senior year, I started a newspaper in our school and sold the first copy for five cents to the famous mayor, James Curley, re-elected while in jail. He gave me five dollars and lots of souvenirs. Our picture was printed in the *Boston Globe* newspaper. I learned this when my mother came raging up from Cape Cod to scream at me for my vulgarity in having a picture taken with the mayor. "Nice girls don't show their faces in newspapers," she hollered. I didn't understand what she was talking about. I hadn't seen the picture and didn't know that what I did was wrong.

After graduating from high school in 1950, I moved to California to study nursing. The next year, when I became ill with gall bladder disease, they were unable to reach my mother to get permission to operate. I was too young to give consent. After doing a spinal tap, the doctors changed my diagnosis to viral encephalitis: inflammation of the brain. Fortunately for me, they couldn't reach her for consent to do brain surgery.

In my second year of school, I met Dr. Langton, an ear, nose and throat specialist. He had seen my name on one of his patient's nursing notes. Thinking we might be related, he contacted me and asked my family history. Knowing nothing about my family, I said I would contact my sister. When I reached her, I was so excited that I didn't realize she wasn't talking. "Are you okay?" I asked. Amidst her tears she answered, "Mother won't be happy with you. Why do you always upset her?"

Taken aback, I felt my cheeks burn. "Are you crazy? Upset her? I haven't heard from her in more than six months. Tell her to call me at the nurses' residence."

Our mother called back within twenty minutes—a first! "Don't you be taken in by that man," she ordered. "Don't you talk to him."

"What? He is a well-known doctor," I said.

"Phyllis, stay away from him and don't tell him anything," she screamed.

"I don't know anything. Who is my family? Why won't you tell me? I'm going to his home on Friday to meet his family."

"I forbid you to do that—"

I hung up the phone while she was talking and started to cry. My roommate listened to me spill out all my hurts from this woman that I never liked and could never reach. In the past, when I was sick, the nursing school couldn't reach her, but Molly could reach her in minutes. Like a flash I remembered that whenever I entered a room where Molly and my mother were talking, they stopped talking. The more I thought about it, I realized that I wasn't family to her. Only Molly was. All these years, she and Molly had been a tight unit, excluding me.

Something awakened inside me that was unexplainable, but real—an epiphany of detachment from her as my mother. At that point, she became Margaret, and I called her that until her death. She never commented.

Yet, I was still puzzled. Why did she dip in and out of my life when it suited her? What did she want? I wished she would stay away. I wanted no part of her.

I went to Dr. Langton's home that Friday and many times thereafter. Over the years, they became my first Langton family. I was included in their family events, and cared for their children as they grew up. We stayed in contact until they moved from the area and I was married.

When my daughter was born in California on March 4, 1965, I called my sister and learned that Margaret had married an Air Force colonel a year earlier. He had suffered a heart attack the previous day. Molly was upset because she hadn't met him. Our mother had put us in the closet again, calling my sister every few weeks when she went to Mass on Sundays. Margaret, of course, never called me. He died in 1966.

The next year, my sister and her family were transferred for her husband's work to San Jose, California for a year. For the first time, Margaret drove from Massachusetts to Santa Monica, California, where I lived, because my sister and her family were visiting me for a week at Christmas.

Margaret spent Christmas Eve with us, speaking little, and retiring early to her hotel. Late Christmas morning, when she hadn't arrived to open presents with us, I called her hotel. I was flabbergasted to learn she had checked out. Totally jarred, I hid in the bathroom to regain my strength before I told Molly.

Molly looked stricken. I held her and wept with her, but was unable to fathom her despair. She nearly collapsed as I helped her into bed. She had desperately wanted to talk with her mother about her birth certificate that she had just received. She needed it to apply for a passport to travel with her husband. But the line for father was blank. That information shocked her since she always assumed that she had a legitimate father and I didn't. She was devastated when she saw my certificate that listed my father as George Thomas Langton.

All these years Molly had protected our mother from my inquiries, but now she was the one who needed answers from her and couldn't get them. "What will I tell my children?" she asked. She remained in bed for most of their visit.

For the next two decades, my sister and I were family to each other. We spent holidays together and other special times. Sometimes we gathered at her home in Ohio and other times at mine in DC. I moved there after completing my Ph.D. in 1968 to take a position as an Assistant Professor at George Washington University. Sometimes Margaret joined us at the last moment, but she was always distant, leaving early.

During those years, my sister's health began to deteriorate from an insidious addiction to prescribed drugs like Valium, Melaril for depression, and alcohol. She carried a long plastic tray with slots for her different pills and set an alarm for when to take each one of them. I was frightened to see the progression of her addiction to prescription drugs and alcohol. When I talked with her husband he told me to mind my own business.

Over time, her erratic behavior increased. She left her job, lost her car when her husband took it away, and finally her phone because she called me often and talked for long periods. She became completely isolated in her home in the country.

In mid-August of 1987, I spoke with Molly from Nashville. "George and I are going to visit you after our daughter is settled in an apartment to attend medical school," I said. She was thrilled and answered, "I want to hear about your new home and all those bedrooms." We giggled like young sisters.

We never spoke again. She died a week later from liver failure, a few days after her fifty-seventh birthday. I felt relief for her—she no longer needed pills and alcohol to numb her feelings. She was free at last of the pain and misery of her damaged life, free from trying to roll a rock up a hill forever like Sisyphus, free of trying to find something she had lost—or never had. I ached with pain and loss deep in my bones.

My need to know more about my family persisted after my sister and Margaret died.

In late 1996, while going through some of Margaret's papers in her attic, I found my baptismal certificate from St. Patrick's Catholic Parish in Massachusetts. A man and a woman with different names were witnesses. My head swirled with dizziness in the hot attic. Why had my mother saved it? Had she wanted me to find it? Or had it just been overlooked? I wanted to believe the first, but I think that even in death, she wanted to block me if she could.

I knew very little about how the Catholic Church worked. If the two witnesses had been sponsors at my baptism, they must have known my family. They might even be relatives.

I called my husband telling him of my discovery, unable to hide my eagerness to take action immediately. Being a slow deliberate thinker, he approached the issue methodically.

"How will you find them and what will you say to them?" he asked. "This might be disturbing news—if they even remember the experience. They would be in their eighties now, if they're still living."

"I called information," I said, "and I have Mr. King's phone number. He still lives in Massachusetts. Because I don't know her family, I'll tell him that my mother died and I'm trying to find her family to share this news."

"Come home. Don't do anything in a hurry."

I scoured the attic in search of more treasures. I found many pictures of my sister and her family, but none of my family and me, even though I had sent her pictures over recent years. Why did she save my baptismal certificate, but no pictures of me and my family? Perhaps the certificate was her way to show me I wasn't invisible, that I really did exist. I would never know if Margaret was a victim, if she was sane or disturbed. But I did know that she hadn't been a mother to me.

In 1996, on Monday of Thanksgiving week, while my husband was playing tennis, I called Mr. King. I felt both anticipation to talk with him, and nervousness that he might actually answer. I carried a tall glass of water into my office, put the phone on speaker so that I was free to take notes on our conversation.

After dialing his number, a soft-spoken male voice answered, saying in the slow, crackling, plaintive manner of a very elderly person, "Hello."

"Hello. Mr. King?"

"Yes."

"My name is Phyllis Langton. I live in Virginia. We don't know each other, but we may have known someone in common. My mother was Margaret Langton who died last year at Cape Cod. I am trying to find her family to let them know. While cleaning her attic, I found a piece of paper, from St. Patrick's Church in Roxbury, with your name on it. The paper is dated April 23, 1933. I apologize for calling you like this, especially if you didn't know her...."

The phone was silent for several seconds. Then he shouted into the phone, "Oh, my, so you're the baby. Are you all right? We always worried about what happened to the baby."

I answered, "I'm no baby and I'm not sure if I'm the baby you are talking about. Could you tell me something about that baby?"

"Well, your mother lived with my Aunt May in 1933 during the last months of her pregnancy. My aunt helped women who weren't married. She let them stay at her place until they went to the Salvation Army Home to have their babies. Your mother left after you were born. I'm sorry to learn of her death."

"Are you sure of this?"

"Yes. I remember that occasion very well. The second signature was of my wife-to-be at that time, Beatrice, who wanted to keep you. But we weren't married yet, and that wasn't permitted. By the way, I'm having my ninetieth birthday next month."

"How wonderful. Congratulations! Since you asked, I'm happily married, expecting a granddaughter in January, and have been a professor for many years at George Washington University in DC. Is there anything I can get for you?"

"No. My son helps me."

"Do you know anything that might help me locate her family?" I asked.

"No. She stayed in her room. I'm sorry I can't help you."

"Thank you so much for talking with me. I hope I didn't upset you by calling without any warning."

"You didn't upset me, but you certainly surprised me. I am so pleased that you are well."

I had mixed feelings about hearing this story. On the one hand, it felt like another slap in the face from the woman who claimed to be my mother, the mother who died refusing to tell me about my father. But I was used to her cold, hurtful ways, like when I tried to hug her, and she pushed me away saying "Don't mess up my face."

On the other hand, I felt compassion for her intense loneliness, and empathy for the pain she carried all her adult life. How devastating to have lived with such a massive burden. One lie led to another, and that was the sad story of her life. Secrets and lies. I, with my own open nature, was one of those secrets, one of those lies.

After talking with Mr. King, I thought I might have living relatives in Massachusetts. I wanted to find them if they were still alive. Now that I had a name to search under—the one I had used openly all my life—I decided to explore new ways to locate my extended maternal family.

In early 1997, I bought a tape of addresses and phone numbers from the Massachusetts telephone company of people with the last name Langton. After reviewing the list, I wrote a letter on January 17, 1997, to forty-eight Langtons.

The responses were immediate and colorful with snippets of their Irish family history. One man offered to send me a copy of a *National Registry of Living Langtons*, 1991 edition. But I still had no direct leads to the family of Margaret Langton.

One evening in late February, when my husband and I returned home after tennis, there was a message on our answering machine: "Miss Langton, I have your letter sent to Helen Langton. I'm your cousin, George Sennott. Your mother was my Aunt Peg. I will call tomorrow." He left his phone number.

I had hit the jackpot! I couldn't sleep that night and chattered to my husband about this stroke of good luck. The next evening, I dialed George Sennott with questions ready. When I heard his soft-spoken "Hello," I was thrilled. His voice had the similar pitch, tone, and Boston accent of Margaret's.

"Hi, George," I said. "This is Phyllis. Thanks for calling. Are you sure my mother was your Aunt Peg?"

"Hi, Phyllis. Yes, I'm sure, and I'm also troubled that our parents hid us from each other. I bet our grandparents and parents knew about you.

My mother and Aunt Peg were close. She stood up for my mother when my parents married in 1941. We saw little of Aunt Peg. She didn't come to her parents' funerals, but she came to my father's funeral."

"Strange. My sister, Molly, died in 1987 at age fifty-seven. Margaret died at age eighty-five, so I'm the end of the line of Langtons I know."

We exchanged stories, and he confirmed my Irish ancestry. There were four sisters. George's mother, Katherine, was the oldest. Then came Margaret or Aunt Peg, Helen, and Mary, in that order. The other sisters had died several years before Margaret. George suggested that we get together soon.

On March 15, 1997, a few days after my birthday, I arrived at Logan Airport, Boston, scared, yet thrilled to meet my family. Walking up the long ramp to where many people were milling around looking for their friends or family, I searched the crowd for men wearing the Old Brogue baseball caps that I had sent to my cousins so I would be able to recognize them, since we had no pictures of each other.

Then my eyes fell upon a husky man of medium height wearing the Old Brogue cap. He wore a wide grin on his face. I almost cried, ran over and hugged him, blurting out, "You must be my cousin, George." Next, I ran to the tall, thin man with a bushy mustache covering his lips, and an Old Brogue Cap on his head, and said, "Hi, you must be my cousin, John." Then I heard from somewhere, "Hey, Phyllis looks just like Aunt Helen." For the entire weekend people told me I looked like Aunt Helen. I was accepted immediately into the family.

George and I found my luggage, and joined the party to celebrate my arrival at the Cheers Bar in Logan Airport. We drank, ate, laughed, and hollered as we matched stories. We had to talk at the top of our voices to be heard over all the usual whoops, hollers, and cheers in the bar. Everyone was aghast when I said I had lived in a nearby orphanage.

The next morning, George and John picked me up in George's huge truck that he used in his roofing business. George was apologetic about the truck. "When I called your husband to ask what you liked and what you were like, he said that you were like one of the guys and would get a kick out of riding around Boston in a big truck. I hope that's okay."

I roared as they boosted me onto the vinyl front seat of the cab between the two of them. "What a million-dollar view of the city," I said.

"You're right. When you see it every day, you forget," George answered.

I felt young, silly, warm and secure with my new cousins. The humor was constant as we exchanged more stories about our pasts. I felt the immense pride they shared for their families. I realized what I had missed all those years. Above all, I wanted to belong to their clan.

They drove me to places the family had lived in Cambridge, including the gravesite where all the family was buried except Margaret, and to Boston where Molly and I, completely unknown to them, had lived, worked and studied only miles from where they were busily living their own lives. They still talked about their disappointment with their family for hiding us. But they were thrilled that I had found them.

Their open-hearted kindness and my open nature were a natural combination. We were totally comfortable with each other. I felt girlish when I saw soft tears in their eyes as we joked and teased while riding around. My eyes were gritty and wet.

We returned to George's house in Winthrop for a brunch with all the family, a birthday party for me and for Laurie, one of George's daughter-in-laws. The cake was covered with loads of candles, Irish Shamrocks and butter cream icing.

Everyone wanted to meet the new Irish cousin from Virginia. Children and grandchildren came from Cape Cod, western Massachusetts, and other local areas. The exhilaration and giddiness were contagious as we tripped over each other, laughing, hugging, precariously balancing food trays. How different from my own childhood. How different from Margaret's life and death.

Flying home that night, wearing the Cheers' T-shirt and cap they had given me, spilling over with the love and care they gave me in those two days—my own Irish Langton eyes, claimed at last, were smiling.

MEREDITH DEVNEY

DOUBLE DATE: 1965

The wind plays tug-of-war with the Cadillac's weight
as it weaves through slushy roads on the outskirts of town.
You and your sister sit snugly between the Lombardi brothers
in the back seat, smoothing your ironed skirts and curly hair
every time you pass a street lamp. Up front their father smokes a cigar
as heat blasts from vents, blowing the stench into your face
and muffling Glen Miller on the radio.

The movie started at 7 but it's half after and you're nowhere near
The Paramount. Aunt Pat's making out with Bruno so Benito
places a hand near the hemline of your skirt but you slap it away
just as his father says—
Takin' a little detour, hope you love birds don't mind.

The car's headlights hit pavement casting a yellow glow
onto a Colonial home. Their father parks the car but leaves the engine
running and Benito yells—*Where you goin' this time, Dad?*
But his trench coat and briefcase have disappeared into the darkness.

That night you sat for hours on the plush backseat taking swigs
of scotch stashed in the glove compartment as Aunt Pat sat
on Bruno's lap and your date's dad did God-knows-what.

Three years later there's a ring on Aunt Pat's finger
and a headline on the front page of the paper—
"Mob Boss of The Enterprise Busted:
Family Man Piccaretto—Papa of Rochester Mafia."

MADEIRA

Every day you're gone I study
the map above my mantle
trying to guess which *pueblo*
you are making your music
and love to at that moment.
This is my secret

and yours
is the Portuguese girl
named Catalina or Luciana
or some other name ending in -na
who owns an exotic beauty
I will never own.
Glossy, black hair
that almost looks blue in the light
and skin the color of cocoa and cream
so that you swear she'd taste like
Hershey's and milk if you could drink her.

You find her in a crooked alley
sitting on crumbling steps
where you first play for her
mint-green or aquamarine eyes.
She guides you to castles and ruins

and open air markets
where you buy *aceitunas* and *uvas*
that she shows you how to wash
with cold water and hands—
your hands over hers—in the basin
of her kitchen. On Sunday
mornings you sit in the coffee shop
down the street and drink
café con leche out of cheap china
stenciled with green vines
as you struggle to communicate
more than a smile.

WAITING ROOM
ELON UNIVERSITY'S HEALTH ROOM

These white walls are vaporous,
a gaseous substance I can't see through
but still I know what waits on the other side:
a crammed room with closed blinds,
desk, bookshelf, an overstuffed sofa
where I'm supposed to recline and tell
a man I just met the cyclic thoughts
turning in my head.

I no longer scrapbook because I fear
the orange handled scissors in my end table drawer.
They're only 53 feet from the foot of my bed.
I stripped my house of pillows because I owned a prime number
of them and I don't trust sidewalks. Cars can easily swerve
over the curb. At night I recite my prayers twelve times
and twice during the day I call ten people I love
to make sure they're still alive.

Irrational ideas run my mind
into a marathon, force my heart to bang
against bone (like the fist of someone inside
wanting to come out) until I can't catch
my breath. I swear the other student
in this room who's sitting across from me
can see my sweater shaking,
hear me wheezing.

I need to focus. Take deep breaths.
Inhale: One white table.
A single *Self* magazine.
The stench of antiseptic.
Exhale: A stainless steel water fountain.
The clicking of computer keys.
Thirteen chairs—I need
to get rid of one—

but now the door is opening
and a nurse is standing,
clutching a clipboard,
calling my name.

PENANCE

Uncle Jim filmed Mom in her floral dress.
Braids fell down her back as you two ran
from the church to a daisy-draped VW van.

Five years later you filmed Mom and her
blessed belly walking Crescent beach
in a green and yellow sundress. We used to

watch the voiceless videos on rainy weekends.
You'd commentate through jumpy images projected
on our living room wall like a CNN sport announcer
as we ate handfuls of Mom's pecan popcorn.

Now you're engaged to a woman who doesn't know
you still watch those reels every weekend it rains.

CASSANDRA ROBISON

LEAVING HOME AFTER A SHORT VISIT

My old mother at the curb, waving her white
handkerchief; I pull away, wave
a white napkin back, honk at the corner.

She is still there, fluttering
her farewell hand like she did everyday
when I walked to school as a child. A few blocks up
the hill I pass the cemetery where all
my family lies: father, aunts, grandparents, great aunts
and uncles, great grandparents I never met.

Ten miles north, my Jeep sweeps across the bridge
at Bemus Bay, past the long wild fields
of the Southern Tier rife with July bloom:
cornflower, buttercup, black-eyed Susan,
pristine Queen Anne's lace, purple clover.
The ripe corn heavy eared and tall rising
like some old grief in my heart.

At the Pennsylvania line,
headed back south to Florida,
I cross into the future 80 mph,
full of hope and promise as a school girl,
wondering how many childhoods do we have?
how many chances to get away clean?

MOVING

Today she forgot her mother's given name,
and yesterday the way home from her other
daughter's house just across town,
as if memory were too fine a thread
that finally gave out after long use.

This is the house she's lived in 30 years,
years she says that jumble like 300
piece jigsaw puzzles she would lay out
on the dining table where night after night,
twirling pieces in her hand, she refound
their rightful place. Years have drained away.

Her life limp. Already she is moving
to the next place through the heavy swell
of time, point to point on a life map—
a wary-eyed blond girl to an aged crone.
Her life closes off, her mind adrift,

and her daughters left on the mooring, waving.
Waving. *So short*, she'd say, *so short!*

SUSPENSION
. . . *Marta Amanda Rosenqvist*

In her latter years—after Ben was gone—
she was a brown wren perched in an upstairs nest
of her middle daughter's house.

Everything small now, as if the old age
required only twigs and thread. Her black
aged Singer hushed away somewhere,
even the knitting needles stashed like secrets
from a former life.

This old Finnish woman, resilient, still plump
with life. How she laughed, especially when
my father told her a story. Oh, Raymond!
she'd say, cocking her head sideways in delight.
Her iron wisps of hair pin curled, her neat
brown dress, her white cardigan.

She would clasp those startling hands—
that had fished the frigid waters off the Aland Islands,
thrown rocks at retreating Russian soldiers,
grasped the immigrant ship rail, upholstered chairs,
sewn clothes for her daughters—
she would clasp those hands, to keep them
from fluttering off. She might reach up
to pat a loved one's face. I think of her nestled

there in three rooms, preening
her feathers all those strange, small years,
suspended between the end of real living
and the real hard end at 90, weightless as down.

YOLANDE HOUSE

LEARNING TO LEAVE

I often feel divorced from my old self, the self of my youth, like her legacy is not my legacy, as though my childhood of abuse and neglect stands outside of myself. I know it to be "mine," as I have the memories and anxieties to prove it, but I left so much behind the night I left home. An essential tearing of my true essence, leaving me years of picking up the pieces, stitching them back together, and hoping the final product is whole and complete.

The night I ran away from home, my sister was in an unusually good mood. She was a bossy child and, although I was ten years her senior, we argued a lot; I often found myself wondering how a four-year-old could win an argument so often. That night, though, she was calm, happy. "Want to play Barbies with me?" she asked just before I'd planned to leave. She made me want to cry. This was going to be so much harder than I thought. Not only was I about to leave my home, leave my mother, and walk out into the unknown all by myself, I was going to leave my little sister. I was erasing myself from her life, by necessity, but it was an unintended consequence of my choice. I would not see her again for a few months, and then for a few years. We would never again have a normal sister relationship. My mother was the link that broke us apart, and we have yet to come back together again.

For the first four years of her life, I was my sister's primary caretaker. I would return home from school to find my mother, newly diagnosed with a chronic illness, still asleep after a late night. My sister would often be asleep, too. I would make sure she was fed and her diaper was changed. Mother would wake up in the evening, sometimes in a good mood but often grumpy and snapping at me for little things. If I had neglected to change my sister's diaper or forgotten to feed her, as an eleven-year-old can understandably do, my mother would punish me, going into a screaming fit that would often include a slap or two.

As I walked out of the apartment building, I momentarily paused, realizing that this was it, the last moment I could change my mind. If I ran back now, maybe I could say I went for a walk. But no, everything was coming to this. Months of talking on the phone with my aunt, my uncle, my dad—all of them assuring me that I had a place to stay should I choose to leave—was all making this moment seem inevitable. Sobbing, I continued walking along the familiar pathways, leading to the highway and convenience store, next to which stood the police station. This is where I was supposed to come the next time my mother hit me.

That night she had hit me for the first time in months. The physical assaults used to come more regularly, but since I had contacted Social Services a year earlier, my mother had learned to control herself—she now rarely hit, slapped or scratched me, making it harder to document the abuse for the police or other authorities. No, the abuse came in other ways now. Worse ways. I had learned to handle a slap or three, a backhand, a rough push, a scratch. I had not learned what to do when she ordered me to vacuum the living room—and, being an obedient daughter, I would—and then hulked there, standing over me the whole time, glowering. This was not a reasonable chore she was asking me to do; this was a replacement for physical punishment, a new way for her to have power and control over me, to take pleasure in my humiliation and anger. I would grit my teeth and glare at the floor, trying not to cry, trying not to show her how much this hurt.

I had not learned what to do when she openly complained to her friend about what an ungrateful daughter I was, while I was standing in the same room peeling carrots. Obedient as I was, I did not feel entitled to complain or stop working, so my anger came out in other ways. The carrots were peeled, all right; by the time I was done with them they were little slivers of carrot stick, the juicy middle, with the carrot roughage discarded in resentful heaps around them. My mother, upon seeing the carrot wreckage, was indignant. She yelled at me, likely using her favored phrases of "ungrateful little bitch" and "fat fucking cocksucker," and told her friend, "See? What did I tell you?"

I had not learned what to do when she delighted in my distress, like when we were at my aunt's house—she was playing a game of cards when I discovered she was wearing my shoes. Disgusted at the thought of her sweat in my own footwear, I asked her to take them off. Her response? She laughed and refused. Then I started pulling at her feet, trying to free my shoes. She laughed even more delightedly and dug her heels in—literally putting weight on her feet so I could not remove the shoes. I cried at her feet, at this point begging her to take them off. This went on for a good ten minutes. To this day my aunt recounts this story as the moment when she realized how messed up my mother was. To torment your daughter in such a way, to take delight in her pain and humiliation. These are the sorts of things that got worse when my mother realized it was no longer wise to take her frustrations out in physical ways.

The night I left, on Easter Sunday, was a rare exception that year. We had just finished supper. I forget what we were arguing about; my mother seemed to explode at the smallest and most bizarre provocation. I know I was sitting in the wicker rocking chair in the living room, watching TV. Maybe she wanted me to do some chore? I do know, whatever she had asked, my response was a simple, calm, "No."

"WHAT did you say to me?!" she screamed, barreling over to where I sat. I looked up, and she had her hand held up high, in a threatening motion to hit me. I glared at her as we locked eyes. The challenge was simple, a game we played over and over that year. It was for power, and she wanted me to relent, repent, to give her the power as the parent; for me to accept my place in life, subservient and silent—a "Yes, ma'am," again and again. But this year I had grown angrier. In the increase in hostility on the home front, I was much more resentful and challenging than this obedient daughter had ever been in the past. And so my response to her question was again a simple, "No," while staring, glaring, up at her.

And that's when the hand came down. My god stood in judgment and found me wanting. Punishing me for my sins, the hand slapped across my face and shook my body. The chair, the earth, rocked beneath me. Everything changed.

I had a plan. Conceived with my supportive family, in secret from my mother, the plan was to leave home the next time she hit me—the next time she performed an action that the law and society would deem clear assault, abuse. There was a police station near my house, and I was to head to it.

But first I had to leave.

Mother's last words to me that day were an indictment to do the dishes, the last horror-inducing chore she would ever foist on me. I did them in a daze, my head reeling—was I really going to do this? Was I really going to leave? I knew I must, that I really didn't have a choice, or that I finally did have a choice, with family support and places to stay. Without that choice, I knew I was headed toward suicide. I already had a plan to kill myself and a way to carry it out. It was my aunt's first phone call a few months earlier that shed light on a new option, a new way to end the pain (or so I thought). A year earlier I knew I could carry on, when the cycle of abuse was familiar and my mother's slaps the height of my agony. But the elevation of the mental distress, the invoked humiliation and outright hostility, the nearly constant hatred and animosity—I knew I couldn't handle that much longer. And so I had to leave. Hands shaking over the sink, rinsing off my final flower-covered plate, I knew this was the last time.

My mother was safely tucked away in her room, talking loudly to someone on the phone, so I knew I was free of her for the moment. I could make a clean getaway. The complication was my little sister, my lovely little four-year-old sister, who was being so sweet and attentive. She wanted me to play Barbies, training her big brown eyes up at me, pleading for attention and love. It broke my heart that I had to leave her behind. I couldn't just pick her up and take her—friends would ask later if my dad was going to take her in, too, and I had to tell them that, no, she had a different father. I promised myself that if the day ever came that she needed to walk away like I did, that I would take care of her, much like I took care of her as an infant while my mom slept for twenty hours a day.

Knowing I had to get my sister out of the room, and not thinking about what kind of damage I would be inflicting on her psyche, I asked her to get something from my bedroom. "Okay!" she cried happily, and started to run down the hall. "Wait!" I said, knowing I needed to buy more time, "How about we play a game? Why don't you count to a hundred before you come back out?" She agreed, and ran off to do my bidding. I stared after her sadly, heavily, and took a final glance around the place I had called my home, my hell. Then I turned to leave.

The next complication was my mom's doorknob decoration of very loud bells. With years of practicing the art of being invisible, I swiftly lifted the bells off the doorknob, moving them so slowly they only clinked lightly a few times. Even those few chimes sent spasms of panic through me, and I glanced up toward the hallway in fear, scared someone would hear. No one did. Then, I laid them delicately across a wooden chest covered with dark flowery material—one of the many pieces of furniture my mother had re-upholstered herself. Then, with the same delicate artistry, I slowly unlocked the door and opened it. I numbly walked across the top hallway of the apartment building, down the sets of stairs, and through the apartment front door.

Once the automatically locking door shut behind me, there would be no turning back.

It clicked closed, sealing my fate. I walked across the parking lot, thankful my mother's window didn't face my direction. Hot tears running down my face, I looked up at the apartment building, still thinking that perhaps I could turn back. I could ring the intercom and explain that I had simply gone for a walk, and then just suffer the punishment of leaving the house without my mom's express permission or approval. I walked in circles on that spot for quite a few seconds, not wanting to linger in case they came looking for me, but at the same time wanting to be sure of my decision. But I knew I finally had to do it, I had to leave, for any change must be better than this. So I continued walking along the familiar pathways to the police station on the corner.

I learned that leaving was the easy part—and that part was incredibly hard. Having to live with this legacy has been so much harder. I am an artistic, feeling person, and I have worked for years to move through the pain of that childhood. I have made incredible progress, but I fear I am nowhere near finished. Likely I never will be done. It would be nice, however, to get to a point where anxiety is not a daily reality and I truly feel that I am worthy of healthy, loving relationships, with friends, family, bosses, and romantic partners. I am still waiting to come into my own, to merge the torn pieces of my self so I can become more than the sum of my parts, so that I finally accept and put forth my best self, free of fear, wrenching off the once comforting confines of a self-imposed invisibility. I no longer need that cloak. Why do I clutch it so?

HEATHER TOSTESON

MAIDS

I don't have one.

Coming to Mexico, I am clearly aware that this is a matter of philosophy more than finance.

But I am also aware that on a weekday morning, I will be the only woman up on our *azotea* hanging clothes who holds a doctorate. A doctorate and, I sometimes think, a wet black skirt slapping the back of my neck as I reach down into my green plastic bucket to pull out a drenched gray lambs wool sweater, a crazy measure of will. *I want it all.*

I have never done so much hand laundering in my life. This is because I don't trust the *lavanderia* with my clothes, although weekly or bi-weekly I send the clothes of the rest of my family there, mainly jeans and t-shirts, *calzones* and *calcetines*. I want it all, and I know my own limits. I wouldn't be able to speak to my son or my lover if I were up here beating the dirt out of their denim.

I know it would be cheaper to hire one of these women. She could beat and rinse and wring for three days for the cost of one trip to the *lavanderia*, where we draw our own clothes out of our duffle bag and heap them in the basket suspended from the scale.

"Hide the *calzones*, Mom," my son says, glancing over his shoulder at the girl who chews gum and reads a lurid romance comic while keeping an occasional eye on the needle. Three kilos. Six. Sometimes nine.

Up on the *azotea*, I wring out a slip, a brassiere. A maid in the third cage from me pulls a dripping synthetic dress from the water, shakes her head, and slips it back, scrubbing harder. I don't know if my presence is self-indulgence or self-mortification. These are *my* clothes I am caring for. When I gather them from the line, I experience a moment of genuine satisfaction. No maid could do that. She would only feel the tightness in her neck, the pull across her back as she reaches higher and higher in the service of someone else. Gathering my clothes, or my son's when he was a small child and not as close as he is now to being a man, I felt grounded. I felt I was giving both of us the security I had dreamed of having as a child.

At home in the States, I was not alone in this. Here I am.

"You have met a culture," my psychiatrist mother teases me when I call her, "which meshes too neatly with your own neurosis. Maybe at last you'll change." She has never forgiven me for saying, at the age of twelve, when asked by a visitor what I wanted to be in life, "A maid."

A maid, let us be clear about this, with a doctorate.

The third week here in Mexico City, I enrolled in a brief, intensive course in Spanish. Among my classmates were two American women, a housewife married to a military attaché at the American embassy and a young Texan who represented Max Factor cosmetics when she wasn't jetting to Los Angeles or Newport. The housewife was taking the course, she told us all, so that she could talk with her maids.

"*Sucio,*" she told them in triumph after the third day of class. "*La estufa es muy sucio.*"

"They say they can't wax the stone floors," she complained to one of the women instructors. "But I think they are the same stones they have in the embassy. They wax them there, and they look wonderful. Isn't there some way—" But the verb *to wax* isn't included in the vocabulary of Curso Intensivo I.

"*Mi sirvienta,*" she said, "*pasa por mi hija a la escuela.*"

Every day she brought a styrofoam cup of coffee from *La Embajada.* She returned after class to have lunch with the Newcomer's Club. "It's only for women who speak English," she said, bustling off. The pretty Swiss and Belgian teen-agers shrugged; the Canadian social workers shifted in their chairs.

Her conversation about her maids came to form the prologue for every class. "We've never had it so good. A big house with a garden—and these maids. If only I can get them to understand what it means really to clean a house. Unless I get them to do what I want, I'm not going to keep them. We've told them they're on approval for sixty days. *Then* we'll buy them uniforms."

"We like *ours* so much," the Texan blurts out, "we've already bought her uniforms. A different color for every day: pink, lemon, green, blue— She's so *cute*."

I winked at the Canadians as I rushed out of the class. "This *comida* business is beginning to drive me crazy," I had already confided in them. "I'm not used to having my day broken in half." However, *comida*, is less a cultural adjustment in my case, rather a practical compromise between my lover's evening teaching load and my son's morning school hours. As is my custom, I resorted to making huge vats of soup—a freedom pot, from which we each dipped daily until we couldn't bear the taste any longer.

But the truth is that it is more than the *comida* that is driving me crazy. As I rush from the metro to the *mercado* to our apartment, my feet seem to beat out the words *la*-bor in-*ten*-sive. "Labor saving," I mutter as I fit my key in the lock. "De-*vices*," I shout as I put the groceries down. "Who's going to help?"

Dead silence. No one is home yet. I put on my red apron, my only one. It is covered with flour, mole, drippings of soup stock and grease. Something has to be done.

I remember an old friend, a man, teasing me years ago as I made cupcakes for my son's birthday party, a copy of Abram's *The Mirror and the Lamp* propped on the kitchen counter so I could study as I frosted. "I keep wondering when you'll have to make a choice," he said. It was true, I hadn't yet. Even as a single parent, I wanted to raise my son as if it were my only task in life.

"Never, if I can help it," I remember saying, swiping another cupcake with a spatula of chocolate, turning a page.

I was not alone in this. I remember a friend, another single mother, rushing home from her last Friday class. "Vacation!" she said. "I can't wait. First I'll do the laundry, then I'll clean out the closets." There was true glee in her voice. Our five-year-olds nodded at each other and slipped out the door. So much love and so much flurry.

But no fury. The fury comes when I do all this for a grown person, particularly a man. Then the pleasure and sense of self-sufficiency and nurture I feel when I look at an orderly house is compromised. Then I feel this is *not* a house I've set in order to permit my child and me to do our *real* life's work. When domestic order is no longer a way of clearing a path to my desk, then I *feel* like a maid. Still, I can't stop, even if I think it is unjust. In my home, I'll pick up after anyone. It is, I can't rid myself of this belief, the only way I *can* get to my desk with my heart intact.

Soon, I am afraid, something is going to have to give. Walking five blocks to the left for bread, three blocks to the right for paper and pens, straight down the road for tortillas and *queso*, I know I'm not going to get home with anything worth having—no energy, no inspiration, no love.

I also know a maid is no answer. At most it would be a collusion based on outrage and necessity.

My Mexican lover in a moment of intimacy told me that his ex-wife needed three maids to keep our two bedroom apartment in order. One to cook, another to wash clothes, and a third, I believe, to mop the kitchen floor and cover all the burners with tin foil. I don't think it irrelevant that along with not wanting to cook or clean, she did not want to have children. She wanted to study and paint. She wanted to find herself.

"That's decadent," I told him angrily. "Now there are three grown people in this place. How many maids do you think *this* means?" I rolled the carpet sweeper noisily by the bed, disrupting his sketching.

"What do you want of me?" he asked, putting down his pen and pad.

"*Fifteen* maids," I told him. "And a divan, and a vomitorium."

"Clear *your* room," I yelled at my fourteen-year-old son. "There are some customs that are *not* going to change."

Love, I say to myself as I chop onions. Love, love, love. I love these people. I love myself. I wipe my eyes. They tear even more from the traces of *jalapeño* on my hands.

"A butler," I announce in desperation on Christmas Eve. "I want Santa Claus to bring me a butler. Can you imagine how many men we would have to interview to find one who would do what almost every woman here does daily?"

"Millions," my son says. "But please, Mom, I don't want to be your butler until you find a real one."

And I, it is clear to me, want to be a mother, a lover, and a friend. But never anyone's maid. This, at least, I and the ex-wife have in common.

II

Unlike many children of the American middle class, I did grow up with maids. Whenever my mother went back to continue her medical training, someone came in to help with the four children. First, Mrs. Gathe, a robust Norwegian widow, who slept, I remember my astonishment, on a wooden board at night. Then, for almost eight years, we were cared for by a young Danish *au pair*. Later, having learned her lesson, my mother only employed daily help. Black daily help—because we had by then moved to the South. Vivian. Mary. Fanny. Since she has lived alone, my mother has chosen to employ a domestic cleaning service.

My father's second wife, an Argentine physicist, has employed the same full-time domestic help for a decade, a couple from Barbados. When they first came, they were each paid about $2,000 a month and given an apartment over the garage; they were also promised help with their immigration papers. The relationship between them and their employers is at this point icy. The husband, as soon as the papers cleared, found work elsewhere, but the wife still comes daily to the house. Their son, who has attended the same public schools as my half-brother and half-sister, is now a student at Middlebury College. He parks a bright red Trans-Am outside the garage in which my step-mother parks her antique Ferrari. When we visit, the maid insists my son make his own bed. She does this in an act of solidarity with me. No child, we both agree, should grow up not knowing how to *do* for themselves.

My step-mother feels differently. "All my childhood," she says, "I never did *anything*. I never made my bed. I never picked up or ironed a piece of clothing. It didn't do me any harm." She wants her children raised the same way. On the maid's day off, her son, if asked three times, will carry his own dish from the breakfast table to the sink. Obviously the capacity, as she claims, still exists. But I watch all this in amazement. When there were no maids in our house, we children were organized in shifts to sweep, to do the dishes, to make our beds. We bartered between ourselves for the favorite tasks. Everyone preferred, for example, sweeping floors to polishing furniture, washing dishes to drying them. But we never, as far as I can remember, felt it was an injustice to be asked to assist. Indeed, the emotional situation between our parents was sensed as so precarious that to perform these tasks was a way of reassuring ourselves that the household, if not the home, was stable.

III

Here in Mexico, maids are everywhere—and nowhere. They open the door to my lover's parents' house at midnight. Neatly dressed in plaid skirts and cardigans, they blink into the headlights, not shyly, and retire without a word. My lover's father is a lapsed Communist, but he sees no incongruity in employing several maids to assist his wife.

Another woman I know, an actress, also employs a maid. The maid stands at the stove heating tortillas while we sit around the kitchen table sipping soup. With a wave of her hand, the actress dismisses the maid.

"*Now* I have a maid," she says, "But before this, I made everyone sit in here with me when I cooked. Now, when I am sick, my daughters can make the food for a dinner party. I think this is good."

My lover points at me and says, "She is a wonderful cook."

"How lucky for you," the actress says dryly.

"She knows me," he says laughing.

The actress is the sister of the ex-wife.

"My *son* cooks too," I say.

"This is a completely female household," my lover says quickly. The actress, her daughters, the female cats, the female dog pacing in her dirty kennel that adjoins the maid's doorless hut. We hear the maid talking as she hangs clothes on the line outside the door.

"Except for him," the actress says. "The maid's son."

I put my spoon down. I have no appetite today.

"I'm going to learn how to do *everything*," my son has recently told me. "How to cook, how to do laundry—so when I get older no woman will ever scold me. I won't need *anything*."

As a child, I admired the maids we had. Like my son, I wanted to internalize the nurture their activities implied. I remember my envy watching my friend Carrie Guttman fold her shirts in perfect thirds in preparation for a summer vacation with her family. Her family had no maid, but at twelve she and her two sisters could take care of themselves in a way that made me desperate for a place in her house. The maid, maybe it was Vivian, sat in front of the television. "Is *this* right?" I asked her, holding up my brother's shirt. "Why don't you go on and try another," she drawled, changing the channel. "One of your father's this time." I did but not out of any desire to care for my father or brother. Although their shirts hung rippling on the hangers, somehow I felt that this would soon permit me to fill my suitcase with my own neatly folded shirts and shorts. It meant I too could go on a vacation with a friend sure that my family would still be there intact when I came back.

IV

We *all* need something from each other. Often when women employ maids they want to preserved the domestic values they were raised with. Even when they work, as my mother did, at presumably masculine occupations, the relationship with the maid is often one of collusion.

"Things were different then," the mother of my Argentine step-mother said sadly some years ago. "We were all friends."

The woman from the Barbados had nodded good-night and left the house silently. She no longer worked weekends. That night her son graduated from high school, but no one had mentioned this.

A friend here in Mexico takes us with him to meet his American wife returning from a vacation with her family.

"Something must be done," he tells her as soon as we are settled in the car. "The maids are eating too much."

"Haven't you talked to them?" she asks.

"*Ham* and cheese," he says. "In the middle of the night."

"Why me?" she asks. "You've been back for three weeks. Besides, you've had maids all your life. You know how to talk to them."

"I've reduced the household allowance already," he says. "I can reduce it even more."

"All right, all right," she says. "I know," she adds after a moment's pause, "I'll tell everyone we're going on a diet. We're *all* getting too *panzona.*"

We had a maid once named Fanny. Having raised six children, she now lived alone in a small house at the end of a gutted dirt road on the outskirts of Durham, North Carolina. Each spring she bought a piglet and raised it in a pen in her garden. Every morning and evening all spring and summer, she carried out to it several gallons of slops. I remember trying once to hoist the bucket she used. In the fall, she had the pig slaughtered and had most of it smoked or made into sausages. She lived off this for the rest of the year.

The week of the slaughtering, she brought several delicacies to share with my mother. The first day, Fanny brought a pig's foot, which my mother consumed with relish.

"I *know* I hurt her feelings," our mother told us nervously the second day, "but really I *couldn't*." Our mother had earlier earned in equal parts our admiration and disgust for developing a taste for scrapple, the contents of which we children could barely force ourselves to read off its plastic wrapper. But even she baulked at pig snout and pig ears in recognizable form.

"*Whatever* she brings you tomorrow," we warned her, "you're going to have to try it. She's trying to be friendly."

"The ears still had *hair* in them," my mother moaned.

"Well, I suppose you could say you have a doctor's appointment," my brother relented at last.

"If you had a maid," the American woman tells me, "you would improve your Spanish. I learned all my Spanish from my maids. The first year, my husband wouldn't let me go anywhere without one."

"How's the diet going?" I ask. "Do you think you can take the car outside by yourself and meet me for a cup of coffee?"

"As long as I'm back by seven. It's my curfew."

This evening, our conversation centers on sources and avenues of information here in Mexico. "Now I talk to my mother-in-law and sister-in-law when I need to know things." Her mother-in-law has recently, for example, revealed that her husband has not had two previous marriages, rather three.

"But when I came here, it was the maid who helped me out. She had been with my husband for years before I came and knew everything. Right after I came here, a woman came one evening to visit, and I knew, I just knew that there had been something between them. I may not be too smart, but my *instincts* are good.

"Of course, he denied everything. But I locked myself into the bedroom and told him to get her out of the house. The next day, I asked the maid. She used to come in the middle of the night, the maid told me. 'And what,' she asked me, 'are two grown people *doing* in the bedroom in the middle of the night?'"

We both laughed. "I was such a child then," she says. She is now twenty-seven. "We don't have her anymore."

"Why?" I ask.

"My curfew," she says, glancing at her watch. "I'll just have to say I got stuck in traffic. The maid will back me up."

V

On New Year's Day, my lover and I have a violent argument about whose turn it is to light the pilot in the boiler. He goes off in a huff to his parents' house. I, for the first time in a year, call my own mother. "You'll love this," I tell her. "I've decided I'm going to get a maid. I'd prefer a butler, but I don't have the time—"

"Eons," my son calls out from the kitchen.

"I'll pay," my mother says. "But only if this guy promises not to sleep with her."

"That goes without saying," I tell her.

But I say it anyway, a few nights later, when we meet with the American and her Mexican husband for a drink. The consequences are amazing.

The conversation began amiably enough.

"American women are used to working harder than Mexican women," the middle-aged businessman told me, "but there is no need to here. My wife, for example, has two maids."

"But when they're not there," she said, "I'm the one who picks up after you." She looked at me quickly for support.

"I work," he said. "When you work, you can hire even more maids. But what are you implying anyway—that I treat *you* like a maid?"

"No," she said, reaching over and touching his hand. He pulled away and sipped his scotch. "But if I'm the one who does their work when they're not there—"

"I work," he said. "As long as I can pay, I will have someone else do those things for me. They are not worth my time. I've done without maids, but I don't choose to."

"When?" I asked curiously.

"I was a Boy Scout," he said. "I did not take my maid with me on camp-outs."

I had a sudden image of the look on his face at twelve as he looked behind him, the crumpled tent on the ground, the bent tent pole in his hand. *No maid.* He must have looked just as exasperated and amazed as he did now.

"I feel the same," my lover said. "I would prefer to have someone do all those things. But this month I can't pay."

"Then, you have to do the work," his friend said with a shrug and a loud laugh.

"It's all taken care of," I said. "A Christmas present from my mother. She's only set one stipulation—"

I told them. The American woman and I laughed.

"That's *not* funny," both men said in unison.

"Your husband is an honorable man, how can you even suggest—"

"But men do sleep with maids sometimes," the American woman said.

"If I were to tell you not to sleep with the *gardener*," the rich man told his wife.

"It was just a joke," I said. "It says more about her life than yours."

"It wasn't funny," both men said again.

I had a Guatemalan friend as a teen-ager. One time we were talking at a party about early sexual experiences, in particular, what our parents had told us about sex. "It happened," he said, "before I had any idea of sex. So it was more than I ever imagined. When I was eleven, my father told me to go into the maid's bedroom and jump on her. So I did."

Now, seven years later, his father dead, he lived in North Carolina with his mother and sister. His relationships with girls his own age were scrupulously egalitarian.

The room was silent.

"He was my father, so I obeyed him. But I had no idea, really no idea at all, what would happen."

Still no one talked. Someone got up and left the room to get a beer.

"You can't *understand*," he said angrily. "It was all different there."

"I fixed her teeth," my mother said weeping. The *au pair* girl had returned to Denmark when I was thirteen, but again and again all through the years we were teen-agers, my mother would repeat this whenever she had had too much to drink.

"I fixed her *teeth*. For *what*?"

It was only years later that she would complete the thought. But even then, I knew. Coming down early in the morning, I had often found my father sitting in the kitchen with our young housekeeper helping her with her homework for the calculus course she was taking at the local university.

"I've set the table," I would say loudly. "Wheaties, the breakfast of champions. Cheerios. Grape-Nuts."

Every week or two in the year that followed, after our housekeeper Lillian, so thin and desolate, had inexplicably left us, I would compulsively rearrange the silver in the sideboard drawer. My mother had always refused to use plastic holders because she said they were vulgar. So every time the drawer opened, the knives and forks tumbled together, all the daily Danish stainless and my mother's wedding silver. "Mom," I would call. "Come and see. Don't you like what I've done?"

"Yes, yes," she said the first few times. Then, later, "Really, I can't be bothered. Can't you just set the table?"

By this time, my mother had started a residency in dermatology.

She had hired a fat ugly black woman to watch my youngest sister in the afternoon. "She's our *maid*," she told us. "Not a housekeeper."

The maid's dialect was almost impossible to understand, so my mother left notes for her before leaving in the morning. I remember the disparity in their script. My mother's handwriting was large and unformed as a small child's, but from the maid's huge hand came a script beautifully small and angular. "Could you please remember to do the wash?" read the note from my mother. "I can remember, but I can't *do* it without detergent," the maid wrote back.

Even now, twenty-three years later, I find it difficult to imagine the full extent of the betrayal my mother felt. Certainly, I saw its consequences. First, my mother took a "rest" in a psychiatric ward, then she returned to her residency. But once she had finished her residency, she only worked part-time. When she finally began to work full-time—in a psychiatric residency— my father, she said, warned her that this would destroy the marriage. "The children need attention," he said. But by this time, my mother did not care how she tipped the scales; they were weighted to the breaking point anyway.

My father, if asked, would say that he loved the *au pair*. I believe that this was true. *Why?* is the question. He had chosen my mother because she was brilliant and beautiful—and one of only fifteen women in her medical school class. As soon as they married, however, he expected her to stay home and raise four small children without demur. My mother expected the same of herself. She returned to her medical training sporadically and only in reaction to her despair at the marriage and his frequent infidelities. Given the dynamic between them, could she *not* have been betrayed? But, as a child of my father, I must ask myself, why did he choose to betray her in exactly this way?

My father's affair took place in the home, and it symbolized a constellation of attitudes toward the home that is still difficult for me to understand. What values, for example, did he expect to instill in the three daughters who were formed by this experience? Under the circumstances, what values could *she*?

Love, he will say, as if that explained the source of his anger or of his need.

We children loved Lillian, the *au pair*, because in our mother's absence she provided us with the attentions we believed a mother should bestow on us. She stood *for* our mother.

"Not in my *house*," my mother would say years later. Then, touching the true source of her desolation, "I trusted her with my children."

She did worse than that, she trusted him with *herself*.

They both did.

Whatever nurture my father thought he was finding with the young Danish girl, it was not strong enough for him to marry her, to build a life on that basis. My father, consciously or not, exploited the weaknesses of both women, both of each of their weaknesses: the *au pair's* dream of love and my mother's dream of advancement; the *au-pair's* dream of advancement and my mother's dream of love.

Upon further thought, I have again abandoned the idea of a maid.

"This is the bottom line," I say, coming out of the bathroom having checked the water level in the toilet tank. "We are each responsible for our own shit."

"I can live with that," my son says. "But will you make my bed?"

ANNA STEEGMANN

ABSCHIED

Living alone for the first time was glorious. I was grateful for my new life where I could eat pumpernickel bread with plum butter for breakfast, lunch, and dinner, and stay up until 3:00 AM reading Günter Grass. I had escaped the tyranny of my parents and my high school teachers, who although officially denazified, had tortured me with their fascist teaching methods. At the University of Münster most of my professors were Marxists. Gripped by the radical ambiance, I joined a socialist cell. Six weeks into the winter semester we went on strike and boycotted classes.

After a long day of revolutionary activity—inspired by Jerry Rubin and the Yippies, we had crowned a pig president of the University—I came home to crash on the sofa. It was November 21, my forty-seventh day of living away from home. When the Dutch Pirate Radio Veronica started to play Barry McGuire's *Eve of Destruction*, I sang along with enthusiasm. I didn't understand most of the lyrics but *Yeah, my blood's so mad feels like coagulatin', I'm sitting here just contemplatin'* sounded great.

The telephone's harsh ring aborted my reveries. I expected my landlady to complain about the noise. But it was my mother. "Your father is back in hospital. He might not make it this time," she said. I felt her weariness through the telephone cables. She didn't sound sad or anxious, just tired to the bone. "You have to come home right away," she said.

My father had been sick for the past two years. Blown up to 300 pounds, he was responsible for his sorry state by his stubborn insistence on gigantic portions of food high in starch, fat and sugar. As he gave up, everyone else in the family gave up on him also. He wanted to die. It was just a matter of time. We had run out of compassion and waited for the inevitable.

I took the bus directly to the hospital from the Moers train station. I dreaded having to see him at *Krankenhaus Bethanien's* Medical Clinic II, a unit few people left alive. The entrance hall was full of rubber trees and snake plants, the standard decoration for every German institutional building. The receptionist on duty was a chubby rosy cheeked matron with big ruffled curls that made me wonder if she slept with rollers the size of Coke cans. She knew me and handed me the visitor's pass without asking where I was headed. I took the pass, and then walked along the long corridor toward the elevator.

The moment I got off the elevator I was in the grip of unconquerable trepidation. The smell of disinfectant, ubiquitous clinical white and the deathly silence, made my stomach queasy. I sped up as I passed by the nurses' station to avoid the spurious cheerfulness of Sister Hildegard. She might invite me to the evening service in the chapel. I had declined her first offer two month ago: "Thank you so much, but I'm no longer a member of the Church. I signed myself out when I was fourteen." She had given me a stern look as if I had personally offended her and made it her mission to bring me back into the flock.

Sister Hildegard sat behind the desk surrounded by rubber plants. Immersed in her TV guide, she failed to notice me. The door to room 142 was left ajar. Stepping in was a Herculean task. Although I had been visiting on and off for the past two years, it had never gotten any easier. As I peeked in, my father's roommate, Herr Wischnewski, winked at me. He had worked at the Friedrich Heinrich coal mine for forty years and had been diagnosed with black lung disease. The doctors had cut out one of his lungs. He had forced me to listen to his sad tale several times: "They opened me up and discovered cancer. The inoperable, progressive kind. There was nothing they could do, so they just sewed me up again." He was waiting for his Maker to take him home and had already saved enough money for his funeral. The drawer of his nightstand contained a list of all people he wanted invited to the memorial service. Like my father's previous roommates, he too would leave in a coffin. Herr Wischnewski, akin to all the other patients I had encountered, was lonely and bored. The patients lived from visit to visit. In between they watched TV.

I forced a smile, straightened my spine and stepped in. "Good afternoon Herr Wischnewski, how are you today?"

He gave his standard answer. "Ready to call it quits."

"It can't really be all that bad. You look so much better than you did two weeks ago." I tried to humor him. Waiting for death was gloomy enough. I went over to my father's bed, shook his hand and placed a bag of oranges on the metal night stand to his right.

"How are you?" I asked.

"Terrible."

"Why so?"

"Sister Hildegard took my sleeping pills away."

"Have you been collecting them again?"

"Sure. I want to die. But they won't let me."

I gave him the once over. My father was a shell of his former self. The blue and white striped pajama hung loose on him. He must have shed a hundred pounds.

"Do you want an orange? I'll peel it for you." I offered in lieu of having anything better to say.

"Turn on the TV, Channel 2 please," Herr Wischnewski pleaded.

I went over to the TV mounted on the wall. *Der Blaue Bock*, a live broadcast of German folk music from a Frankfurt tavern, started.

"Turn it up," my father and Herr Wischnewski begged in unison.

"Do you want an orange?" I yelled, my voice competing with the rhythmic clapping and the audience's singing along with the theme song.

"You look pale. I'm sure you could use a vitamin boost."

"I told your mother, I wanted waffles. Didn't you bring any?" my father shouted over the music.

I did not approve of my mother's habit of smuggling homemade waffles doused with confectioner's sugar into the hospital. "That stuff is poison for you."

"Your mother doesn't think so. I don't know how she does it, but the waffles are still warm when she gets here."

"I'm not my mother," I reminded him.

"I know, I know," he sighed.

Avoid self righteousness and arguments at any price, I told myself. *No need to be right all the time.*

"Will you take me to the patients' cafeteria after the show?" my father pleaded. "I have a craving for a piece of cake. Some *Herrentorte* would be real nice."

"Take me too. I could use a cigarette. Have not had one in a long time," Herr Wischnewski shouted.

My father knew that I could not lift him out of bed to put him in the wheelchair. He knew I would not let him have any of the sweets that put him into a diabetic coma in the first place. *Both men are dying. Are they truly joking or are they just pretending to have fun?* I thought as I cranked up my father's bed and fluffed up his pillow. Now he had the perfect angle to watch TV. I took a chair and moved it closer to his bed. All three of us were facing the TV. "Let's enjoy the show," I said.

At *The Blue Ram* the proprietress and the head waiter were engaged in a comedy routine. Herr Wischnewski burst out laughing. My father chuckled. I failed to see how anyone could find this funny. The jokes were predictable, the Frankfurt dialect irritating. At home I could be watching Beat Club on Channel One. The Steve Miller Band from California was scheduled to appear. I was curious to check them out. Instead, I was subjected to lame jokes and syrupy melodies. How was it possible for this show to mesmerize twenty million Germans every Saturday afternoon?

I glanced at my watch. I'd have to stay at least another half hour, most likely forty-five minutes. My father and I had nothing to say to each other. Talking was dangerous; most conversations ended in an argument over politics. He would accuse me of being a Bolshevik and I'd accuse him of being a Nazi. Watching TV together was the only safe activity. "It's Billy Mo, Anna," my father yelled. "The fat Negro. Sit down and check him out."

I sat down. Billy Mo, a trumpeter from Trinidad, was a huge star in Germany. A dark-skinned pop-eyed man with an enormous set of white teeth, Billy Mo looked like a caricature of a black man. Always appearing in a Tyrolean costume did not do anything to endear him to me either. Still, I hated it when my father called him a fat Negro. It smacked of racism. How could I be kind to a man who made racist remarks? Herr Wischnewski adored Billy Mo. He clapped along and knew all the words to the song.

A man came from Las Vegas.
He offered me a thousand dollars.
Told me "You're going to be a big star."
None of it was true.

My father, an enormous grin on his face, joined Herr Wischnewski in belting out the refrain. Billy Mo, fat and jolly, waved his plumed Tyrolean hat in the air. It was painful. I picked up one of the magazines my mother must had left on the window sill. She visited every day with treats. Brought her knitting, her crossword puzzles, and reading material.

"Don't read," my father said. "Sit next to me."

I pulled my chair closer.

"Not like that. Sit on the bed."

He had never asked me to sit on the bed. I had never volunteered to do so. Billy Mo finished his song to a thunderous applause. The headwaiter handed him a *Bembel*, an earthenware pitcher decorated with grape vines, a gift every guest received. I sat down on the bed, my upper body stiff like a soldier's. I didn't want to interfere with the IV hookup, but mostly I was afraid to get close to my father's sick man's smell.

After eight-and-a-half torturous minutes, Sister Maria, a nurse-in-training, came to my rescue. She made me get up from the bed to give him his insulin injection. I stood next to the bed. A new act, a brother and sister duo, promising stars in *Volksmusik*, took to the stage. They sang *Schwarzbraun ist die Haselnuss*, a song I remembered from summer camp.

"I'm glad to see you're having a good time, Herr Tersteegen," the young nurse teased him.

"I'd have a much better time if you let me hold on to my sleeping pills, Sister Maria," my father said in his best flirtatious self. "Why won't you let me do away with myself?"

"*Aber* Herr Tersteegen," she protested as if he had made an indecent proposal. "You know that's against the law."

"What about the laws of compassion then? Don't they teach you those in nursing school?" His voice had suddenly lost its playfulness.

The young nurse frowned in exasperation. "I'll be back with your medicines at dinner time."

"Put in an order for pancakes with lots of extra sugar and apple sauce on the side," my father shouted as she left the room.

"Don't forget my beer and *Schweinshaxen*," Herr Wischnewski added.

Sister Maria, half way out the door, gave the men a stern look and said with a voice at once teasing and reproachful: "*Aber bitte, meine Herren.*"

I jumped up from the bed and followed her to the hallway.

"Sister Maria, how is he?"

"Didn't your mother tell you?" she asked.

"I didn't get a chance to speak to her yet. I came straight from the train station," I said.

"That's right. You're studying at the University of Münster, aren't you?"

"Yes I'm a freshman. I've been there almost two months, forty-seven days to be exact."

"Your father is so proud of you."

Proud? My father? That was hard to believe.

"You bet. He brags about you all the time. All the nurses and doctors and most of the patients on the floor know that his oldest child, his only daughter, is the first one in the family to attend university."

This was news to me. During my last visit he had offended me: "Well all right, you made it to the university. But you'll fail. I see that coming. It wouldn't be the first time." The visit had ended in an argument. "Just because I got left back once, you don't have to hold it against me for the rest of my life," I had screamed before storming out the door.

I put Sister Maria's comment on the backburner, to ponder later. Then I asked: "So how is he?"

"He's doing very poorly. We are worried he might not survive the amputation of his leg Monday morning."

"He knows?"

"Yes he does. Pray for him."

"Thanks, Sister Maria."

She rushed off. I dreaded going back in. Should I have mercy and get him a piece of cake from the cafeteria? I decided against mercy. The rising stars of German folk music finished their act. The headwaiter thanked them and handed them their gift jugs. I was mad at my mother. Why hadn't she told me about the amputation? I was no longer a child. I deserved to know the truth. This might be the last time I saw my father alive.

I forced myself to sit on his bed. "Did I miss anything?" I asked.

"It's almost over. Do you want to stay for *Sportschau*? The MSV is playing Köln. It promises to be an exciting match. I made a bet with Herr Wischnewski and I hope to win five Mark."

"No way, Köln will win," Herr Wischnewski butted in. "There's no better soccer team than the 1st FC Köln. Ask your daughter to get us some beer and salt sticks. You can't enjoy a good game without them."

"How true," my father sighed.

Waves of nervousness coupled with fear made it impossible for me to sit still. The impulse to run out of the room took hold of me. To not give in to it, I held on to the side of the bed. It was a crucial moment. Maybe the last time I'd see my father alive. I should say something meaningful, act in a way I wouldn't have to be sorry for the rest of my life, but I couldn't come up with anything.

Zum Blauen Bock was coming to an end. "Did you enjoy the show?"

I asked.

"I just pretend to," my father said.

"You and I are really good at that sort of thing," I surprised myself saying.

"You bet," he agreed.

I looked at him from the corner of my eye. Did I see tears welling up? Was my father getting sentimental or was I just imagining it? I had to leave. Get away from this room. Away from this hospital. My hometown. Get back to Münster and my exciting new life as quickly as possible. I couldn't deal with my father being so emotional. We were enemies after all. He was a Nazi. I was a Socialist. What would happen to my anger and loathing if I had to see my father as a mere human?

"Time to go," I announced. He took my hand and covered it with his enormous farmer's hand. The last time he held my hand, I must have been nine years old. "Stay a little longer," he said while he squeezed my hand.

"I can't," I said and pulled my hand away. Then I rushed out leaving the smell of death and decay behind.

He died Sunday night. Before the amputation of his good leg. All our relatives came to the funeral. Many strangers also. I didn't know he had friends. My mother cried during the sermon. At the grave, a male choir of veterans, their uniforms decorated with war medals, stood at attention, saluted and sang *Ich hatte einen Kameraden*, the traditional lament of the German Armed Forces.

> *In battle he was my comrade*
> *None better I have had*
> *The drum called us to fight*
> *He always on my right*
> *My good comrade*

Everyone was sniveling. I, stoic, like the good soldier my father trained me to be, did not cry.

LYNN HESSE

MURDER: FOOD FOR THOUGHT

Milly woke up from her afternoon snooze with a jerk. Sitting in her favorite lounge chair, she gazed from her living room window at a world out of focus. She rubbed her spectacles on the edge of her cotton blouse and said, "Son, is that you?" Wondering if the mailman had delivered a letter from back home, the Georgia transplant swore the stubborn earth of Missouri clung to the inside of her relatives' envelopes. She stuck her glasses firmly on the bridge of her nose and watched the mailbox. The gravel road radiated heat from the July sun. It seemed to her like the objects slid into a viewfinder. Defined. She decided to walk the rutted dirt driveway after watching *Oprah*. The letter wouldn't be going any place.

A thud came from the back bedroom, her son's room. Was that Joey? No. He had left for town after lunch. The fried grease smell from making bacon gravy clung to Milly's clothes. It was a pleasure to cook for a healthy man who liked to eat.

Holding on to an armrest, she pulled herself out of the chair. Arthritis in her hip joint made the muscle spasm, and she rubbed the spot of pain in a circular motion. It must be critters scratching around in the crawl space she heard. Her husband never had boxed in the foundation thirty years ago because using little more than ingenuity—money always being meager—his enthusiasm waned toward the end of the project. As a consequence the house sat in the middle of twenty-five acres where spiders, snakes, and mice took refuge under the floorboards.

There it was again, a scurrying noise, maybe inside a wall or the chimney.

The stove timer went off.

"Blasted pills. Can't get a thing done for taking meds," she said to the unconcerned air. She shuffled across the room and had passed the hallway on her way to the alcove kitchen before the shadow in the hall registered. "Joseph Eric Sharp, you better answer. You hear me. Enough. A grown man shouldn't play tricks."

The old woman knew her son's undiagnosed hearing problem was a convenient disability. It fluctuated in severity depending on the length of Milly's to-do list and the demands of her whimsical nature. She stuffed a handful of pastel pills in her mouth while using one corner to puff out the words, "Are you typing on that one-eyed monster? Computers. I don't get the fascination."

When Joey didn't answer, she changed the subject. "I know you worried leaving me here with Jason on the loose. Poor Jason." She remembered teaching him Sunday school ages ago at Marvin Methodist. Was he six or seven then? No matter. He was kind of stand-offish with strange parents. They rarely poked their heads out of doors—let alone attended church. He must be thirteen or fourteen now. "Such a shame."

All those days surrounded by loud, rambunctious children. Gone. She counted her blessings and counseled herself: Others were less fortunate. Think of Jason's father. Dead. Decapitated. For the love of Jesus.

What kind of life would Jason have now? An unloved child, grown in hate-filled soil, was a pitiful waste of sweet potential. Unwanted, even worse. She wouldn't judge him.

"Mrs. Sharp, I won't hurt you." The voice spun her around, and off-balance, she grabbed the table and gingerly sat in a kitchen chair. Wheezing and trying to catch her breath, she watched Jason's measured approach.

His dark bangs shielded his eyes, and the four-inch hunting knife in his hand seemed to grow longer as Milly stared at it. "I'm scared, Mrs. Sharp. I did an awful thing."

"I know, Jason…but it will be all right. I'm here." Milly gripped her hands in her lap so hard her knuckles turned white. "God is with us."

He exhaled and collapsed in a chair like a deflating balloon. "I don't know where to go…what to do. I'm tired."

The knife blade lying on the table flashed silver and blue streaks as the florescent lighting above Jason's head flickered. Last week she'd complained about the faulty switch, but Joey, slow like a mule, hadn't fixed it. Milly flinched when Jason moved forward extending his free hand and closed the few feet between them.

Jason withdrew and wiped his hand on his sci-fi T-shirt. "You're afraid of me. I guess I can't blame you." He drummed the table top and studied the family photographs. Pictures on the bookcases, an entertainment center, a low hutch, and coffee tables showed the Sharp clan happy and robust. "I always thought you had a pretty smile. You could be Julia Roberts' grandmother."

He folded the blade blunt side down against his out-stretched leg and slipped it in a front pocket. The crème-colored handle poked above his jean pocket like an extra thumb.

Milly's tongue was glued to the roof of her dry mouth.

Nodding at the family portrait on the wall, he said, "I hope your family knows they're lucky. Some people like me never had a real family. No chance."

Jason's face closed to an unreadable mask.

A shiver of panic ran down Milly's calves. She intended to ask him to give her the knife, but a lump of fear blocked her vocal chords. Thank God, the police had the axe. She prayed the horrible murder scene would vanish from her imagination. She laid her glasses in her lap. Her mind went blank, "Are you hungry?" spilled out. "You look half starved."

"Yes, ma'am. Could I have a scrambled egg? That would be great."

Milly nodded, replacing her glasses.

"You remember you made me breakfast one Sunday morning when your Buick broke down half way to church. Mr. Pauley gave us a lift back to your house. It was raining too, but my lucky day."

He leaned back in the chair and gazed at the stippled ceiling. "The eggs were so good. So yellow...like daffodils cooked in butter, no brown flakes. I'll never forget it. Perfect. Mrs. Sharp." His voice went flat. "He beat me every day of my life."

Milly stood up and tried to straighten her bent spine. "Jason, I'm so sorry. I never...so terribly sorry."

She stroked Jason's shaggy hair and readied herself. "Please. Let me have the knife. It makes me nervous." A tic pulled at her cheek as she smiled. "I want to be able to concentrate on my cooking."

She opened a drawer beside the old refrigerator as the icemaker jarred on and ice cubes avalanched into a bin inside the freezer. "Just put it in the drawer, right here, and I'll whip up these eggs in no time."

She lifted the egg carton from the refrigerator, leaving the door open until Jason, tall and lean, deposited the knife in the drawer and walked back to the table. His shadow seemed to linger over Milly as she cracked the eggs into a red mixing bowl. Bracing her large hips against the counter, she felt his black eyes watching her.

"I've been on the run for days. Broke into Dean Shepard's old place and took some food he left in the pantry. People just up and leave everything. The divorce must have freaked him out."

Milly glanced at him. He was rocking back and forth in the straight back chair with his hands tucked under his armpits.

"I haven't got anything to leave, and I still don't want to go. Mom tried to save me before she died, but her sister wouldn't take me in. Should have run away, escaped, but where would I go." The only sound was Milly scraping the spoon on the pan before he said, "Oh God, I killed my own father."

"Out of ashes comes goodness," Milly said, and folded the napkins into triangles on each plate. After saying grace, she and the young murderer ate in silence.

When Milly asked the boy if he wanted another cup of coffee, he shook his head and studied his hands. "I'm ready, ma'am. Go ahead now. Call the sheriff."

"Jason, look at me." She dug into her apron pocket and pushed a small tin cross across the table. "I won't let them hurt you. I promise."

ALEXANDRINA SERGIO

BABY OF MY BONES

I
Baby of my bones
  and the bones of my mother's mothers
  and the wasting bones of long-gone gray gone-frail mothers
Whose breath rolls out
  to dare the world to harm the baby of our bones.

No place in my being is deep enough to hold you close enough
Baby of my soul
Baby of the soul of my mothers' mothers.
Child of my child.

II
In the time you were mine
  there was just you and me
  in one hour that was all time:
More precious than happiness,
  a gift of forever.

In the time you were mine
I heard the echoing whisper
  of all that was and is and is to be.

I touched your newborn hair still damp
  and brushed to kiss your tight shut baby eyes
  and beheld your wondrous baby fingers.

In the time you were mine
I told you things I knew.

An hour of all time was enough of all time
  because there was just you and me
And somewhere deep in you
 and in me
 lives the hour
 and all that is worth knowing.

III
The hour was gone and you were gone,
Taken to where other voices would hush the night sobs,
Other arms would stretch to draw the breathless,
  tippy first steps,
Other hands would build the loom
 and show you how to weave the tapestry of your life,
 adding their own threads as well,
All but one bright strand,
 the very first
 laid down by just you and me.

IV
At every age
In every place
I see you.

Yesterday you were the beach baby,
 floppy white hat askew,
 crowing with delight at the extravagant legs of a hermit crab.

Tomorrow you will be the dust-streaked Little Leaguer,
 tossing cap to heaven,
 leaping and whooping in the glory of a Home Run.

Today you are the child in the park,
 Plummy cheeks, rapturous glistening eyes, belly laugh scattering to the sky,
  sausage legs kicking and stretching to the sun,
 Swinging with the unfettered joy of the immortal moment.

V
Children's laughter and Mothers' prayer,
With tidal swell and predawn drum and temple bell,
Are one in earth's chant.

Your laughter and my prayer too,
Child of my longing,

Baby of my bones.

I READ OF YOUR DEATH

Young years ago
I refused you.

Now appears something
like an eggshell,
A puzzling thing
broken open,
empty,
its fragile inner skin
dry threads.

The story I read
is that of a stranger
with your name
who journeyed beyond
what I ever knew,
upon whose dying
I discover
a newly barren husk,
part of me
I didn't know was there,
part of me
I couldn't know would break.

SHIREEN CAMPBELL

BENDING TIME

No one can prepare a parent to hear that a child is seriously, perhaps fatally, ill. In mere minutes of diagnosis, time itself may become unstable. Such diagnosis throws present and future into chaos, casts doubt on memories, and threatens to rewrite the past.

April 10th, 2001

"Can't you tell that isn't a space? Are you blind?" I engage both clutch and brake again. The white Lincoln ahead of us has stopped and idled at the halfway point of three entire parking garage floors before turning left to snail upward another level. Now, it sits, the blue-white head of the driver barely visible above the steering wheel as she ponders whether or not to park in a spot clearly covered with yellow stripes.

"Relax, honey. It's only ten till." My husband Jeremy pats my right thigh. I tense my quadriceps and shift my thigh to the left.

"We can't be late. These specialists have tight schedules."

"Shireen, we're on time," Jeremy looks over at me, but keeps his hand on the truck seat, "and we'll be out of here in an hour."

Sixty minutes later, we only wish we were bickering in the Ford F150.

My son Jonathan is struggling as hard as a three-month-old can against the echocardiogram. A technician is attempting to map his heart functions, but Jonathan screams and kicks. The older child being tested in the other half of this small room, divided by a plastic curtain, begins wailing.

"Honey, shh, shh. It's ok." I stroke Jonathan and bend over to hug him on the gurney. Electrode goop smears on my chest as my dress rides up in back: Jeremy quickly pulls down the hem. *Who cares if my butt shows right now?* I furrow my brow at him; he furrows back. Dr. Sherman, the senior pediatric cardiologist we met for the first time today, comes in. He's short—and I mean short, as in five feet, three inches tall—but commanding.

After glancing at the read-out on the technician's machine, he turns to us. "Can't you give him a bottle, quiet him down?"

Jeremy responds: "No, he's breast fed, and we didn't remember to bring one."

"Look at that heart rate! We've got to calm him down." He turns back to the technician, and they confer quietly. Jeremy stiffens. We don't look at each other.

Maybe nursing will help. I force my right breast up out of my neckline, recline sideways on the gurney, and rub the nipple across the baby's lips. Jeremy starts to hold a green striped receiving blanket around me, but gives up. The technician is busy with her probes and machinery anyway. Jonathan latches on and sucks, shutting out the cold and the noise and the strangers who keep touching him. Now, as he settles, the technician begins her measurements.

The echocardiogram screen features greens and blues and reds and yellows. Periodically, the technician freezes a frame and measures the distance between two blobs, then moves her probe on Jonathan's chest. Blue gives way to red gives way to blue again. *Is that what a heart looks like in action? Is what I'm looking at good or bad?*

Over the hills and far away
Teletubbies come to play

I snap toward the noise. A video has begun playing on a TV mounted high in the other child's corner. Purple, lime, yellow, and then a smaller red being spring out of a dome.

Time for teletubbies
Time for teletubbies

Oh, that's what they look like! Now the tubbies are introduced, each waving to the camera. *Which one's supposed to be gay?* I can't understand their speech, but watch anyway. It hurts to look at the video slumped sideways, but Jonathan seems hungry.

Another doctor, twenty years younger and even shorter than Dr. Sherman, enters, and the technician asks him to look at the screen. He smiles and points. "That's good. That's really good. His valve is fine." He turns to us. "Your son has the best possible version of his defect."

Defect. As in defective. Jeremy and I nod as if we understand. We don't.

January 10th, 2001

Jonathan had been born a few days late, but healthy, on January 9th. Early the next morning, around 2:30 a.m., I remember sitting awkwardly on my adjustable bed, gazing at my son. I was supposed to be nursing him, but not really succeeding. I stared at him, tiny, so alert. He gazed back, and I cried and smiled and snuggled him close. We rested in scented semi-dark—roses from Jeremy, a carnation and miniature rose arrangement in a blue baby shoe vase from my in-laws, an open double-decker of Whitman's from a friend. Except for squeaky footsteps and passing med carts, the hall was quiet. *Hi sweetheart... I'm your mommy. Do you know me?* At Lamaze we'd learned that newborns know their mothers' voices immediately, familiar from months of muffled conversations. *Will I be a good mommy? Who will you be?* Jonathan's small face suddenly squinched, mouth opening in silent cry. *Sing a lullaby, quick.* I remembered few. "Rock-a-bye baby?" *No, that's dumb—what's a cradle doing in a tree top? And then it all falls down. Why would anyone sing **that** to a baby?* But he was still squinching. Unable to remember other choices, I rocked him and sang

> Rock-a-bye baby
> In the tree top.
> When the wind blows,
> The cradle will rock.
> When the bough breaks,
> The cradle will fall.
> And down will come baby,
> Cradle and all.

My teary croak should have driven anyone to tears, but Jonathan's face relaxed and his eyes closed. I continued.

Twenty-five minutes later, when a nurse came to check bleeding and give me a welcome pain pill, I was sniffling as I held my sleeping son.

"Are you ok? Have you peed yet? Does this hurt?" Her hand pushed firmly on my deflating balloon of a midsection.

"I'm fine, just stiff. Numb tailbone, but I've gone to the bathroom twice. . . . He's so sweet."

She smiled down at us. "What a pretty little boy."

April 10ᵗʰ, 2001

My pretty boy has finished really sucking, but continues to lip at me. *He's got to be ok. But the doctor said defect. Can't think about it.* I crane back up to the screen.

"All done here." The technician deftly removes electrodes from Jonathan's chest, then wipes the sticky residue off his chest. "You can pull his clothes on and go back to the examining room."

I would rather keep watching the tubbies.

Minutes later, we wait in the small examining room where we started this consultation. I hold Jonathan, now quiet in a red and yellow striped onesie and fleece Pooh pants, in my lap. Jeremy stands, cradling my sweaty, cold right hand, and we stare at the drawing of a heart on the wall. Dr. Sherman enters. He leans against the examining table. He looks at us.

"Some children have heart problems that don't require surgery. Sometimes a minor defect requires no care. Other times it requires only regular observation or perhaps medication." He pauses, then speaks even more deliberately. "Your child, however, has a congenital defect that requires immediate open heart surgery and lifelong medical care."

Jeremy gasps, slumps. My right arm wraps around him tight. Silent sobs are shaking his body.

"What is his defect called?" I ask, my voice too high but clear.

"It's called Truncus Arteriosus." Dr. Sherman shows us a large laminated picture of a healthy heart, then superimposes a sheet with Jonathan's defect on top of it. He talks us through the specific features of Jonathan's condition. Jeremy regains his voice and begins to ask questions. I stare and nod without hearing the answers. I do hear the big message, however. Without surgery, Jonathan would most likely die of congestive heart failure by his first birthday.

Dr. Sherman is still speaking, his tone now lighter. "Usually this defect is diagnosed at birth. I'm amazed that your son is in such good condition for three months old. He's grown well, which is excellent news for the surgeon." (I have since learned that our hearts are the size of our fist. A three-month old baby hand balled up is the size of a golf ball.) "But he is a pale, sweaty baby because his pulmonary system is being increasingly compromised. We need to operate as soon as a suitable homograft can be found and before more damage is done."

As our session finishes, Dr. Sherman gives us an American Heart Association Brochure—*If Your Child Has a Congenital Heart Defect*—and dog-ears the pages on Jonathan's "because it's helpful to have this when explaining it to relatives." We exit through the general waiting room, where beige sofas and coordinated chairs hold the cardio-impaired—balding, white, and gray headed people and their relatives. Jonathan's stroller feels heavy on the thick carpet. No one drives in front of us on the way out of the parking garage, I think.

I manage to finish a call to my mother as Jeremy drives us toward home, but break down in the middle of a call to Jonathan's godfather. Hanging up, I gasp and gulp. Jeremy is inside a pharmacy, filling Jonathan's prescriptions for a diuretic and a heart medication. *How could this be?* Did we miss something earlier? Always sleepy, initially drugged, hormonally wobbly, I remember the routines but few specifics from his early weeks. I was with him almost all the time. On a reduced teaching load, I left Jonathan only to teach a literature seminar at my college on Monday afternoons and hold office hours on Thursdays. We took forty-five minute morning walks through the neighborhood, the baby in a snuggly on my chest, our two dogs straining against their leashes. I sat in a worn recliner and positioned him on my bent legs, facing me. I could read, watch him, doze.

And his pediatrician hadn't noted anything wrong at first. I reported that Jonathan was stuffy at his one-month check-up. This is common for winter babies, so the pediatrician recommended elevating his crib head and using a vaporizer. The first big clue came at Jonathan's two-month check up on March 9th, when Dr. Albers lingered as she listened to his chest.

"I think I hear a murmur. Yup, there it is." She smiled and told me that many people have heart murmurs and it means nothing. "He's fine. I'm sure he'll be able to play sports and everything. But just to be safe, why don't you come back in a month, and I'll listen to it again?"

Jeremy loves gadgets: I do not. But he had convinced me to get a cell phone about mid-way through the pregnancy "so you can call me in case." I acceded, but my subsequent track record—two lost cell phones in a little over three years—suggests resistance. The moment I left City Pediatrics, however, I was dialing his office.

"Hey, Shireen, how was the check up?"

"Bad. . . . Well, I mean, Jonathan's 50th percentile for weight and 75th for height, and he handled his shots fine, that's all good, but Dr. Albers heard a heart murmur. We have to take him back in a month so she can recheck it."

"Did she seem worried?"

"Well, I don't know." I braked hard to avoid rear-ending a dented hatch back that swerved in front of me, then stopped at the red light. "Watch it, you ass . . . jerk!" Since Jonathan's birth, I'd been trying not to swear in traffic.

"Huh?"

"Sorry, somebody just cut in front of us." The light turned green, and I shifted from first to second, tailgating the offender. "Anyway, Dr. Albers didn't seem worried, but then she's not going to scare parents unless she has to. She did say that heart murmurs are common and often don't limit activity." I heard Jeremy typing. He was probably writing code for some web page even as he talked.

"Well, there you go. That's true. I think my mom might have a murmur, or maybe one of my other relatives."

"Jeremy, this is serious. Can't you call your mom and find out?"

He did so that night. She did not have a murmur, but Jeremy asked around and found a number of mutual acquaintances who either had one or knew someone who did.

Should we have pressed for more testing then? Jeremy did some web surfing and reported that heart murmurs in infants are fairly common. We suctioned thick yellow mucus out of his nose sometimes, but elevating the cradle head did ease his night breathing.

Busy with work and learning to balance motherhood and work, I brooded only intermittently about Jonathan's heart murmur until April 9th, the day of his next appointment. Dr. Albers listened intently.

"The murmur's still there . . . and I think it's louder." She pulled down Jonathan's blue fleece shirt—too warm for the weather—and turned to me. "Just to rule out anything serious, Mrs. Campbell, let's check with a specialist. Let me see if I can get you an appointment."

She left the exam room. I held a fussing Jonathan, patting his back in the light, rapid way he liked. He burped, relaxed. A child was shrieking nearby. *A toddler getting shots? At least Jonathan hasn't had any shots today.*

"Good news," Dr. Albers smiled as she re-entered the room. "The Singer Clinic had a cancellation, so I was able to get Jonathan in tomorrow." Slim, blonde, elegant in cream twin set and brown wool trousers, she dated and signed a referral.

"They're great—the best in the area. Again, I don't think anything is seriously wrong, but we'll all feel better when we know more about this little one's heart."

And today, we know. Once home from the clinic, we make and receive endless phone calls and visit with Jeremy's two business partners, who bring us sympathy and a random selection of groceries—pasta, macaroni and cheese, chicken soup. We show them the AHA diagram in *If Your Child has a Congenital Heart Defect.* Jeremy then mentions some on-going projects, and the three of them begin strategizing about how to handle Jeremy's coming absence. After they leave, we cry and hold Jonathan. That evening, Jeremy hunches at the computer, collecting information about truncus arteriosus. Preferring ignorance, I cannot look at what he uncovers.

Instead, I look at Jonathan's baby pictures.

In February, a winter storm had hit our area. Because our street crews don't plow, don't even have plows, any accumulation shuts roads down, and any snowstorm means playtime. In the morning after the storm ended, Jeremy and I bundled Jonathan in a fleece one piece, extra pants, coat, red hat, and mittens, then loaded him in our jog stroller and went to explore the white world. We walked to Monroe Road, a four-lane arterial one block from our house. It was smooth, undriven.

"Whoa." Jeremy slipped a little, but caught himself. A step ahead, I turned to smile, then thudded on the Oakhurst Baptist Church lawn.

"You ok?" Jeremy was trying to hold the stroller, to help me, and to avoid falling himself. Toto, our big black mutt, nosed me.

"Yes, it's soft in the grass." I made a snow angel before getting up. We crept two more cautious blocks down Monroe, then turned right to loop back through our neighborhood. By the Lakeview Apartments pond, ice crisped willows cloaked the large, usually stinky green dumpsters. We asked a man scraping his windshield to take our picture, in which we beam optimistically and Jonathan stares. Snow falls diagonally, upper left to lower right, and loads the glossy green leaves of the large magnolia tree behind us.

My family is big on such snapshots. These record both holidays and more spontaneous moments, such as when my brother Eric danced in the mud. My in-laws tend toward a more formal visual history through framed studio shots of coifed, well-dressed children. Jeremy and I try to bridge the gap. So, one Saturday near the end of March, we took Jonathan to "sit" at a kid's photography store. The adolescent photographer propped him up against various colored bean bags.

"Jonathan . . . Jonathan! Hi sweetie!"

"Little buddy, look at Daddy!"

He stared at the photographer's bright toys, at our goofy faces. What did he see? How far could he see? None of the five poses was great, but we bought two anyway: one a full-length shot that emphasizes his baby body, the other a head shot in which he gazes at the camera, an earnest Gerber baby with red wisped hair and deep brown eyes, skin pale, slightly blue around the bridge of his nose. Until tonight, I hadn't seen that blue.

December 2008

For months after his surgery, I could not remember the three months before Jonathan's diagnosis. The early optimism of new parenthood lost, I worked to regain equilibrium and looked to a future in which Jonathan was our son who just happened to have a heart defect, not our son-with-a-heart-defect. By July of 2002, while hanging his first official portrait next to his infant brother's in the stairwell of a new home, I realized that I no longer saw the blue before I saw his soft face. Time had been reordered again.

Jonathan is about to turn eight. His is a medical success story—a healthy, happy kid with a slim scar on his chest—but denies him or us the closure people want from such stories. For Jonathan lives with a heart that requires periodic work—open chest surgery—in order to function. When kind friends and colleagues ask, in hope, if "it's all corrected now, right? Maybe one more surgery and that's it?", I sense time shifting again from its linear progression. I am thrown back to that moment of diagnosis, back to the moment when present knowledge erased our Before.

I imagine that time normally works for parents in two ways. They experience linearity as their baby becomes a toddler becomes a child becomes a teen. In nostalgic counterbalance to this progression are memories of the surly thirteen-year-old's first steps or first word. For me, the mental move forward and move back work imperfectly. Look forward too much, and I see surgery for Jonathan; look backward, and time stalls around the period of diagnosis. Mostly, I concentrate on the immediate here and now. At present, Jonathan's health is excellent, and we are on a once-yearly status to visit his pediatric cardiologist.

Sometime between age ten and age fourteen, our surgeon has explained, Jonathan will outgrow his graft and need a replacement. After his ninth birthday, I will begin studying my son. *Is he winded too easily? Does he seem tired?* Jeremy will tease me for being paranoid; I will be. Over time, we will perceive that our son is slowing, weakening. His heart will murmur loudly to the naked ear, and we will let ourselves admit that it's time again.

II
SEX, LOVE, DIVORCE
& ALL THAT STUFF

DAVID HARRIS EBENBACH

BEGGING FOR MERCY

Gary is still asleep, Sunday morning, when Elaine comes across the places on his computer. They are bookmarked in his web browser, with innocent names like "Post1" and "Post2," but when she opens one with a dim early-morning curiosity, the room becomes small around her, as though the lamp, the bookcase, the plants on the windowsill, the walls themselves are crowding around her to look over her shoulders for themselves. Even before she sees it, she knows she is going to see something.

Then, on the screen is an image of a man in an undershirt and boxers. He is bound, bent over, a red ball stuffed into his mouth. Over him is a woman in shining black leather, her sharp heel hard against his back. Elaine's own mouth hangs open. Strapped to the groin of the woman is an enormous, arching dildo, also black.

Elaine giggles involuntarily, like a reflex, and then that's washed away. A kind of terror takes over, hums in her. She looks around the room, at the old photograph of her and Gary pulling a canoe out of a lake, at the high school graduation picture of their son, at the racquetball racquet leaning against the wall, at the mini-stereo, at the shelf of exercise and fitness books above the shelf of old medical reference books above twenty-five years of collected issues of *JAMA*. Everything is the same as it was. When she looks back at the screen, that, too, should be what it was, should be just a spreadsheet or the *New York Times* online, the e-mail she'd been checking before getting bored and poking around, but instead it's the image of the man, and of the woman over him. Elaine reaches out and touches the image, for some reason, and then pulls her hand away.

Scrolling down, she sees there are links to "femdom pictures," "male submissive bondage pictures," "pain videos," and even stories—"cuckold humiliation," "tranny domination," "rape." All the length of the page there are flashing thumbnailed images of men being beaten and wounded and pushed to the ground. Women using those dildos on them. She leans forward and squints at all of them. The men are pale and flabby, mostly. Maybe Gary's age, but not as fit. Elaine scrolls to the top again, where it says "Beg for mercy—Get none."

There is a sound from the bedroom down the hall. Elaine, who hasn't even asked Gary if she could use his computer while hers is down, closes the browser window in a flash, her heart pounding. She jumps up, turns and goes down the stairs, needing to put herself in the kitchen, which they have so recently redone. "Elaine?" Gary calls as she rushes down the stairs.

In a few minutes he appears in his bathrobe. He rubs at his matted, mostly gray hair. Elaine can barely look at him. She is busying herself with slicing bread and beating eggs at the large butcher block at the center of the room.

"French toast?" Gary says, yawning. "What's the occasion?"

Elaine laughs as though what he's said is very funny. She can't make herself say anything. She feels that if she looks directly at him, she will find that he is bound and bent over and speaking through a gag. She will see the woman behind him, wanting to fuck him like a man. The eggs froth at her vigorous efforts.

Gary sits heavily in a chair. "Man. I guess I should go bring the paper in. Jesus. I still can't believe that dinner last night." They spent the evening at the Folsoms', the most painfully boring couple they know. All the way home they wondered aloud why they had gone in the first place. She glances at him now, like sneaking a look at the sun, and then her eyes dart away again. He is a terrifying figure to her in this moment. "Are you okay?" he says now.

She shoots another glance. "Just fine," she says. "I'll be right back." And she moves briskly off to the bathroom between the kitchen and the garage. In there, in that windowless place, she stares at herself, her pale self, in the mirror. She touches her pubic bone, tries to imagine what she would look like with one of those long black things arching up off her. She yanks her hand away again, as though in sudden pain.

She finds a way to act normal with him as the day progresses, saying little, relying on the habits and rhythms of more than two decades of marriage. So much of that, Elaine realizes, is a kind of mindlessness. She needs that mindlessness today.

That morning, they drive to a curtains store next to the mall and arrange for some new drapes to be delivered, and then go to the grocery store and to a frame shop, where the painting is waiting for them. They bought the painting on a St. Thomas stopover during a cruise, taken by the fact that it was so bright and tropical, full of oranges and greens. Now it will go in their living room, over the white couch.

Gary is unsure about the frame. "I think it's too dark," he says. It's called beech veneer. "What do you think?"

They're standing right in front of the woman who helped them pick the style, and Elaine feels awkward discussing this in front of her. "I don't know about that," Elaine says. He looks at her with a searching frown. He often sends food back in restaurants, when it is unsatisfactory for one reason or another.

"I was never completely sure about this color," he says, and Elaine watches him looking at the picture, which the framer is holding upright.

"I think that, when you get it home, you'll be able to see it in its proper context," the woman says, a little defensively.

Gary raises his eyes to her, arches an eyebrow. Elaine must have made a mistake about that website. It can't be his.

"What do you really think?" he says to his wife.

"Let's try it out at home," she says. "I think that's a good idea." And the framer smiles. It's a conspiracy of women against Gary.

"Okay," he says, rubbing his chin.

When they get home, they hang it over the white couch, and stare at the picture from different places in the room. Now Elaine thinks that the frame might be too dark. The eye is drawn to the edges.

"I don't know," Gary says. But of course he does know.

Elaine feels a surge of anger. He never said he was unsure about the color *before*. Why didn't he just pick the right color in the first place, if he had a feeling about it, instead of waiting until now to be upset? She doesn't say anything, though, keeps her anger to herself. She keeps picturing that woman on the website, and it keeps her in check.

In the afternoon, Gary watches a game on television and swears at the set, and Elaine makes phone calls. She has work to do on the computer, but hers is still down, and she isn't ready to go back to his study yet.

Later, for dinner, Gary grills chicken outside because the fall is still holding on, the winter at bay for a while longer. He can't stand to miss a grilling opportunity on a mild Sunday. Elaine watches him from the kitchen window. He has spent the afternoon throwing foul language at the television set. In the past, she has heard him raising his voice at telemarketers, at burly contractors who drag their feet. He once stepped *toward* a man who tried to mug them after a show in the city, managed to stand him off. Gary has never left a contract negotiation with less than what he was aiming for. Now he stands out in the cool of the falling evening, stabbing casually at chicken breasts that hiss on the grill, talking into the cell phone in his left hand. It seems clear that there is some mistake about the website. It can't be his. Yet it must be his.

"You've been strange all day," he says when they sit down to eat. He frowns as he says this. "What's going on?"

"Nothing," she says, chewing. The chicken is slightly overcooked on the outside.

"I really don't like it when you're like this," he says.

She stops chewing. Elaine has never been *like this*. It would be impossible for her to have been like *this* ever before. "I don't know what you're talking about," she says.

"You've been mooning around all day."

"Don't be a jerk," Elaine snaps, and his eyes flare up, fill with emotion. But is it indignation, or something else? The unknowing makes her look back at her plate.

At night, she watches him as he sleeps. As she has observed before, he goes through phases; for a long time he will be perfectly still, his set face almost grim, and then with a kind of violence he will suddenly heave himself up and take a new position in the bed. He has always won their nightly wars for the covers.

Eventually she pulls herself out of bed and walks down the hall to his study. The computer is still on, though sleeping. She wakes it up and, sitting in the dark, opens one bookmarked website after another. Each one is nearly the same, with the same kinds of pictures, the same kinds of words. And now the shock is less, and the terror is quieter, but in their place is a heavy kind of dread and sadness.

Elaine tries to remember the last time they had sex. On this site, even with all the cruelty, still there is the fact of these women touching these men, their nudity, maybe even their naked courage. She thinks back to a time. Nighttime, dark. It was cold in the bedroom, but that could easily have been air conditioning. She remembers that there was a kind of white noise in the room that could have been the air conditioning. She was cold as he kissed her legs. Very soon he was inside her, strong enough to be up on the flat of his hands, and through the darkness she stared at him then as he moved with his face taut, his eyes closed. She had liked the kissing of her legs, only wished it had been warmer for that part. With the white noise and the temperature and the lack of light, the room could have been alone somewhere in space.

She touches her pubic bone again, feels the stiffness of her pubic hair through her pajama bottoms, and then she goes inside. Those hairs, at least, are not gray. She feels how her vagina is closed. She is looking at these pictures and cannot begin to be aroused. It's like her vagina is a mouth that refuses to open.

Elaine gets up and goes downstairs. It seems like a time for a strong drink. She leaves the lights off in the kitchen, can see well enough to mix herself a vodka and orange juice, to finish it, and to mix herself another.

"Mistress Elaine," she says.

She walks to the living room, where it is too dark to see that the frame of the new picture is dark.

She remembers the way Gary haggled on the price of the picture itself, really got it down, but afterward he still felt cheated.

"We should have paid less," he said over dinner, with some bitterness, in a way glaring at Elaine. "We were suckers."

She finishes her drink and goes back upstairs. In the study she gets the racquet, still in its rubbery sheath, and then she walks to the bedroom to stand over Gary as he sleeps.

"You worm," she says, quoting.

She brings the covered racquet down on the covered shape of his body. Maybe it isn't very hard, but he wakes up.

"What—?" Gary says, jerking partway upright.

"Beg for mercy," Elaine says, and she swings the racquet hard. He is protesting, sputtering, churning in the bed, and with her right arm she is bringing the racquet down on him as hard as she can. The room is raging with their movements. At the same time, her left hand is under the waistband of her pajamas, her fingers looking for answers. In the fury of this scene, is the mouth of her vagina going to stay closed? Or does it have something to say about all this?

EBONI HOGAN

GIRL #1514

My father always told me,
"No matter what you choose to do with this life,
make sure you are the best at it."

It took me 3 years of NYU theatre training
at $45,000 a pop to get where I am.
Naomi. Girl #1514.
I am not a phone sex operator.
I am a fantasy conversation specialist.

This is not for the faint of heart.

This is for the wilted women
who sit lined up in cubicles
like vegetable stands.
The bruised fruit,
irate lesbians,
the daughters of incest,
bodies in all stages of bloat and decay.
On the line, they are California blond, tits for days,
with a tongue so eager to please.

They are brick skinned and unimpressed.
Commune in break rooms to compare notes on the latest sucker
to blow his wife's paycheck on a lil' audio suck-and-blow.
Mr. I'm-Not-Gay-I-Just-Have-This-One-Fantasy.
Darth Vadar, who calls just to breathe heavy.
Clint from Arkansas who likes midgets and amputees,
and the one we call "Noose" who fakes his own death every time
because the sound of a young woman crying
gets him off.

My father didn't raise me like this,
but Brooklyn's been babysitting
and she doesn't provide much warmth in the winter months.

If you can't understand not eating for two days
because you had to pay for text books,
shoplifting tampons from Walgreens
and stealing toilet paper from Starbucks—
humiliation is not listening to 25 men a day jerk off;
humiliation is having to pawn family heirlooms
so that the rent check won't bounce again—

If you can't understand *that*
than *this*
is not for you.

This is for the hand-me-down women who call in anonymous tips
when one of their own ends up in a suitcase under a bridge in the Bronx.
Make sure her son receives her final check
and her boyfriend does time for his crime.

I just thought you might like to know the truth.

My name is Eboni.
I have a severely distorted sense of self worth.
I'm working in it.
I do this while watching the Tyra Banks show on mute,
eating Cheetos and painting my toenails.
I don't do this because any part of it turns me on.

I just can't hold a job for longer than three months
because I'd rather stand mouth to mouth with a mic
than fight check to check any day.

When I love,
I love like a brick through a window
without any regard for who might be sleeping inside.
I speak sometimes when I should be listening
but when I'm listening,
I hear *everything*.

And that's what makes me sexy.
And that's what made me good at that shit.
The best.
And that's all my father
ever asked for
out of me,
anyway.

DANSE SAUVAGE

Since I personified the savage onstage, I tried
to be as civilized as possible in my daily life.
—Josephine Baker

Take a lesson from Josephine.
The way she rolls her eyes
like a possessed voodoo priestess.
All teeth and ass,
spinning and winding
like someone slipped Spanish Fly
between those coltish legs.
Woman never set foot on African soil
but moved like her blood was on fire,
like jungle vines choked her spine.
France licked her off their fingers
and begged for more.
More chocolate truffle shuffle,
More bon-bon burlesque.
You could learn a trick or two from Madame Josephine.

Because you don't sound like the black girl I called here for.

Can't hear the pork belly sizzling in the skillet,
Grease popping on swinging breasts,
Hot comb cracking the code on nigganaps—

Moan for me.
Moan like a negro spiritual,
like your eye was on the sparrow,
like Texas back roads caught in the throat,
like you been eating gravel by the fistfuls since birth.

Can I call you "Jasper?"

Mark the spot where there was nothing but head left,
but I hear black girls don't go down
so you gonna have to get down,
get down on some Princess Tam Tam,
Zulu Lulu fat back shit.

Let me call you "Auntie."

I like them black as watermelon seeds,
hips wide enough for the birth of a nation,
teeth white and straight as klansmen in yearbook photos.
Got no time for a tragic mulatto.
Puts a damper on the festivities.

It's not hard.
Follow the leader.
Halle Berry rode Billie Bob something vicious
and he bought her a tub of ice cream
and named a rest stop after her.

Shuffle along.

Superhead booty-clapped her way to a book deal
and child services still took her son.

Drop it like it's hot.

Josephine turned water to malt liquor
And fed the multitudes with the fruit of her skirt.
But that was before they sold banana clad replicas
to the children of Paris,
called it idol worship.

I heard your pussy is just God's way of saying,
"Muthafucka, what!"
That you are breasts, thighs,
drumsticks, gizzards,
beer-battered.
Lips big enough
to suck Europe
out of Africa.
That you were fat,
ugly as a knot
but still managed to be Willie Lynch's wet dream.
That you fancy yourself complicated
but turned out to be easy.

And you damn sure don't sound black to me.
For 45 cents a minute,
Assatta Shakur better be on the other end of this line
wearing nothing but pancake syrup and a smile.

Let me hear you moan for me, baby.
Like the red Mississippi,
Like toes scraping across
the top of dirt, just a-swingin'.
And we will call you "Jezebel."
We will call you "Hester Prynne."
We will call you "Josephine."
And you can have my 45 cents
every minute for the rest
of your life.

BLACK-EYED SUSAN

These
Black-Eyed Susans,
blooming under bridges
and beside creek beds,
whirl-wound in the spoil and
stink of the East River,
lids peeled back in revelation,
will always be too beautiful,
too difficult to look at
without cringing,
too dangerous,
for this world.

So
the people will read a wisdom tooth,
a hipbone stretched like a wet bow.
The fluorescent arrows will illuminate the unmarked grave,
but they will not know how to tend to you
without snapping you at the torso.

But it is said that Black-Eyed Susans forgive neglect.

They will peel your wings sticky
from this strange cocoon—
a lone suitcase placed roadside
on the Hudson River Parkway.

When a woman's body is found on the road,
the rubber neckers will never know
that she had a long standing feud
with the coffee machine in the break room
and hated the morning shift because men tend to be quick to the punch-
line
when they're ducking the boss in the men's room.

How's a girl supposed to feed her baby
with men clocking 30 seconds,
not even a thank you?

You will never know how many
would see your charcoal visage on the local news.
The sketch did the splendor
of your blackberry mouth no justice
but it was still unmistakable.

Dial the number on the screen,
tell the nice lady on the other end
that yes,
this one,
I know her.

No, I don't know her real name.

This made it hard to
google-you, cnn-you, new york times-you,
hoping to be told that not all of you was in that tiny parcel,
but it was and somehow this seems all the more vicious.
The certain packing peanut crunch
as you were folded like honeymoon lingerie
into a suitcase barely large enough for a weekend getaway.

When we empty the contents of your locker,
we return to your family only the things they need to know.
You will always be too dangerous to handle with
open palms
and closed minds;
will be quick to sketch you another fast life pitched from the fast lane.
Some man's good will donation, this city's detritus,
another train-crash-trick-ho-what's-her-name
who got what her paycheck bargained for
in the end.
We make trash like this useful.
We create compost heaps to cope
with the things we cannot preserve,
pristine.

No matter who you were,
you did not deserve to end up there.
Your disemboweled locker
spilling roses and unopened cards,
a cross heavy with lilies and candle wax,
the evidence that you were holy,
will remain holy
and we will bloom
in the wake of your
shifting shadow.

VALENTINE

I have a habit of being too honest with you.
Details of me become she
so I tell you that the man
I loosely refer to as my boyfriend
would sooner give me his kidney than a Hallmark card.
Two February 14ths have taught me not to take this personally.

You were born with the gait of a dinosaur fossil.
Palsy padlocked muscles in a pose
that does not easily lend itself to lovemaking.
Your only lovers have been
breezes, voices,
and a visiting nurse
who took your virginity in one calloused hand
as mechanical as if she were changing a catheter.

If I were your Valentine, you would sing me to Sicily
where we could tiptoe across kisses at the top of the Eiffel Tower.

I tell you that the Eiffel Tower is in Paris.

To kiss me anywhere,
or nowhere at all,
in a space that does not exist,
is enough.

I am sorry that this girl could not be real for you,
though she has real-girl fears and fades like perfume on collarbone.
I'm sorry that you continued to search for her,
refused all other options of redheads, horny housewives

and barely legal's to be loyal to her,
even after she changed her schedule so that she wouldn't have to say
"I love you, too" anymore.
Words that mean "thank you"
or "same time, same place,"
pass like the 1st of the month,
bounce like checks.
Words she   and   I
can barely afford to spare
for the man we loosely refer to.

You have to go now.
Time for your medication.
By now I know the sound of the alarm
your mother sets so you don't forget.

This much is true.

Sometimes I need you,
more than you need me.

FRANK SALVIDIO

MÉNAGE À TROIS

1. *HER FOOL*

A fool, I loved you at first sight, although
I knew you terminally married from
The start to one I must admire, one who
Feared not that anyone could take you from
His side. And still I fashion my rough rhymes
And wait upon you patiently when he
Is not at hand, to celebrate past times
I knew you were doomed and present days I see
Must end. Why do I linger at the last
To contemplate my borrowed life with you—
Still married to a half-forbidden past
That was as false to me as I was true?
There is no other course that I can choose,
Because, in some sad way, you are my Muse.

2. *FALSE AND FAIR*

O False and Fair: false to him, false to me,
Betrothed to both—to one in law, in mind
The other, none in heart. We are three
Who live as two, as you are so inclined
To us—vain men who weary ourselves out
To serve you, each to share you in his turn
As you determine—keeping both in doubt
To whom, or when or if you will return.
And so you trade us, with your distant smile,
And think, perhaps, that you are true to each
One on his turn, content with both, the while
We struggle for a heart no heart can reach.
And thus the hasting years have hurried by,
And still we serve you, and do not know why.

3. *CANTO V*

You said, "If Dante has his way, I will
Be in the storming winds of Canto V—
Eternally deprived, wild voices shrill
With fear around me—dead, yet still alive
In unfulfilled desire, regret, and pain
Of longing, tormented by the sight
Of what can never be for me again,"
Then asked if I would share your endless night.
Alas! There is no need for me to die
To know that pain. I see you close at hand
Yet unattainable, and know that I
Have been condemned not by the dread command
Of his avenging God, but you: there is
No further need to die to suffer this.

ENGLISH 379 REVISITED

Not openly, as others loved, loved we,
Lovers by night who dissembled by day,
Were eager to debate a simile
Or parse a metaphor, but balked to say
A word in harmless badinage, nor dared
To tease or touch, or even be alone,
Till candled night enclosed us—bodies bared,
Our books aside, all inhibitions flown:
Now, though no more the lovers that we were,
Dissemblers still are we: in company
Convivial and bright, smiling we share
Our moment, touch and part, lest any see
That had you had less conscience, I more will,
We had these many years been lovers still.

CONFESSIONAL

I must confess to have a felon's hand,
By art or stealth to steal possession back
From you, although past passion now when bland
Desire supplants excess and hope the rack
Of fervency. And so I play the friend
To secretly seduce your pledge away
And gratify a futile lust whose end
Cannot be worth the friendship I betray.
How vain it is, how past performance base,
That I attempt what I cannot complete,
Who seek to occupy a former place
And force myself to an assured defeat.
Thus serpentine, deceitful, perjured, lewd,
I slide this course that cannot come to good.

KATHARYN HOWD MACHAN

IN THE PRODUCE AISLE

"I don't know anyone else
who's got a baby"—plaintive
voice across clean cushy stacks

of napkins, tissues, sandwich bags.
And here you are, a full
forty-five, your silver shining

cart fat with clean lettuce, beets.
Leaning to reach for red-ripe
tomatoes, you hear astonished

other words in another voice
and twenty years disappear like a meal
cooked for a dozen on Sunday:

florescent tubes turn to trade-wind sun,
conch chowder replaces radicchio,
and there you are, meeting

sin again, his eyes above a lone
thin basket, his warm tanned hands
poised to pick a perfect plum.

FORGOTTEN

like the watch you bought
when your husband wasn't looking,
the one studded with tiny crystals
pink as a Chautauqua dawn
when you wore white down to your feet
bare to the dew of a century's grass

you danced through in holy Palestine
recreated in pale miniature, the lake
where discarded gods took shape
as ducks and frogs and herons and loons
and you held the sky in both your hands—
one for old moon, one for new sun—

and the young man you would never touch,
his shoulders sure, his eyes a story,
threw a stone into the water,
the clear stone you had given him
the time he played your father's music
and you stood there dying like stars.

I REMEMBER WHEN YOU TOLD ME

I was a crocodile, submerged
and waiting for my prey: you,

hapless husband merely trying
to be lovable, to be good. You

said my silver tears were false
and that you knew my heart

was ready to kill anything
unlucky enough to wander:

lunge, strike, drown. You
spoke so certainly, so sure

my open mouth was toothy proof
that you were right, so justified

in straying from our riverbank,
in tasting other tender flesh.

JACKET

It's hung in six of my
closets so far, sometimes
wrapped in dry cleaner's plastic,
sometimes just draped
with the glitter scarf
I wore with him in Lasalle.

Cut to the waist, long sleeves,
a zipper underneath metal
snaps, soft raspberry lining
his mother sure-stitched in.
Even before he made it
mine, it gleamed with years
of steady use, meant to
survive through bend and carry,
winter's rain in Marseilles.

It fits me, but I'll never
wear it, though the reek
of his smoking is gone.
I'm saving it—like
a poem, a crushed flower—
this history
of dark brown leather
with strong curving arms,
for the daughter who followed
after our love, after
the night his fist began
my flight forever from France.

LEMOYNE'S SUNFLOWER

Thirty years ago she traveled
to the south of France alone,
only a bag of purple cloth
for shoes, good dancing slippers.
Midnight in the small hotel,
green-shuttered window opened wide,
she watched the moon reveal its face,
then hide again in high-swept clouds
that disappeared by dawn. Aloof
except when music called, she
ate good bread, drank simple wine,
and one moment at a morning market
bought a brooch of shining petals
on a long thin perfect stem.
I might have guessed this had a story
the new owner says with a nod.
But she doesn't know
about the lavender, long warm purple
filling his arms, the man who offered
his small stone house and fields of flowers,
golden crowns on sturdy stalks
that faced the light of each new day
she tentatively lingered.

MARIA NAZOS

LOVE POEM TO A TREE

After he and I stayed too late at a party between parties, I said I was through
with the fighting, for there are too many fights

in this world. Say it to the tree, he said. The tree's shadow quivered in the
window like an orgasm in the dark, and his hair was wild

nighttime vines, and I said to the tree, "I want to love you," and he asked
me to say it again, and so I said, "I want to love you,"

which I thought the same as telling him, because everything is connected.
But then he went back to Iowa. And I feel the empty

hiss between my shoulders. How difficult to speak to a world whose beauty
reflects blank loss: from the breakwaters, to the sand dunes,

to every face, wanting them to tell me he'd be back from the gold-choked
cornfields. But none of it replied. The world seemed a hollow

canyon without echo I'd call into for him. Until he's back. Present in
everything. Even that tree: now I can speak to you again—

I hate this earth for burying you standing up. Demand to know why. And
so the glittering dunes refuse to answer.

And so the deserted lobster pots on the docks refuse to answer, and the fishermen with skin like old boxing gloves I've searched, hoping to find

yours underneath, refuse to answer. I keep saying, "I want to love you." But words are impossible to say to the one

who was never here. And so I kept saying, "I want to love you." Until I came to love this strange world. With or without you in it.

THE FIRST PERSON

I've been the man who has fucked four times a day, you said, struggling to get
your pants back on like a better-fitting skin.

And I've been that woman, I wanted to say. Though that woman seems
faraway as the *I* was from the *you,* until I'm only sure it's possible to escape

not through your skin, but by shifting focus from the first person to third,
then back to gain perspective, like a camera lens

zooming in and out. Like an eye pupil exposed to dark, then light, then
dark—Rilke said metaphysical. I call it plain goddamned human.

This woman and the man—because perspective has changed—are walking
the blond dunes. She's afraid to graze his hand.

They've found a tiny puddle. Upon further examining, the tiny puddle is
filled with fish the color of the sand dunes and why,

she's thinking are those flecks of rainbows in the water, why do we try to
slip out of our bodies with this drunkenness, sobriety, happiness,

melancholy, with this escape to the world's edge, and into someone else's
skin? Why this emphasis on time when it doesn't exist?

By now, the water has expanded and the woman's no longer sitting before
the puddle, but in it, and the pool of water

formed a tail, and more of the strange, muted fish shot through the tail like tadpoles through the tail of a much darker, bigger tadpole,

and darting under the glittering flecks of sand when they saw the man and woman's shadows—there were dead horseshoe crabs the color of coral.

Then they realized it wasn't a puddle, but the ocean expelling itself into the dunes. That the pools would grow

deeper and wider and more frequent. Pretty soon, there would be water everywhere, which makes sense, because we are water

anyway, aren't we, that is one thing we all are, which is what united us. Which is why I can slip back into the first

person, the first person, and the trickle of water grew louder and I was still afraid to touch you, afraid of the old way: my anger, the dead

crabs, the people we were who were not us, not us, as much as who we were about to become—the way an ocean will soon separate

us, and while the rainbows danced, and you made concentric circles in the sand which I pressed my head against. Until a shining

cord hung from my belly: a necklace I had always owned but you were too transparent to see in the right light.

WENDY BROWN-BÁEZ

MY GREEN CARD MARRIAGE

When I think back to the months immediately after Michael's death, my emotions seem raw, brutal, vivid, disorienting. There was the grief of his passing and missing his presence, despite the last years of depression that had settled like a grey pall over our lives. When I met Michael, he was full of vitality, charisma, and enthusiasm. He was warm and gregarious in ways I longed to be but found I could not. I didn't know how to greet people (kissing the cheek) and I didn't know how to make people feel comfortable. Michael's humor was irreverent, honest, self-deprecating, and arrogant all rolled up together. It made people instantly bond with him: students in a psycho-drama class, workshop attendees learning to pray to the beat of a drum, strangers at a highway cantina in Mexico, stalled motorcyclists along an arroyo in New Mexico, dancers in a club, hikers along the river. He never failed to make a new friend wherever he traveled, offering espresso he cooked up on a one burner propane stove, sips of mescal carried in a plastic jug in the trunk of the SUV, tokes from a glass pipe bought from a street vendor in some small desert town. Later, he might bring home people he had met in a bar at two in the morning when I had to awaken at 5 to get to work and I found his warm-hearted gregariousness less amusing. Later, I would take the mantel of his spirit upon me deliberately, approaching strangers to talk despite the clench in my stomach of shyness, dancing alone no matter what others thought, willing to make a fool of myself, crying in public, offering kisses when introduced to strangers.

There was also the grief of the relationship, the memories of our ecstatic falling in love, when we slept the night through with our arms around each other, when affectionate tenderness wove through our days, when we stayed awake late pillowed against each other, laughing, reveling, telling stories, complaining at how others were so straight minded and didn't understand. All spiraled downward. I became the care-giver, he the needy child; I the therapist paid to listen in the coin of a home provided for me; he the patient who had to dredge the same silt of his past over and over again without solution. Michael had plans for suicide. As thoughtfully as a person who is slowly leaving mental stability for the wild imagination of insanity can, he executed his plan to exit the torment that he had suffered from for years.

And of course there was the grief of the future, the relationship we would never have, the golden years I had hoped we would spend together, the concept of family and community and comfort that would keep us warm, keep us safe, keep us protected from loneliness and heart-ache. I finally had a companion. And then as his sickness took over his behavior and words, I was more alone than I had ever imagined.

Our closest friends knew a touch of what was happening, but the most outlandish of his behaviors he reserved for the confines of our condo, the wee hours of the morning, the whispers next to me at daybreak when he held me tightly and asked me not to leave him, when he shook with panic at the thought of getting out of bed. I could not even find words to express a slow state of despair, fear, and inevitability that was overtaking me. I did not want to see Michael institutionalized, I didn't care if he told us that he was happy those months he spent in a mental institution after his first suicide attempt in college.

I often thought that if his parents had responded then, if they had had the wisdom to demand that he get help, be evaluated, if they hadn't thrown up their hands at their wild, intractable, quicksilver, vivacious, but irresponsible child, if they hadn't chalked it up to culture shock and personality flaw and genetic make up, perhaps Michael might have received the help he desperately needed. And felt the love he craved, the assurance that his mother cared enough to travel from Italy to visit him in the hospital. His roommate had returned unexpectedly after planning a week-end away to find Michael stretched out on the bed with a stomach full of pills and Michael said he would never forgive him for saving his life.

Because of meeting Roger, I had gone into therapy. Roger was a gay Hispanic artist living with HIV. His urgency to not only live but to do something worthwhile for the community with his talent stood out in sharp contrast to Michael's constant moaning and complaining, self-centered analysis of his own problems, a spoiled rich kid mentality that he could not shake off. Michael didn't have to work for a living. Roger craved work, his art, his gymnastic classes, his love of children, to negate the fear tiding in the back of his throat that he might not have long to live. He made every second count, each minute a tribute to the creative muse, each encounter precious and deep. I met Roger during a week-end workshop and it was as though I woke up out of a long sleep. Did I have the right to throw my life away? Michael didn't want to live and I was spending all of my time trying to convince him otherwise. Why? What was I doing?

I believe it was my Angels who got me out of the house to house sit for a mutual friend of ours so Michael could wrestle with his demons. He lost the will to go on. But I am convinced he took his life in a courageous decision not to burden me any longer. He didn't want to live in a mental institution. That might have been amusing for a couple of weeks but Michael craved freedom. He would tell me that he didn't know where he was headed until he got into the car. Then, inspiration would take him down new highways, to new towns in the desert, to visit old friends where he was received as a prodigal son, to cross the border where he could lose himself in drink and song.

It was the information that he had purchased a gun and hidden it from me for two years that alerted my therapist and unnerved me. I couldn't live in the apartment knowing a gun was there, somewhere. Despite all of the times I had cleaned out his junk, the pile of old glasses frames, the calendars of years past, the broken bits of flea market *recuerdos* from Italy and Mexico, I had never seen a gun. There were not that many storage places. Did he keep it in the car, under the camping equipment? Did he periodically bring it into the house and store it under the bed? I had to go and circumstances evolved to push me out the door. I would not be the one to find his body. And for that, I am eternally grateful.

When I first met Alejandro, I was in this altered state. The veil between worlds was torn and my emotions careened between relief and sorrow, reconnection to myself and recognition that my heart was torn into pieces. I met Alejandro at Roger's booth at the Espanola Art Festival. Roger had already confided in me about their relationship, that Alejandro was a sophisticated, elegant art dealer from Mexico City, that their relationship was intense and "*peligroso,*" dangerous. Later I would understand that falling in love with Alejandro was like a bungee jump, like bursting into flame. At the moment when Roger introduced us, the desert skies were hot and dusty. Alejandro was wearing sunglasses and Roger asked him to take them off so I could see his deep dark eyes. He whipped off the sunglasses and I reached up a hand and caressed his cheek. This was a gesture so unlike me, so out of character. With Roger I felt safe enough to cry on his shoulder, let him hold my hand while I choked out a confusion of emotions. Many of our mutual friends had hugged me during the memorial service, but to reach out to stroke someone's cheek whom I had just met was an instinctual reaction that only later I would understand as a form of recognition. "Oh, so you have come back to me," was the meaning of that gesture. That night, I had a dream that Roger asked me to marry Alejandro in order for him to get his green card. But I didn't see him again for nine months. Despite several invitations I made to both of them to come for dinner or to escort me out to celebrate special occasions, we were unable to meet again until they had broken up and I was moving on to my own creative projects.

I was creating a bilingual poetry performance and looking for Spanish speakers to participate. With some poems, I wanted my voice and the Spanish to interweave back and forth, stanza by stanza. With other poems, I needed a background of voices, enacting people in the *mercado,* for example. My close friend Victoria, the woman for whom I had been house-sitting when Michael died, taught languages and had agreed to be the female ensemble member. When I emailed Alejandro and mentioned that I wanted to invite him to a poetry performance that winter, he emailed back that he was in Mexico and was sorry to miss it, he loved poetry. So I asked him if he would like to be in my presentation and he said yes, he would be back in Santa Fe by spring.

He sent me the link to his website and I opened it to find his portrait. He was extraordinarily handsome, dark, with a confident smile that I would learn could sell ice to an Eskimo. I would also learn that he was an incorrigible flirt. I knew that Michael had been my true love and doubted that I would ever love anyone with that intensity again. Nevertheless, I showed the website to my girlfriend and announced: "That's my new boyfriend." Her response was "Oh la la!" Oh la la! indeed. Later he would tell me that when he received the email, he didn't remember exactly who I was but doing poetry together sounded interesting. "When I came to your apartment and we met in person, it felt as though we had known each other forever," he later told me.

Alejandro made each rehearsal an event. We would have dinner, drink tequila, act out our parts with lots of horsing around. He was gay, and he would greet us, male and female, with kisses on our lips, sweep us off our feet into his lap, and tease us with sexual innuendoes. It was so much fun, we barely could remember our lines, but the performance did happen. His current boyfriend arrived from Mexico in time to help create the stage setting. A long table was covered in a colorful Mexican woven table cloth, a cut paper panel of the Virgin de Guadalupe adorned the center, and *velas* ran along the edge. After each poem, whoever was on stage lit *velas* and, after the last poem, the altar was dedicated to the women who had disappeared in Juarez. It was Alejandro's birthday and I gave him the flaming red-tipped golden roses that had been on the altar, emphasizing "flaming" when I told him they were for him. Alejandro and I egged each other on to be flamboyant and outrageous. He was good medicine for my grieving heart to emerge as a performance poet. What a time we had!

It was just the beginning of our friendship. I knew he worried about his immigration status and that it was inevitable that he would ask me to marry him. One day I gave him the key to my apartment so he could come and go and use the computer or just have a place to chill. He also informed me that he was HIV positive.

When he finally called to ask if I would marry him, I hesitated for just a second. "What, do you want a church wedding?" he joked. I laughed. "Maybe."

I knew I was in love with him and I would do anything to take care of him and protect him. He was receiving medical care at the local clinic and they had told him that as their funds were being cut, he had to work towards his green card and the best way to do that was to get married.

Later, he would ask me in front of his counselor, "You married me to help me out because we're friends, right?"

"No," I replied, "I married you because I love you."

He thought I wanted him to become my real husband, that I thought I might change him to go straight, that I wanted a complete relationship. I never could explain to him that I loved him as the man in my life but I understood that we were sexually incompatible. I had lived outside of the box for years. I now had a marriage that was outside of the box, but it was still a marriage. I often wondered if Michael had had a hand in bringing us together. It was companionship that I was missing most of all.

I will never forget our wedding, a fine warm October afternoon on the lawn of the bed and breakfast across from the courthouse. Victoria and his boyfriend served as witnesses and I called a friend to take photos for the immigration interview. I wore a lace blouse and black skirt and Victoria Secret underwear. He wore a green jacket and a tie of a Gauguin painting of bare breasted women in Tahiti. He slipped a ring on my finger that I had bought for six dollars, a simple silver ring with a malachite stone, and I slipped on his finger a silver band that he had brought back from Mexico. When the judge said to repeat "Til death do you part," a shiver went through me and I realized that I was taking a vow I meant to keep. We might never sleep in the same bed. But we were intertwining our lives in a way that was irreversible and permanent. Michael may have been my true love but we never took a vow to honor our commitment to each other. I believed the vows Alejandro and I took. For better or for worse. I just didn't believe it meant I had to stay with him no matter the cost. After a while, he had to return to Mexico, the HIV status more than we could afford to pay an immigration lawyer to overcome, where I visit as often as I can, although not as often as I like. When we tell people we are husband and wife, they are startled, disbelieving, but finally, they like it, they approve. We provide a counter-balance in some indefinable way. I travel in Mexico as a married woman. I like the sense of security, of identity it gives me. A new identity. Alejandro's wife. Or a secret identity, my gay husband. We love each other, of that I am sure. We might have lovers but no one else can take our places. And when we are able to be companions, it is a blessing and a joy. Yes, we have fought, kissed and made up. Yes, we have been cruel and jealous and stubborn. Yes, we have comforted and given loving support and guidance. Yes, we are a married couple, just not the kind you expect. I am hopeful that as time goes on, we will find more ways to give and to receive, more ways to stretch beyond the box, more ways to perfect the meaning of friendship and grace.

III
REINVENTION

NICHOLAS SAMARAS

THE CULTURE OF MOVING

Yes, I had a childhood I was kidnapped from.
Yes, I longed for home. There were beds, but they
never became familiar. I grew adept at assuming
other people's accents. I was an FM Radio
inflection that said, "Hi, I'm from nowhere."
People never understood why my presentation
didn't fit my biography. Though I lived in exile
from my life, all I ever wanted was to be sincere.
So, I held what was perishable, and cherished it.
I held memory and imagination. I reflected
the land I was living on until the world grew
expansive, until my country became possibility.
In the weft of the world, I learned to sleep with grace.
Because I was no country, I was every country.

TWINNING THE KIDNAPPED CHILD

Because there are always two of us
Because there is my life before

and my life after
Because every thought is sense

of who I was and who I am
Because memory is not trusted

Because this house is not trusted
Because we second-guess every step we make

Because, on foggy nights, the moon is ringed ghostly
Because moonlight is stolen light from its source

Because this is a private club
and we are always talking to ourselves

Because no one is talking to us
no one answers the haunted questions

Because we are twinned by circumstance
and don't look like anyone else for explanation

Because who the hell are you
is who the hell I am

TWINS

We differ.
Each day, I ask the mirror to lie.

Breathing cataracts on the glass,
with fingers to the fogged surface,

I know at last of a limit
where the image gives

up on itself
at the joint.

I ask for nothing
but the boundary of my skin.

Through the rainy window
framing the wet garden,

colors mute and glisten.
In a window pane,

I am the faintness
of what is returned to me.

In the leaded glass, always
the ghost-image of you,

somewhere else,
the distance bringing me

to the end of myself.
My breath inhaled,

held,
holding.

WORD GAMES FOR KIDNAPPED CHILDREN TO PLAY

You know it's not your name, but you pretend it's your name.
You answer to that name on the outside,

but you refuse that name on the inside.
Every single calling, you refuse that name on the inside.

You do this to stay alive. You do this to keep
the shell of the house quiet and keep your skin on yourself.

On the real inside, you remain your own twin,
the outside yourself and the inside yourself.

You don't tell anyone these words.
You just learn which person to be for which scenario.

You learn the words of your captors' biography
but they are never your words. You just mimic them.

You learn to parrot their history of towns and houses.
You parrot their strange relatives. You vow to erase

everything once you're able to find yourself.
If it takes years, you remain patient and look for your out.

You memorise each continent and country you're hidden in.
You memorise the hedgerows and alleys like a trail of breadcrumbs.

You see you don't have the means or the right words.
You see you have no choice but patience.

In the meantime, you impersonate your life, you say the words.
You know it's not your name, but you pretend it's your name.

You say "yes, sir" and you say "thank you."
You become the consummate actor, consummate actor

and smile for the house of strangers. You smile for the long
succession of teachers in the long succession of schools.

Until escape, you look out the glassy windows always. You
never say the words on the inside. Until freedom, you live

only on the outside. You play the word games.
You answer the roll call.

You know it's not your name but, for now,
you pretend it's your name.

EDGE OF THIRTEEN

This was the way we drank
the sunlight of sub-teen years,
living near each other as childhood
expatriates in the foreign rank:

Welford and Greenham Common, hitched
in humped hills and kilted sheep-pastures.
I remember best the country colors
and tend to blur the rest, how we bitched

with each other in our exclusive society.
Coffee-colored from California—
that unfamiliar country—
with the first, small afro, Robert

was the popular one, guiding us in games,
striding the farmer's field-mare,
taking girls into the back-woods and rolling
the dice for kisses, rolling for the blood between us.

Robert, I admired you
for I was the smart nothing,
but even you used to beat me up, pin me
to the ground daily, feed me grass or leaves and laugh.

I choked on the ritual. To be included, I'd be
everyone's spar, anyone's round.
How I hated the word *precocious,* flinched
at the headmaster's voice, begged for amnesia

to pinch me from the edge of thirteen.
But I remember best the easy way
the girls tilted to you, the back-woods play.
I've nearly forgotten the rest

except how I wanted to be you, Robert.
I'd practice smacking the glassy air
with my finger-snaps, just
bopping down the empty road, trying to be black.

AFTER THE CHILDREN HAVE GONE TO BED

Ian, do you remember Dark Shadows
when we used to sit on the floor
with a crimson blanket around us,
watching the Vampires suck
the fair ladies with rubies around their necks
and us, sucking the television tube daily?
Still fresh from England, we were two brothers
who quickly adapted to the Californian shows.
The Monsters still march forth, and children grow.
Sepia years now, Ian—
and they're bringing back
the old programs for the late hours
and I recall the in-between
where we grew apart into our own lives
and you stayed young through time
with the dream of drugs and the learned American rhyme.
I laid a flower on your name, Ian.
You always played Vampire too frantically.
I always thought you were insane.
Yet now, they rerun Dark Shadows across my screen
and I cannot resurrect you:
brother smile, darker version.
So I ask you instead if you remember
while I sit here in the late hours, aglow
with my tuck-me-in liquor,
the room in a blue halo,
still a place for you within my blanket,
up from the great slide of time,
an ageing me distantly saying,
Pass the biscuits, Ian . . . .
Rerunning you here with me
in blue light, stopped adolescent, over
and over again, laughing at my side.

EMILIO DeGRAZIA

THE OTHER BROTHER

I never knew when my other brother would be there. When I was still a child he left the house in the middle of the night, and he's never returned to show his face. When your parents have a history of not getting along, it's understandable that he'd stay away. Their quarreling also made an outsider of me, an adopted son of sorts not shadowed by the outsider's need to reconnect with biological parents. Kids like me give up on their parents, but not on the brother left behind, the outsider like myself.

Most of the time I shut the door on the thought that he exists. But once in a while on a city street I see a youth staring at me, then glancing away as my eyes find his. The eyes are always the telltale fact, their soft brown set deeply behind thick brows exactly like mine. From the eyes you move out to take in the shape of the face, to see if you fit, the cheeks, small chin, tight unsmiling lips. But I return always to the eyes, the brown sadness, vulnerability, and wonder in them.

The sense of familiarity with a stranger can be profound, as if the link of identity inheres not merely in genes but in a history that's shared. More than once I've tried following a face like mine, but he always gets lost in the crowd just before he turns to reassure me that he has forgiven all of us. I do not know what there is to forgive. I know only that his story is tragic too, his ghostly presence in my life explained only by other ghosts. His story comes to me the way a human form becomes visible in the fog when you're alone on seashore, looking for a house with a light because there's a terrible storm coming on.

I'm not sure when his appearances first became felt. Looking back I'm certain I missed him most of the times our paths crossed, but I especially recall the market stalls on the Rue Cler in Paris. My father had insisted that I go to Paris to study for at least a year, and insisted on paying my way. So there I was one morning on the Rue Cler, and there he suddenly was, a youth about my age standing in the silence next to the white-aproned fish-seller who was holding up a giant squid for everyone to see. I'd never really seen squid before, so I paused to take a good hard look. The youth saw me and smiled just as I turned to walk away. That's all there was to it at first, the same eyes, thick brows, and forgiving face, and this time something I had not noticed before, the black hair parted on the right just like mine. Three years later, as I was thumbing through the pages of a travel magazine, I caught myself in time. The young man pictured there was watching boys playing soccer in the streets of Beirut, Lebanon. His eyes, the parted hair, and the same forgiving calm that seemed permanent on his face arrested me long enough to make the connection: Was this the same young man, the fish-seller's assistant I'd seen on the Rue Cler? What was he doing in Lebanon?

I let the notion pass, even though I couldn't escape the eyes that seemed fixed on mine as I set the magazine down, or his clean white shirt. I'd never been to Beirut, knew it only vaguely as a place on a map, hadn't played soccer since I was a schoolboy, and there was the fish-seller's assistant watching me as I walked away from the travel magazine face-down on the table.

The impression the photograph left on me was permanent. In real life and in movies we're always too late to catch up with the images passing by. Most of them we let go thoughtlessly, and a few we want to chase down so we can gaze, take them wholly in. I was almost sixty years old when I realized that I wanted to do that to my own life, turn it into a photograph that would stand still long enough for me to get a good long look at it. The photo of the young man in the travel magazine stood still for me that way, even though I foolishly left him behind on the table in a dentist's office years ago. Here I was, a successful lawyer with three grown children and a gracious wife asking me to retire before our sunset years turned entirely gray, and there he still was, a young man in a bright white shirt watching boys play soccer on a street in Beirut. I'd given up soccer for tennis when I was twelve, made the university varsity team the year after my return from Paris, courted several ladies before marrying my favorite, raised my family, gained my partnership in the firm, paid off my debts and mortgage, married off two daughters and a son, and am looking forward to my first grandchild by him—all of this while the face of that young man in Beirut kept that same smile fixed on me, as if that color photo in the magazine was a negative with the black and white reversed.

About thirty years ago there was another encounter in a London café. I was stunned when I saw him there, for a moment thinking it was Paris instead ten years earlier. It took me a few minutes to right myself and gain the courage to nod at him, a gesture he returned with the confident smile now familiar to me from the Rue Cler and that travel magazine I carried in my mind. From the way we kept glancing at each other I could see that we both were waiting for the other to make a move, and I regret now that I lacked the courage to step over to his table and introduce myself. But what would I have said: Who are you and what is the link between your life and mine? No, he would have thought I was interested in something else, and I was not. When I finally left the café I saw myself in the mirror to the right of the front door, white shirt and no tie. Yes, we were both dark-haired and just under six feet tall, and no, I was not seeing myself when I looked at him. He nodded and smiled when I threw one last glance over my shoulder just before I left.

My mother had no clue, or if she did she kept to herself. Whatever my father had done in Pigalle before they met was for her to guess, and she preferred the facts that allowed her to carry on her daily life. She had more than enough to do without cluttering the bed and living rooms with useless discards from our pasts. She passed away with a smile on her face, her life by standard measures happily married. My father felt her absence more deeply than her presence. I often found him wandering in the house and yard, his face full of brooding, as if he had lost something, couldn't remember exactly what or where he had laid it last. He became careless and slovenly, spending whole days in his bedroom. I wondered if it was his way of returning to his dumpy place in Pigalle.

I went back to Paris too, determined to celebrate my fiftieth birthday by revisiting the haunts I had visited when I was so full of wonder as a young man. I found the stalls along the Rue Cler unchanged—the heaps of oranges, apples and pears, the ripe strawberries and mounds of lettuce and mustard greens, the oddly shaped eggplant, the grilled chicken, the wonderful loaves of bread filling the air with aromas that made breathing a pleasure. All these wonders seemed at once ancient and fresh, outward and visible signs that the earth's generosity was enduring and unmoved by the noisy progress congesting the widest Paris avenues.

One morning I went in search of the fish-seller's assistant, the ghostly brother I had walked away from both here in Paris and later in the London café. What should I look for in the faces I found there? I was beginning to suspect that my own face was hardly the one that had stayed with me when I returned from France some thirty years earlier, that it had become unfamiliar, gaunt and rough like my father's. I lingered long at the seafood stall, studying the two men and the boy selling the fish. The older man was too short, his smile too wide, and the other's nose, high brow, and curly hair I could not by any stretch of the imagination trace back to the fish-seller's assistant whose eyes had filled mine with such a profound sense of recognition years ago. And the boy—he was too young, and almost blond.

As I walked the Paris streets the next few days I tried matching faces with the picture I had in my mind of the youth watching boys play soccer in the streets of Beirut. Perhaps someday, I told myself as I sat alone on my bed in the hotel, I would go to Beirut. It was said to be the Paris of the Mideast.

At that time I was only dimly aware that Beirut was going up in smoke, the momentary epicenter of the unfamiliar wars in that vague region of the world.

On my return home from Paris I interrupted my father's slumber with a little white lie.

"Dad, when I was in Paris I spent a whole week in Pigalle."

"You saw Amalia?" he blurted out, still half-asleep.

"Amalia? Who's she?"

"Never mind," he replied, coming to his senses. "She's gone."

"Where did she go?"

"She went away. To Morocco, somewhere over there."

"Why did she go away?"

"Because she had to, that's why. You never mind."

"Why didn't you go with her?"

He seemed momentarily paralyzed by the question, as if to answer it he had to rear his head from some pillow he had slept on decades ago. We never told him outright, but father was slipping, getting a lot of things confused.

"I couldn't go with her, that's why," he said. "Everything was ruined."

"Ruined?"

"She had to go. It was an act of God, a terrible act of God. I'm not going to let her hold me responsible. Besides, your mother was waiting for me here."

So Amalia was pregnant and had to go away, and my mother was waiting at home for the man who one day would marry her. The mother who did not exist as mother yet because I did not exist, for whom the lovely woman slouching off to bear her child in the Moroccan sun did not exist. So I began to see it whole: This unborn child would become the other brother I saw in the fish-seller's stall, then again by the strangest chance he would appear in the photo of the travel magazine, then later in the London café.

"My, my," I said out loud to the deepening confusion of my father, "we do get around."

"Around?"

"All the way to Beirut, Lebanon. You ever been to Beirut, Dad? The Paris of the Middle East."

"Huh?"

"I guess we really are alike, Dad. I've never been there either."

I checked with travel agents but there was no getting there, not with the wars going on and on. I took a sudden interest in the large atlas I had hauled from place to place in my life. The success of my career had locked me in place, my circuit the city of Chicago and environs, all my sallying forth from there to vacationlands far safer and less spectacular than the lakefront with its parks and monumental views shrunk to ordinariness by the daily routine of business as usual. I opened the atlas to France, tracing the most obvious routes from Paris to the French coastal cities facing the Moroccan shore. From there I measured the distances across the Mediterranean, turning quickly to a comprehensive view of the North African nations. With my outstretched palm I spanned the spaces from Morocco to Egypt, dwelling on the names of desert places I never knew existed before. And from Cairo I spanned the distance to Beirut, my palm covering Gaza, Israel, Jordan, and southern Lebanon as my finger reached for Beirut.

How much there was in these teeming spaces that I had never seen, would never know! My other brother had made a passage from the Paris of Europe to the Paris of the Middle East—thousands of miles traveled by truck over desert sands, or perhaps by ferry past Malta, Crete, the Cyclades, Cyprus, past crowded taverns on beaches washed by warm ocean streams, past towns perched on white cliffs looking down on sailboats silent against the sky. He had wandered through crowded bazaars, the air fragrant with the scent of savory and cloves, the eye dazzled by mounds of colorful vegetables and fruit. His journey had required courage, daring, cleverness, resourcefulness—and an energy I had mortgaged to a future that never arrived. I envied him. I shrank as I realized how courageously he had lived the life I lacked.

The need to find him deepened as my sense of the vast spaces between us grew. True, he had experienced a life I wanted to appropriate, in part because our connection, whatever it was, made our life a joint venture giving me proprietary rights. These rights were useless to the extent that he was not present to me. But something deeper, less vulgar, made my skin crawl when it ran through my mind: Call it blood. This became my father's story the moment I learned about his Amalia, mother of my other brother but also stepmother to me. His blood, the way his genes inscribed the familial lines on our faces, gave each of us the same cast of eyes and hair, the same chin and lips, the same body structure and weight, perhaps the same shy reticence when we encountered each other in a London café—this blood sense running deeper than any identity conferred by names, nations, or religious beliefs. I never knew and never learned my other brother's name, and I never felt the need. What we have runs deeper than names, is profoundly more enduring than all the words you will finish reading here soon.

You can imagine the shock I felt last night when I came out of my favorite neighborhood restaurant. I'd had a quiet, solitary dinner, the one night a week affair I'd promised myself after my father died and my wife went to live her own suburban life. When I stepped outside the lake breeze seemed as fresh as the clear twilight that cast a calming spell on the downtown streets. And there, almost nose-to-nose with me on the sidewalk outside the restaurant, he was. The white shirt, the same eyes I knew so well, the familiar lines above my father's brows, the ones I faced in the mirror every morning, the small curl of his sad smile so full of forgiveness and regrets, the face, in short, of the youth selling fish on the Rue Cler, the one in the London café, and the one watching the boys play soccer on the streets of Beirut. I was speechless, and in that long moment I lost him again. He turned abruptly and walked away, and by the time I called out to him my words got lost in the city noise. He quickened his pace as I followed him, and because I've always been afraid of being thought a fool I never actually ran to catch up to him. Still I shadowed him, turning this way or that down another street, hoping at least to see where he'd end up. Then, as suddenly as he'd appeared, he was gone. I know now that he turned left where I turned right. A train screamed by overhead, so crowded with shadowed heads I thought it was headed for a concentration camp.

In desperation I tried the archives of the library, row after row of travel magazines lining the steel shelves in the lonely dungeon beneath the reading rooms. Finally I found him again, watching the boys play soccer on the street, his face darker in the dim light, his smile sadder, more resigned. Carefully I tore the page out, folded it, and put it into my shirt pocket. I have him here still.

There were other sightings after that. He appeared in full color in a weekly news magazine, one of seven civilian casualties of war stacked like cordwood as two soldiers stand idly by, weapons in hand. His shirt was bloodstained, his face one of three plainly visible, the only one wide-eyed. The eyes caught me immediately, and from there I found the other familiar lines. To be certain I unfolded the photo from the travel magazine and laid the pages next to each other. The match left me so speechless and confused I stopped walking by the restaurant where I had seen him before.

I kept watching the news on TV. He was there only a moment, and this time he couldn't have been more than ten years old. Gunfire had made rubble of a house, and a tank stood next to an olive tree as a soldier, his back to the camera, marched him down a dirt path. He was the middle boy. He had beautiful brown eyes, this time full of fear and pleading when he turned to look at me.

My father always has the last word, so the night he called to tell me he had something important to say I hurried to his side.

"What time is it?" he asked as I walked in.

I didn't know.

"Never mind. It doesn't matter now."

He was afraid he would die soon, and there was something I needed to know. Amalia again, the six months he spent with her in Pigalle. She never made it to North Africa because she and her ship were doomed. It sank in a squall that hit the whole coast, blasting away even the roof of his hotel in Marseilles. Everyone on her ship died in the storm.

"But it wasn't my fault," he said. "I had a ticket too. I had made up my mind to go with her. But just before the ship was to leave I ran back to the hotel. My wallet—I had left it in the hotel. All the money, what there was of it—and the picture of your mother. Everything. I ran like a wild man to get back to the ship. But there I was on the pier watching it pull away."

It didn't matter who was on the ship or that the ship sank. It didn't matter if my father was on the shore watching the storm come in.

Because here we still are.

CARLOS REYES

AUTOBIOGRAPHY AS FANTASY

The small tan spot
on my upper right arm

I am almost sure it
is a spider bite.

I can imagine skin dis-
coloring, a stain spread

from a black widow
bite in Panamá,

maybe an agitated spider
in my own bedroom.

By now the spot is large,
a dream island

in the Caribbean, but
my doctor says

it is no more than an age spot
albeit a rather large one.

Another doctor insists
that the piece of metal

embedded in my knee
is a bullet,

though I was never shot
that I know of.

Are you sure? he asks.
In fact, "the bullet" is

the most abiding mystery
of my autobiography

and the favorite myth
about me, a plant

I tend with care
in the garden

of an ordinary life.

SEEING TIME

When I look in the mirror
all I see is time.
                    —Mario Benedetti

She said *I always go*
for guys with blue eyes.

I never noticed my eyes
in the mirror were blue,

never saw any color in them,
saw only time.

Now I see blue, walk out
into the world, my vision clean.

No more clogged tear ducts.
Me. The world. All there is.

Rubbing the sleep
away

I open block-light drapes
face the atomic sun,

the blue, an azure sky
not found in nature,

a blackness that turned
grey, turned from grey to light.

I ask myself where I've been
and do not answer yet.

Yet. I am not ready
for someone's vision of my life

though I see clearly
through window panes.

I dissemble then,
answer them at last.

My life, I made it up.
I made it up so real

I can't unmake it,
nor do I care to.

You can take me, or you can leave
me flamboyant

autograph bigger than my ego,
bigger than the moon.

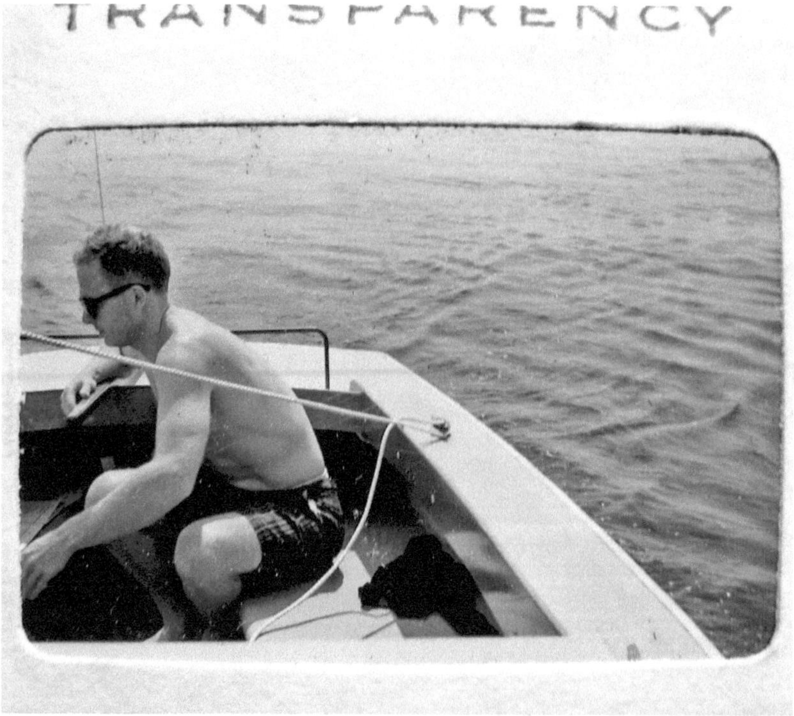
TRANSPARENCY

STEFAN KIESBYE

WATER PARK

They're nice to me and they don't want to be near me. While we rake grass at the superintendent's house, they stay amongst themselves, two raking, another lifting the grass into the back of the E-Z-Go. It's not like they want to offend me, and maybe if you asked them about it they'd say that it's just in my head. But when I join them, they slowly stop talking and don't start up again until I have left to take care of the strip of lawn along the driveway.

The park is one hundred and fifty acres, "a good size," Dan, the super, says. Two years ago they built a small water park with slides and a wave pool, but he wishes he could build an eighteen-hole golf course. We only have a nine-hole disc-golf course, and the disc golfers come just before dark, when the gatehouse has closed for the day. They get stoned or drunk and play and we have a hell of a time getting them off the course in time to close the park at nine o'clock.

I like the park best in the mornings, when it's still a bit hazy, and no one else is around. I drive along the trails to pick up litter. Bunny rabbits scurry along or just sit in the shimmering grass and stare back at me. Bushes and trees I can't name smell sweet before it gets hot, and if you stop the cart, the trees seem to take a step toward you, as if they want to gently block your path, unscrew your head, clean it out, and keep you there.

During breaks I might sit on one of the docks by the lake and watch the fish, mostly bass, swim in the murky water. At first sight, it doesn't seem like much of a lake, but towards the middle it gets real deep. In the evenings, anglers stand along the shore. Sometimes they even grill their catch. People used to swim in the lake, before they build the docks and put up picnic tables everywhere. Now signs tell visitors it's forbidden to wade or swim.

When the other rangers are bored, they drive the E-Z-Go over to the water park to hang out with the girls, though they don't call them girls. They call them 'chicks' and 'bitches.' They show only contempt for them, but can't stop going to our water park, where the girls show off elaborately painted toenails, killer tans and a suave attitude. They call us 'immature.' It's never 'stupid,' 'dumb,' or 'gross,' it's always 'immature,' as though that word gives them power over us.

My mom never mentions the park. She might say, "How was work?" or, "How was your day?" but she doesn't mention the pavilions, the pond with its new fishing docks, the vault bathrooms, the lodge or the waterslides, and when I tell her about them she finds a way to steer our conversation away from the park. She's a tall woman with wide hips, taller than I am. In the summer she wears jean shorts, and there are some green and purple blemishes on her legs she says she got when she was pregnant. I can talk to her about the rangers, the guys I went to high school with and who she knows from the time they still hung out at our place. She's curious about where Karl is going to college, if he's still playing football, or if Fred has a girlfriend now, but when I tell her that Karl was fishing plastic bags and bait boxes out of the pond with a pole he'd made from an old broom and a ski-stick, she hurries into the garage, because she "forgot to take the dry-cleaning from the car."

In Michigan, it's cold for eight months, and the rest of the time it feels like you're inside a carwash. Dad is a Ford-guy, we are a Ford-family. He drives a Taurus, Mom drives a Sable, and I decked out my Focus with money I earned plowing snow. It makes 240 horsepower and Dad helped me put in the supercharger. He's become quiet, and he didn't say a word when I said I wanted to work at the park for the summer. He nodded gravely, just as if I had explained relativity to him. But even though he lets me go on about work, he never answers. He just says, "Oh, that's interesting," or, "No kidding," and he seems relieved when I finally leave the room and get into my car.

We live outside Ypsilanti, in a two-story house in an older subdivision. Last fall rainwater ruined our ceilings, and every storm breaks off strips of the cheap siding. Whenever Mom cooks, my bathroom smells of whatever she's preparing. The Richardsons from next door moved away last year, and many of the families we used to invite for barbecues in the summer are gone. Every month, another 'For Sale' sign is driven into one of the lawns, and each year, the cars in the driveways get a little shabbier. Dad says that the developers knew how bad their houses were, and that they were building a future ghetto. "Give it another twenty years, and you can buy crack from our neighbors," he says.

I wanted to go to the U of M, but didn't have the grades. So now I take classes at Eastern and hope I can transfer after my sophomore year. I'd like to be a mechanical engineer, I'd be happy to work for one of the Big Three, which my dad now calls the Big Two-and-a-half, but I'd love to work for BMW. Their sedans are sweet. I'd just love to drive an M5 and have girls ride with me in the back. I'd even go to Germany and learn the language, though I'm not good at languages. I took two years of high school French and I sucked. "*Voulez-vous couchez avec moi*" is about the only phrase I remember and I didn't learn it in school.

Last week Dan asked me to supervise a new gate attendant. Not that she really needed my help, but Dan wants everything just so and she'd never sold vehicle passes before, so I sat with her for an hour. She was from California, a swimmer on a scholarship at Eastern, and her blond hair and skin looked as if she'd bleached them forever. But sort of pretty, in a serious kind of way. Rachel wanted to work as a lifeguard, but those positions were already filled. She asked me about the park, she'd never heard of the park before a friend of hers applied, and I told her about the trails, the pavilions that always get trashed on the weekends, and the disc golfers.

When Dan stopped by to see how we were doing, she suddenly said she'd heard about an accident here at the park a few years ago. I had no idea why she was asking, she'd said she didn't know the park. She was from California, after all. "Someone drowned?" she asked.

"Yes," Dan said real quiet.

"Even though you had lifeguards?"

"It didn't happen in the water park," Dan answered. Whenever we want an extra day off, or whenever too many workers call in sick, or people complain about the concession stand's expensive food, he lowers his head as if there's a strong wind blowing, and his voice slows down. He doesn't want to become angry and shout or brush someone off, so he answers very slowly and politely. "We didn't have it then. It happened at the pond."

"How?" Rachel said. She wasn't trying to be mean or annoying, she just wanted to know.

"Well," Dan said. "A boy drowned." And he paused. "Let's just say it was a very tragic accident." Then he showed her how to order the different tickets so nothing gets lost. He didn't even glance at me once.

At my brother's funeral I wore a black suit my Dad bought for me at the Men's Wearhouse. We went together, he needed a new one, and the whole affair lasted about ten minutes. I'd been clothes-shopping with him before, and he could be very vain. He loved shoes and had gazillions of expensive ties, but at the Men's Wearhouse, he just tried on the first one the salesperson handed him, and before the guy had a chance to look at Dad's back or pants and suggest alterations, Dad said, "This one is fine." I'm sure he didn't want me to believe he was worried about the way he looked at his son's funeral.

The day was hot and sticky, and our house was full of people who, when my parents were around, fell silent or lowered their voices, but otherwise talked and ate as if it were someone's birthday. Everyone seemed itchy and uncomfortable in their suits and dresses and nobody could answer my gaze longer than a second. Only Grandma, my dad's mother, hugged me and said, "You're still here, you're still here."

Classmates of Ron attended the ceremony, singing "Amazing Grace." Our pastor had tears in his eyes, and Dad had to lead Mom away halfway through the ceremony, because she cried so much. You could hardly hear the pastor's speech because of her.

I had a girlfriend back then, Caysee, and the night after my brother had drowned, she came over, and we kissed and hugged, and she was all in tears and wouldn't let go of me. By the time of the funeral, each time I tried to kiss her she giggled or made helpless little sounds and moved her lips away. When Mom left the ceremony, Caysee left it too, and two days later she called and said it was over between us and I shouldn't think badly of her.

On Court TV, when criminals show remorse, the jury starts feeling bad for them, and the judge seems inclined not to punish them too harshly. As if by crying and asking for forgiveness, the world becomes again the way it was before someone got mugged or killed, as if by weeping, the world becomes better again. Maybe that way, people think the world is still working according to the laws they learned. Maybe if you don't cry, they start doubting themselves.

Our park is well hidden on Wellington Road, three miles outside of town, just at the border of the township. If you don't look hard for the brown and white signs you'll never even know it's there. But it's the only thing to do for kids in the summer, the only thing in a thirty-mile radius. Some days we even get busloads of kids from Toledo.

All the rangers and attendants and managers in the water park, those who've worked here since junior year in high school, know my brother's story and don't ask anymore, and either by will or because they've gotten used to it, they don't remember details. My brother was well liked, played in a jazz band and ran track for our school. If he hadn't died, he would have played

Dr. Higgins in *My Fair Lady*. He could sing real pretty.

But this girl from Eastern kept asking about Ron. When Dan left again that first day I met her, she said, "Why didn't he tell me what happened?"

I shrugged.

"Do you know who drowned?"

"Yeah, I do. But that was three years ago. They don't let people swim in the pond anymore. It doesn't look like much, but it's real deep in the middle."

Rachel was quiet for some time, staring at her toenails, which were done in red, with white, blue, and yellow flowers painted on them. She didn't look very girly, so I asked who'd painted her toes.

"My roommate," she said, suddenly smiling. "Do you think they look cheesy?"

"No, they're fine," I said.

"So how did the boy drown?" she asked.

"Why do you want to know?"

She shrugged. "It's creepy. Kind of cool." She laughed, shaking her head at what she'd said. "Do you mind telling?"

She really has no idea, I thought, no idea at all. And I said, "He was a good athlete, but he couldn't swim."

"Then why did he go swimming in the pond?"

"He wanted to save his brother," I said. "His name was Ron."

The car I had back then, an old Escort, was keyed the first day of school after my brother's death, the headlights were kicked in. They never found who did it. I left the car just as it was, only replacing the lights, and the next day the windows were smashed in. I transferred to Belleville that same fall, my father made the arrangements. On advice of my old school's counselor, he also paid for sessions with a shrink, Al Larsen. He was a decent guy, maybe in his thirties, maybe a bit older, with pale skin, quivering lips, and beard. Whenever he took of his glasses, which shrank his eyes, he looked like a bearded frog. After I told him the story of Ron's death, he said, "That must be hard for you," and I felt relieved because finally someone was talking about me and not only of my brother. I said yes, I had been afraid when my car was smashed and I didn't play roller hockey with the other guys anymore, on Sundays, in our school's lot. But the guy looked at me in this blank way, eyes not blinking and without expression. "That's not what I meant," he said, and then asked, "How are things between you and your parents?" His computer in the back of the office was running, and every once in a while, an e-mail would come in with a 'bing.' Right after he asked, another mail arrived, and he went over to mute the sound.

"So his brother was drowning and he tried to save him?" Rachel said.

I would have liked to ask her out right there in that gatehouse with its sticky floor and the bees always coming through the window. I wanted to drive around with her, maybe to Ford Lake or Ann Arbor, maybe go see a movie. It was nice she wasn't from here, and nice that she was asking me all these questions without knowing that I could answer them all. "No, Ron's brother wasn't drowning," I said. "He jumped out of their inflatable boat and started screaming, I can't move, I can't move. And then he let himself sink under water."

"And?"

"Ron jumped after his brother. He must have. Nobody knows how it could have happened so fast. But when his brother came up again, it was all silent. No screaming, no thrashing, nothing. The boat was empty, and Ron was gone."

Rachel noticed the rhyme and repeated, "Ron was gone," and laughed, I think, despite of herself. She shook her head as if she could shake off the laughter, but kept laughing. "Ron was gone."

And I laughed too, it was so good to see someone laughing about it. I was happier in that moment than I had been in a long time, and she looked pretty laughing. People stopped at the gatehouse window and paid for the ticket and I showed Rachel how to handle errors by printing a receipt and how to fold our leaflets. She had big and strong hands, nice hands, even though she was biting her nails.

The shrink, after I told him that I thought my mom blamed me for Ron's death, asked what my opinion was. Did I blame myself?

"I guess," I said.

"You guess?" His eyes were strangely focused, almost like those of the disc golfers when they leave the course at nine or after nine and are all stoned. Their eyes jump at you, look really mean, and yet somehow they are not seeing anything, there's nothing behind those eyes.

"Yeah," I said. "If I hadn't played with him, he'd never have drowned."

"It could have happened anyway," Al said. "Do you and your folks believe in God? Some people believe in fate, or that God takes people when he decides to."

"But that would make me his tool. That'd be pretty fucked up," I said. "I was pretending I was drowning, that's all. Nobody made me. I just did."

"Do you ever wonder why?"

"It was fun. He was always so worried and scared, and I knew he would get all upset."

"Did it ever occur to you that he might love you?"

"I don't know. I guess," I said.

We had good times together; Ron wasn't a pain in the ass or anything. He was pretty cool, knew a ton about computers and cars and designed a website for me. Apart from running track, he was more of a geek, but a popular one, not one of those pimply nerds with grimy glasses and a gut. He was pretty, even though he was real thin and didn't play football and didn't know how to swim. He was two years younger than me and bugged me that summer about showing him how to drive. But my Escort had a stick, and I didn't want him to ruin the transmission. It was an '89 GT and pretty fast, and I said he should buy his own car and I would teach him alright. I mean, we played pranks on each other as kids, and he was always there, but when I thought of my family, or told friends about Mom and Dad, Ronnie was never part of that. We got along, though, didn't fight much either. When I told him to shut up or get off the phone, he usually would, and most of the times he'd be in his room anyway.

Dad cleaned out Ronnie's room even though Mom cried and hit him with her fists when he did. He got rid of the posters, the CDs, the Cleveland Indians blanket he'd won at a church raffle, and even Ron's photo albums. He didn't want to erase him, but he didn't want Mom to spend her evenings locked in Ron's room, and he didn't even look at the things he threw out. Nobody has used the room since—we don't have many visitors. My uncles and aunts and grandparents all live close by, in Manchester and Saline. Dad bought a bed, a wardrobe, and a desk, but there's nothing in the wardrobe, and no one ever sits at the desk. Mom refuses to clean the room, and Dad doesn't take the time. Ronnie's room is dusty and empty.

The next time I saw Rachel, she came out of the water park's staff room. I was running change to the gatehouse, and she spotted me and came over to say hello. She looked very cool in her bathing suit and white shirt—they'd let her lifeguard because one of the guards had busted his shoulder playing hockey. Her eyes were a bit red, maybe she'd been in the water all day, and she jumped from one foot onto the other, as if she had to pee, but I guess she was just nervous, and I thought she was pretty that way. Her hair was almost white and held back in a pony tail, and she blinked her eyes because of the sun behind me.

That night we went to see *Charlie's Angels.* Even while the movie was still playing, we were already bitching about how silly it was, but somehow it was really fun, and we moaned and groaned and rolled our eyes in the darkness, and everyone was shushing us, and we just kept laughing harder. Afterwards we went to Big Boy's and she said she would like to lifeguard on a real beach out in California or in Myrtle Beach or Miami, and Ypsilanti suddenly felt very small, and for a moment I saw our park and I saw pictures of the ocean, and my souped-up Focus looked real silly, and I thought that if not for that scholarship, Rachel would have never come to Eastern, or Michigan, for that matter. She was only here for a short time, and I wondered if I would ever make it to Germany, or if I would buy a house somewhere here and still drive over to the water park and watch families spread out their blankets near the concession stand and stuff their faces with nachos.

"I'd really like to get a tattoo," she said suddenly. "I just don't know where." She dipped one of her last fries in a big heap of ketchup, and sucked the ketchup off the fry before chewing it. There weren't many people left at Big Boy's, it was almost closing time.

"Oh," I said.

"Do you think that's stupid?"

"No," I said. "I just don't think that I could wear any one symbol or picture for the rest of my life. Or a name. I mean, if you don't like the person anymore, it's still there, and you're constantly reminded of them."

"I'd like a shape, a simple one," she said. "Maybe a triangle, a circle, or a square."

"A square. Simple," I repeated stupidly.

"Yeah, a black square. Doesn't have to mean anything. Just a square."

"'Hey, what's that mean?'—'Why, I love squares,'" I said, and we both laughed.

"Yeah, a square," she said.

We both ordered strawberry milkshakes, although the waitress seemed really annoyed, and while we were waiting for them, I said, "I'd like to see somebody tattooing his body onto his body."

"What do you mean?" she said.

"The shape of his body tattooed onto his skin, just a bit smaller, so it fits. His fingers are drawn onto his fingers, his arms onto his arms. Well, the face would be difficult."

She looked at me, as if I were completely nuts, but smiled real sweet, and said, "The eyes, yeah. The nose—you could do that."

"And one thing would be missing. You know, he'd have the whole body tattooed on his body, but one hand would be missing, or a calf. And everybody would look at the missing limb, because it's just missing."

"That's creepy," Rachel said. "Like tattooing your skeleton, I mean, all your bones, onto your skin."

"Maybe," I said. "But there would be two people, only one is incomplete."

Rachel put her hands on my ears and shook me and laughed, and there was some of her fry lodged between two teeth.

When I dropped her off that night, she said, "That was fun. Let's do it again."

I said, "Any time," and meant it.

But there was no other time. The next day at the park she was all weird. When I came to work in the afternoon and looked for her in the staff room, she didn't look my way, just turned around when I knew she'd seen me. She just turned to another girl and kept talking. Maybe someone had seen us together, or maybe she had told a friend about me. And of course they would have told her about Ron. Whenever I ran into Rachel that afternoon, she passed by me, as though I was only a customer, someone you don't want or need to know and don't see anyway.

The night of the funeral, I'd gone driving around, speeding on back roads, trying to feel anything special when I thought of Ron. Fireflies exploded on my windshield, swarms of them, their squished bodies glowing for a second or two, before turning into smudges. When I came home around one or two in the morning, Mom was still sitting in the kitchen, a glass of pickles and a jar of mayonnaise in front of her. She'd put bread and lunchmeat on the table too, and I could see that she hadn't touched anything. Dad's plate was full of crumbs and he'd left it on the table, and hers was clean, and she sat there as if she were waiting for something to happen, as if she were waiting for the mayonnaise to make sense.

I sat down across from her, because she was sad, and I was responsible for it, and I had not wanted to make her unhappy. But she got up real quick, as if the table had suddenly gotten hot and burned her arms. And she looked at me with her mouth open, and for a long time, no words came. Finally she spoke, but it was a hissing noise, like a hot kettle. Maybe she didn't want to wake Dad or maybe she was afraid of what would happen if she raised her voice. At first I couldn't understand, but she was repeating what she said, over and over again, staring at me as though she were frightened.

"Why don't *you* cry?" Mom said. "Why don't *you* cry?" Although there were no tears coming, I was sure she was crying. And I stared at her, didn't respond, didn't go upstairs to my room, but waited for her to stop, waited until she was all cried out. Then I poured her a glass of iced water and sat it down in front of her.

"Thanks," she said, and got up, leaving the kitchen to sit by herself on the back porch, without the water. She never asked again afterwards, but she didn't need to. When I sit on the fishing dock by the pond and the other rangers come by, I can hear them ask the same question. And I wish I could have cried with Mom after the funeral, wish I could have told her that I never wanted to hurt Ronnie and how much I missed him. Maybe she would have slapped me, maybe even beaten me, but then she would have hugged me and cried for Ronnie and for me. I knew I would have been forgiven.

She wanted to see me cry to find her peace or to be consoled or to be reassured that the world was still what she thought it was, that I was still who she thought I was. I never cried for Ron though, and that night I just emptied her glass into the sink and went to my room. I didn't cry for him. People can smell I never did.

I'm
sorry —

The egoist

DEIDRA K. RAZZAQUE

THE NAME YOU LOST

They call you thief, problem, delinquent, nuisance, liar, threat.
These people in the echoing courtroom, in the shabby police station,
in the narrow aisles of the grocery store.
And me, in my house at night, when you steal my old blue bicycle.
We discuss you in cramped offices filled with computers and telephones,
study files inches thick, and make angry gestures in the air.
You have become synonymous with sighs.
Your name is the sound of someone walking out of a room.
We say we want to help you but we are not patient teachers.
How to save you from your own destructive hands, we ask one another.
We worry about society. We wonder when to leave you alone.
You are fourteen years old and you know
too much about guns, and so little about love.
Maybe you learned this life from your father,
with his own habits of stealth and liquor, with his withering fists.
Maybe it was your mother who taught you defiance.
She wanted so badly to forget you that she bled into another country.
Or maybe you act as you do simply because your own, fine name
is hardly ever said with a smile. It has become a coat
we'd like to hang in the winter closet.

But Omar, this name you lost,
you could still take it up, live it fully.
You could stun us, thrill us,
silence our unkind chattering.
You could become to yourself everything you wish,
and to us, a hopeful story we tell.
Once there was a difficult, uncertain boy, we would say,
but one day he remembered who he was.

So Omar, let's thread together all the meanings of your name
until they form a blanket. We'll throw that blanket over
the wary delinquent, the crying thief, the hungry liar.
We'll let him sleep.
Then you, Omar, you can ride far on my bicycle.
Ride to a place beyond your reputation.
You can find new parents with their gladness intact.
You will become their first son and they will teach you how to plant and
how to harvest.
In that other place, Omar, you will learn, you will grow,
you will become elevated.
People will fill rooms to hear you speak wisely;
you will be profound in your eloquence.
Sometimes you will have strange dreams of a different sort of life.
In these dreams you will know how to wield a knife
and make strangers do your bidding,
and you will find money in your pockets that is not your own.
But in your real life you will follow the prophet
who is your own insightful self.
You will look people in the eye
and they will feel blessed by your presence.
They will ask, and you will be so happy to tell them
your own, fine name.

TODAY

After 30 years of crying I wrote my father a letter.
And it was amazing.
The fact of it, the act of writing, and everything I said.
And moreover, how I feel in this moment, after it is written—
seven typed pages of white paper, sealed in a standard envelope.
Stamped, and gone from my life.

The day has gone on, too.
There have been strawberries in it, and laundry;
the hum of cars playing their quiet song against the road.
And my father is in it, too, in a way he has never been before.

In a few days, he will know that I crave mushrooms with
melted Havarti cheese, that I wake at dawn to walk the empty streets
or to write words so bloated with promise they blind my sleepy eyes.
In a few days, he will know that I love him,
even though I have never learned his sisters' names
or how he feels about winter.
This love snuck up on me, surprised me so much that
my arms have become sparklers.
Little shocks of light drip from my fingers.

And while my father reads about this daughter he does not know,
bees will worship the purple coneflowers.
My own daughter will eat marshmallows,
gumming them and laughing with delight.
Green tides will move toward rocky shores and retreat.
In every place we could call home,
people will argue and make love and pick wild berries.
They will wake up and hope to be at peace.

Some days do hold miracles, lacy as seaweed, rainbow-chasers,
beautiful to whomever will behold them.
I am twisted inside out by the marvel of words
that gushed from my own leaking pen.
For so long, each letter of every word I have written to my father today
was a bead of rage or fear, loneliness or resentment.
The stringing of them nearly choked me.
They were a noose of rot around my sunburned neck
and I could not witness their strange beauty.

You always hear whispers of the transformation—how the garbage of life
sometimes blooms as daisies and pepper plants.
Today I watched this happen to the ground where I was standing.
Coral-colored, the edges washed in blue—
a flower I have never seen before sprang up
and dared me to look upon it.
There it is, yawning lazily yet unfatigued,
resting beneath the yellow sun.

IV
INVERSIONS

NATALIE HANEY TILGHMAN

GREEN

Eloise heard horror stories on her first day of work. Under the fluorescent lights of the break room, her female coworkers—white, gray-haired hippies with crow's feet that started where their eye liner stopped—descended upon Eloise's table and unwrapped their tofu pitas.

Each case manager shared a story. There was the malnourished runaway who lived under Wacker Drive and used all her panhandled money to go to Sunday matinees. And the homeless pregnant woman who visited her social worker in a different fur coat each week, all gifts from "a boyfriend." Eloise learned that one client, a recovering alcoholic and born-again Christian, was particularly trusted, even given a receptionist position at the day shelter. She streamlined the check-in process because she never forgot a face or a name. Then one day in December, when the workers were in a staff meeting, she stole all their wallets and bought $4,000 worth of shoes at Neiman Marcus.

"Most of the charges were on my card," sighed Jane, the clinical supervisor. "It took me two months to get them reversed. That's your first lesson, Eloise, never self-disclose to these women."

"No matter how much you trust them," a case worker added.

"You are…" It seemed as though Jane was about to mention Eloise's age. "Green. And they know it."

Eloise nodded but kept her eyes fixed on her salami sandwich. Her coworkers were all jaded. Already, she felt that she didn't belong.

That evening, Eloise rode Bus 71 home from the day shelter, even though her coworkers advised against waiting alone at the stop.

"You'll get mugged," one warned her.

"The Gangster Disciples hang out on that corner and deal cocaine," another one said.

Eloise hardly noticed two men with cornrows, who stood watch on the corner smoking cigarettes. Another Chicago winter was already bearing down and she shuffled from one foot to the other to stay warm. By the time the bus came, she had lost feeling in the tips of her fingers.

The bus sighed and pulled away from the corner. Eloise looked at her reflection in the window. A twenty-five year old Korean American woman with high cheek bones, almond-shaped eyes and silky hair stared back at her. As a child, Eloise studied her reflection a lot, and by the time she was three, she knew she looked different than her parents—red-headed Marlene and blue eyed Tom—because she was adopted. Marlene, a school librarian, had introduced the concept of adoption to Eloise through a children's book. Marlene found a book for every difficult issue that Eloise might encounter in life—death, menstruation, sex—and subscribed to the theory that published authors could say just about anything better than she ever could.

Marlene told Eloise a more detailed adoption story when Eloise reached fourteen and hungered for more information. The call came one Saturday in March when Marlene had just finished planting in the garden. She had reached the phone on the last ring. After four years of adoption interviews and waiting, a baby, three months old, was theirs: an orphan. Both parents had died in a car accident in Seoul one week before and the relatives were unable to care for another child. Marlene had called Tom away from painting the barn door and they celebrated with a bottle of wine in the empty nursery. "It's simple, really," Marlene told Eloise, "We were over the moon with joy."

Eloise was not embraced by everyone. Each summer, she rode with Tom and Marlene to Kentucky to visit Grandma Pullman, the family historian and Eloise's namesake. Tom tried to make it fun for Eloise, taking her into a nearby mining town to buy lemon drops at the country store and helping her to catch butterflies in the tall grasses behind Grandma's house. But it was a trip that Eloise dreaded. Grandma never seemed to accept the fact that Tom and Marlene could not have biological children. The topic usually came up when Grandma thought Eloise was asleep: "What is she, Tom, a Vietnamese? God, your father would roll over in his grave if he knew you brought one of them into your house."

To make matters worse, Eloise had to sleep in Tom's old room, surrounded by yellowing photos of the Pullman clan. She tossed and turned at night, imagining generations of light-skinned Pullmans on the opposing wall staring down at her, disapproving. Where's your Pullman nose? How come you don't have freckles?

Eloise noticed two black girls in school uniforms sitting across from her on the bus. They played patty cake, singing: "I went to a Chinese restaurant to buy a loaf of bread, bread, bread. The waiter asked my name and this is what I said, said, said. 'My name is Eli Eli Chickali Chickali Pom Pom Beauty Extra Cutie. I know karate. Punch you in the body. Oops! I'm sorry. Don't tell my mommy.' Chinese. Japanese. Freeze!" The heavier girl with braids thick as rope blinked first and lost the game.

Growing up in rural Illinois, people frequently thought Eloise was Chinese. Marlene said they didn't know any better. Eloise herself barely understood what it meant to be Korean. So when Eloise met Susan Kim in high school it was just a matter of time before she sought out her friendship. Susan, who wore the foreign scent of *bibimbop* unabashedly, invited Eloise to her family's restaurant, the only Korean restaurant in Rockford. It was peppered with bamboo plants, little Buddha statues, and pictures of crowded city streets, probably in Seoul, where everyone looked like Eloise. The girls sat across from one another at a small table divided by a barbeque pit. A sweating tea pot and two empty cups were brought to the table with the menus. Eloise's heart sank when she saw that the menu was written entirely in Korean. She squinted to make out the little pictures that danced across the page in a sequence that somehow translated into "barbeque pork and rice." Even if she could have read the menu, she would not have known the first thing about ordering—the only Asian food she'd ever had was cashew chicken from the Three Happiness Chinese Restaurant near Marlene's school.

Susan seemed to sense Eloise's confusion and took the lead, ordering for both of them in Korean. The staccato language rolled off her tongue. Eloise wondered if Susan and the waiter were talking about her because the man kept looking at her and smiling. Pardon my friend, she could imagine Susan saying. She's not really one of us.

When Eloise returned home later that night, Marlene was already asleep on the couch with a book in her lap. Eloise stood in front of her with a warm doggy bag, sensing something was not right. It took Eloise a moment until she realized what it was: the smoky scent of barbeque pork was out of place in the Pullman house.

Eloise waited in her cramped office the next day for her first client to arrive. She had added a few personal affects: her M.S.W. diploma from Loyola and a picture of Marlene and Tom. Eloise also kept a framed quote from Mother Teresa on her desk:

We think sometimes that poverty is only being hungry, naked and homeless. The poverty of being unwanted, unloved and uncared for is the greatest poverty.

As Eloise sipped tea out of her travel mug, she glanced at the clock. It was 9:37 and there was still no sign of her client. Through the thin walls, she heard Judy's voice in the social skills workshop. "Hey, ladies. Good morning. First, business matters: you can talk to the front desk about getting a locker if you don't already have one..."

Eloise scanned the intake form for a third time: Nelly Fadden, Female, Caucasian, twenty-years old. Under "health status," someone had scribbled: presents with symptoms of depression, complains of headaches, does not admit to drug use. She noted that her client was unemployed but formerly an artist. The word "artist" stood out. Not many women at the shelter described themselves as artists. Ever since she was young, Eloise had been naturally talented at sketching and painting. When she felt left out at school, Eloise drew the sky, the students, the teachers, and the playground. Tom and Marlene had encouraged her with lessons and did not get angry when she announced that studio art would be her undergraduate major. Eloise truly admired people who used the word "artist" to describe themselves and what they did every day. It was risky to make art for a living.

Eloise was about to put the papers back in the folder and prepare for her next client when someone tapped on her door.

"Come on in," Eloise called out.

A woman with a bird's nest of blonde curls piled on the top of her head pushed the door open. She hesitated in the doorway. Slightly overweight, she wore ripped jeans, a pink cotton sweater, and a necklace of soda tabs. Black liner ringed her eyes.

"Hi...Nelly?" Eloise rose with her hand outstretched.

The girl eyed Eloise and did not offer her hand in return. With the less than warm greeting, Eloise decided to change her approach.

"I'm your social worker, Eloise Pullman. You can sit right here."

As Nelly lowered herself into the seat, Eloise noticed her face. Her cheeks were rosy but dark bags underlined her eyes. Being on the street had aged her at least ten years.

"So Nelly, how did you hear about us?"

"Clarissa. Do you know her?" Nelly didn't wait for an answer. "She comes here to take showers, and she's trying to get off the streets so she can start her own business. She makes jewelry out of bottle caps, stuff she finds in the trash. Really nice stuff. She made this for me...." Nelly motioned toward her necklace. "She's just gotta lay off the crack. It messes with her mind. Makes her all depressed and shit. Anyways, she said that someone here helped get her necklaces to some shop on Armitage Street and that she has sold like five necklaces for like $80 each..."

Already, Eloise liked Nelly. Her honesty was refreshing.

"Right. We can help women to develop skills and make business connections. Why are you here today, Nelly? How can we help you?" Eloise smiled, even though Nelly had yet to make eye contact with her.

"I don't know. I guess I thought someone could help me here. I want to get back on my feet." Nelly looked up. Her cold blue eyes softened for a second. "And I don't know what else to do."

Nelly noticed Eloise's glass jar of root beer barrels. "Can I have one? I love these."

"Of course," Eloise said. "They're my favorites too. So, you're an artist?"

"I never said I was an artist. Who told you that?" The muscles on Nelly's face tightened.

"Well, I am just looking at your intake form, here..." Eloise tapped the end of her pen on the desk to fill the silence. The fragile connection might snap if she wasn't careful.

Nelly picked at a scab on her arm for a few seconds. "Right, yeah. So okay, I used to be an artist."

Eloise probed deeper, trying to understand what caused Nelly to turn to the street. But it was too soon or maybe she had already pushed too far— Nelly was not ready to share. Eloise backtracked and gathered information about a typical day in Nelly's life. She learned that Nelly spent most of her day looking through the garbage for aluminum cans to sell. Sometimes, she found little treasures, too, like a chandelier earring with aqua beads or a paperback copy of *Arabian Nights*. These finds kept the day interesting. For meals, Nelly used the money she earned from selling soda cans. She frequented all-you-can-eat lunch buffets in diners downtown, stuffing her coat pockets full of rolls, little jams, and gold-foiled butter pads when no one was looking. During a typical day, Nelly traveled quite a bit: from the tree-lined neighborhoods of Lincoln Park to the scrap metal buyers near Cabrini Green. Sometimes, when she had extra change or could sneak under the turnstiles, Nelly took the El. But that was a luxury, and usually, she just walked. At night, Nelly preferred being with the street kids because even though most of them were stoned out of their minds, they were not crazy like the ladies in the overnight shelters. She could have philosophical conversations with some of them and a few were really talented musicians and artists. When her friend Brian from Minneapolis was sober, he could play any song from memory on his clarinet. And somehow, he always managed to find a literary magazine or used newspaper that he would share with Nelly. If it was really cold, she went to the shelter or rode the Blue Line from O'Hare to Forest Park and back, letting the clacking of the wheels over the tracks lull her to sleep.

As the session drew to an end, Eloise promised that they would work on improving Nelly's situation. Nelly nodded, managed the start of a smile, and moved towards the door. Eloise noticed she had a tattoo at the nape of her neck. It was two Japanese characters that Eloise knew well. They made the word *kiki* or crisis.

"Hey, Nelly," Eloise called out from behind her desk. "Nice tattoo. Japanese for 'crisis.' With danger comes opportunity, right?"

"Are you Japanese?" Nelly returned.

"No, I'm Korean, but I took an introductory Japanese class in college. I think I got a C+ so don't quiz me or anything. Does it mean something to you, the tattoo?"

"I guess it just kind of sums up my life. Like a motto or something." Nelly huffed and walked out of the shelter.

Over the next few months, Eloise increased her counseling caseload to six other women, all in various states of despair. It could be draining at times, hearing their stories of rape, domestic violence, addiction, abuse, and sickness. Some of the women seemed like Velcro balls that kept rolling along and picking up more and more troubles. And although it wasn't professional to think this way, Eloise favored Nelly over her other clients. She gained rapport with Nelly quickly, giving her a sketchbook and telling her to keep a journal of drawings each day. Nelly was always hesitant to share her drawings, but that didn't bother Eloise. She knew that artists could sometimes be secretive. The drawings Nelly did share were reflective of her journeys: a steeple of a church in Pilsen; the worn faces of street kids around a blazing bonfire; fruit stands lining Maxwell Street. Her pen recorded everything with bold, unafraid strokes. One picture showed a Vietnamese café bellied up to a gold domed mosque. The drawings captured why Eloise loved Chicago, the city that spread its arms wide and welcomed outsiders, misfits, those without homes.

There was something that Nelly held closely, though—her reason for being on the streets. Nelly refused to discuss the subject until one afternoon in the early spring.

"How are you feeling, Nelly?" Eloise asked as she opened Nelly's folder.

"Like crap," Nelly said. She rubbed her eyes like a tired child. "But what's new?"

"So you've been feeling like crap for a while?"

"Try my whole life." Nelly braided and unbraided a strand of her hair.

"Can you remember the first time you felt this way?"

"When I was four years old," Nelly said with a bit of hesitation. "Our neighbor called the police on my mom because he found me playing in the yard with a bag of blow. My mom was so stoned. She didn't even notice. The police took my mom away and I got put in a foster home."

"A foster home. For how long?"

"I don't know. I lived some of the time with this lady, Missy, in Oak Park. I swear her life revolved around Jerry Springer and chain smoking. I don't think she even knew I was there."

"That must have been hard."

"Yeah, and she had this older adult son. What was his name?" Nelly paused and looked towards the ceiling for answers. "I can't remember his name. Anyways, he had acne. They would always fight about money and Missy would leave the room. I hated that son of a bitch."

"Why?" Eloise asked.

"Because he molested me. And I was just a little kid." Nelly said this as though it was an obvious fact, something that Eloise should already know.

"Nelly, I am so sorry…how terrible. I mean, I can't believe. It must be very difficult. Can we talk more about that? Can you tell me what happened with Missy's son?"

"No."

"I think it might be helpful, given what you've been through…"

"No."

Eloise wrote a reminder in Nelly's file to revisit the subject in a later session. She felt unsure of how to proceed. This wasn't something she learned in grad school.

"So how long did you stay with Missy?" Eloise tried.

"Until the DCFS moved me to another place. My mom never got straight so I stayed in the system until I got emancipated. When I turned eighteen."

"Then what did you do, when you were emancipated?" Eloise made notes in Nelly's file, but her mind was elsewhere. Instead of thinking of Nelly, Eloise was thinking about herself. It was not the first time she contemplated what her life would have been like if she had never been adopted. She often imagined herself living in the dirty, rat-infested Korean orphanage, a prisoner for life. If she ever escaped or ran away, she would be forced to roam the crowded streets of Seoul looking for a chance connection or opportunity.

"Mrs. Shelly—she was my art teacher at Proviso. She helped me get a scholarship to the Art Institute…for my drawing and painting. We put together a portfolio and everything."

"Oh, Nelly, that's fabulous. It's so hard to get in there. What an opportunity! How'd you like it?" Eloise was having trouble concentrating. Remember your role, she thought. You are the healer, the professional.

"The teachers were cool. The studios were nice. The kids were spoiled shitheads, though, drinking their $4 coffees and moaning about their lives. What bullshit." As she told her story, Nelly remained unmoved, like a news reporter reading off the teleprompter. She picked at her chipped nail polish. "Yeah, but class was awesome. I took this art history class and we got to go to the museum. Did you know that Michelangelo might have been gay?"

"So what happened? I mean, with school. Not with Michelangelo."

"I left. At Christmas, the place closed. All the little brats went home to mommy and daddy. The dorm got locked up, the cafeteria, the studio—all closed. I didn't really have any friends to stay with. So I left. Left the dorm, left school. Just left."

"Nelly. Wasn't it too much to give up? Your art?"

Nelly looked over Eloise's shoulder out the window. She squinted as though trying to make out something in the distance. "I don't expect you to understand this, okay?"

"Try me."

"I realized nobody gave a shit about me," Nelly said softly. "Nobody cared if I passed or failed. Fuck that—nobody cared if I lived or died. I had nowhere to go, nobody to go to. I didn't belong anywhere. So I started to live on the streets."

Eloise could no longer control her racing thoughts. She pictured herself leaving the Korean orphanage and knocking on relatives' doors only to be turned away. She saw Susan asking her what her Korean name was. She heard Grandma Pullman's condemnation: "Where's your Pullman nose?" I never belonged anywhere either, she thought.

When Nelly stopped talking, the room was silent, except for the noise from next door where the social skills class was practicing interviewing in pairs. Silence had always made Eloise uncomfortable. But it was something more than the silence that moved her to speak.

"Thank you, Nelly, for sharing what must have been some extremely unpleasant memories for you."

Eloise knew that she should just stop there and end the session for the day, but she let her own emotions boil over. "You know, I haven't told you this, but I am adopted. And though our stories are different, I feel moved by what you shared. My birth parents died in a car accident in Seoul when I was a baby…I never knew them at all. This is all I have to remember them by."

Eloise held up her hand and pointed to the thin gold band with a chip of jade on her finger. "So I know how hard it can be to feel alone and out of place."

Marlene had given the ring to Eloise when she turned twenty-one. It was one of the few belongings that traveled with Eloise from Korea. The social workers at the adoption agency had passed it on to Marlene in a cardboard box that also contained a grainy picture of Eloise's young parents standing side by side on a street lit by neon store signs. The photo was shadowy and the faces blurred, but it was framed and placed on a dresser in Eloise's room from the time she was a baby. Eloise had been overjoyed by the gift of the ring, but tempered her reaction so as not to hurt Marlene. Much later, she learned from a college friend that Koreans believed jade held healing, medicinal powers.

Eloise searched Nelly's face for some sign of connection or empathy. Nothing could crack her stoic mask.

"I gotta go," Nelly said.

"Wait, Nelly. Is everything okay?"

As Nelly gathered her bag, sketchbook, and coat, Eloise became conscious that she might have made Nelly uncomfortable with her story, but it was too late. Nelly was leaving. She hurried clumsily out of Eloise's office, her coat trailing on the ground behind her. Eloise could only listen to the sound of Nelly's snow boots on the stairs and then in the hall as she rushed towards the exit. "Bye Nelly. See you tomorrow," she heard the receptionist say, and then the shelter's front door slammed shut.

Eloise stayed at the shelter late that night so she could finish her case notes on Nelly. It was difficult for her to admit, but it might have been a professional mistake to share her own story. Still, there was nothing she could do now.

The shelter was quiet except for the ticking of the clock on the wall and the tapping of Eloise's fingers on the computer keys. The clients all left the shelter at five, hauling bags, carts, and suit cases as they headed to a soup kitchen, shelter, or evening hideaway. Like owls, they disappeared soundlessly into the gray twilight.

At 8:11 p.m., Eloise's stomach started to growl, and she packed up her planner and travel mug to head home for the day. On the way out, she grabbed a book on adult foster children to read before her next appointment with Nelly. Outside of her office, the lights were off but Eloise made her way instinctively to the back door. It was a closer route to the bus stop from there. She pushed hard on the door and was greeted by the earthy smell of spring rain. As she turned to lock the door behind her, she fumbled with her keys.

Suddenly, Eloise felt a presence behind her.

"Ms. Pullman?"

Eloise swung around to see Nelly. She wore a black hooded sweatshirt and both of her hands were tucked into the large front pocket. Her eyeliner was smudged, like charcoal that had been rubbed by a fingertip.

"Oh, god…you scared me, Nelly. I'm so glad it's you," Eloise let out a sigh and smiled. "Are you okay? I thought when you left earlier...."

Eloise stopped when she saw Nelly remove something small and shiny from her pocket. It was a knife.

"Give me the ring, Ms. Pullman," Nelly murmured.

Eloise felt sweat condensing above her lip. "Now, Nelly, if something upset you, we can talk about it. It's me, Ms. Pullman. We're friends."

"I said to give me the ring."

She waved the knife in the air and moved closer. Eloise noticed that Nelly's eyes were red around the corners, as though she'd been crying.

"You don't mean it, Nelly. I know you. You don't mean it." Eloise's voice did not sound like her own. It was removed from her body, floating above her. "You wouldn't hurt me."

"Don't talk. I can't listen to you talk any more. Give me the fucking ring."

Nelly's gaze held steady. Her face remained emotionless. Eloise knew now that the danger was real.

Eloise was conscious that tears were sliding down her face. "You know it's my birthmother's. I can't. Please. Here, Nelly...Take my wallet. And my cell phone...." Eloise dropped her wallet and cell phone on the wet pavement.

"I told you, no more talking."

In a quick movement, Nelly grabbed Eloise's hand and twisted her arm. She now faced the back door of the shelter where a sign read, "Welcome, please use our front door."

"Okay, okay." Eloise winced.

Time moved in slow motion. Eloise slid the ring off her finger with her teeth and placed it on her flat, sweaty palm. She reached back towards Nelly. Warm fingers plucked the ring off her palm.

"Don't move," Nelly repeated. "I want you to count to ten before you move."

Eloise numbered each exhale: one, two, three.

The pressure on Eloise's arm then disappeared, and the alley walls echoed with Nelly's quick footsteps. Eloise quickly whirled around. Her pulse pounded at her temples and her legs softened beneath her.

Betrayal overcame Eloise like a biting wind. It was a gray evening and still cold, even though it was almost April. Eloise noticed the alley was lined with neglected, overflowing trashcans. Near her feet, a green weed poked out of the cracked pavement. And for the first time, Eloise read the words scrawled in spray paint on the alley's brick wall: "go home bitch."

In the distance, Eloise saw Nelly running away down the alley toward the main street. She did not look back. Her hood had fallen off, exposing the familiar tattoo.

SUSAN O'DOHERTY

LIZZIE FARRELL GETS HERS

Lizzie hunches forward on the sofa to receive the cup—an actual cup, she notes, with a saucer—taking care to keep the foot with the bad sock buried under her other leg. Lizzie has perfectly good socks at home, which she could have worn if she'd had any hint that Cassandra would enforce a no-shoes rule. In Lizzie's neighborhood it is considered rude, lower-class, to make your guests uncomfortable for the purpose of protecting the floors or furniture. Lizzie's mother used to poke fun at Mama Julie, who took in foster kids, for her "pretensions," her plastic slipcovers and the runners snaking like crabgrass through the "high traffic areas"—"Sure, she's saving it all for the Queen's visit," her mom used to say. And here is Cassandra, with a brownstone in Brooklyn Heights, making everyone expose their socks so the floor won't get scuffed. Even Mama Julie didn't have that kind of nerve, certainly not when adults were involved.

Somehow Cassandra manages to thrust the cup-and-saucer combo at Lizzie without seeming to touch the cup itself, and without jiggling the coffee. Lizzie tries to imitate this sophisticated gesture, but just as she lays her hand on the saucer Cassandra opens her mouth and a stream of unrecognizable words spews out, cursing from the sound of it but impossible to understand. Is this happening, or is Lizzie having a stroke? Drug flashback? She has jumped and exploded the very real, hot coffee all over herself and the sofa before she realizes, from the French au pair's quick dive behind them to yank Theo away from the electrical outlet, that Cassandra was yelling to Celeste, not at Lizzie. Cassandra takes in the spilled coffee, flares her nostrils, and disappears into the kitchen. The coffee has scalded Lizzie's legs through her one pair of nice pants. It is soaking through the couch fabric, too, not beading. This is real velvet. Crap. Lizzie feels her eyes well up.

Cassandra returns with a wet dishcloth and thrusts it at Lizzie without looking at her. *Am I a shade darker than you?* That's what the old Lizzie would have said, before she had Louis, who is several shades darker than anyone in this room. Before she had to care what people like this thought of her.

When Cassandra first issued the invitation, Lizzie was so excited by the idea of going to someone's house that she didn't realize she wasn't included. She should have—these are not the kind of women who hang out with women like Lizzie—but it wasn't until she saw the look on Cassandra's face that she realized Cassandra had been speaking to Barbara when she said, "We all get together for coffee Friday mornings while the kids play. This week it's at my place—why don't you join us?" Lizzie said, "Sounds great!" at the same time Barbara, standing behind her, said, "Oh, I'd love to, but we're going to the Vineyard," so Cassandra couldn't even claim that there was only room for one more kid. Not that space is a consideration in this house.

Lizzie could tell she was supposed to say, "I'm sorry, I misunderstood," and slink away, mortified. And she—the new Lizzie, who really is trying to do what's expected—might have complied, if she had anyplace else to go, anyone else at all for Louis to play with. But she has reached the end of the line.

The kids in the old neighborhood would be calling names even if she was clean as fresh wash and Louis was the color of a pillowcase. "Crack whore" and "nigger bastard" are just easy handles, payback from their parents for when Lizzie was beautiful and promising and mean. All the kids make out with anybody now, black, white, boys with boys, threesomes, and most of them look high—ecstasy, she guesses, not crack anymore, but Lizzie was never a crack whore; she and Anton were in it together, would still be together if Anton hadn't seized up, stroked out, and ended up in the nursing home. Hell, she would have followed him there, shared his hospital bed, let him drool and pee on her all the time, if not for the little surprise package that sent her reeling into rehab and back into her mother's unwelcoming arms.

She visits when she can pull carfare, the old ladies make more of a fuss over Louis than his own grandma, and she knows Anton perks up at the sight of him whatever the nurses say. The nurses throw around terms like "persistent vegetative state" and regard Lizzie with pity and even contempt (this white girl doesn't know shit) because they don't know that the left corner of Anton's mouth turns down when he's pleased, that his eyebrows lift when he wants to laugh. *See, they're the ones who don't know shit,* she tells Louis when Anton makes his faces.

And in the meantime, she's working on herself. The rehab place sent her into counseling, "to deal with her anger." She's supposed to be figuring out why she was always so mean to everybody when she was growing up, and then later, in the rehab groups. Always putting people down, zeroing in on their weak spots, showing no mercy. So far, they haven't uncovered any dark secrets, though the counselor is still hoping. Lizzie's own theory is in two parts:

1. She could get away with it. She was beautiful back then, before it all caved in—first losing all that weight, and hair, and then the teeth when she was pregnant ("Poor prenatal nutrition," the hospital people always said, with a sniff, and of course it was true, but if Lizzie had known, maybe it would have all been different, maybe) and then her face just sort of collapsing—and smarter than everybody else. That combination had allowed her to hustle in Bloomingdale's for years. Back then, all she had to do was throw on jeans and one of Anton's t-shirts and she looked like she belonged, like a model. When she'd bump up against some rich old fool, usually a guy but sometimes a woman, they were pleased to make contact with her. They thought she was Somebody, and maybe she'd go home with them, and liberating their wallets was child's play. So she never had to do it for money, never was that desperate, whatever the kids say or their parents want to believe. And even now that she looks a hundred and three on a good day, even with half her brain cells blown away, she's still better looking than those losers in the group, and she can still think, and the endless 12-step babble about higher powers and "suit up and show up" makes her want to jump out a window which she can't do because of Louis, so she pushes on the steppers instead. That lardass Marlene, especially, bringing in donuts for everyone and making them have group hugs and saying, "Thank you for sharing," after the six zillionth repetition of which Lizzie had not been able to refrain from pointing out that Greg hadn't "shared" as much as vomited all over the group, and if Marlene hadn't traded in her heroin addiction for a dependence on Krispy Kremes she might be able to tell the difference between nourishment, which goes in, and puke and crap, which—that remark was what landed her in the counselor's office. Despite the counselor's best efforts, Lizzie hasn't been able to identify any childhood figure Marlene reminds her of except the assholes she went to school with who she straightened out the same way.

2. Which brings her to the other explanation, more interesting to both

Lizzie and the counselor, though for different reasons. Despite all her smarts, Lizzie never knew she wasn't supposed to act this way; that other people were nice to each other at least half the time. Lizzie comes from a mean family. The counselor's ears prick up when they start down this road, but she hasn't yet been able to put her finger on any person, or any incident, and cry, "Aha! Abuse!" as Lizzie knows she is longing to do. Sure, her father beat her for sneaking out and drinking with boys, and her mother slapped her around for being fresh, but even the counselor knows these are ordinary punishments in her neighborhood and that most of the kids grow up okay, go to community college, become secretaries and mechanics, or, if they're really angry, bullies, bouncers and cops. The Farrells never went overboard with the beatings, never broke bones or knocked out teeth as some parents did. They were just mean, her parents and her brothers and sisters (except for Timmy, who somehow opted out, decided when he was about ten that he wasn't playing, but everybody in the neighborhood was afraid of him anyway, on principle, because he was a Farrell). They made fun. Don't wear your new vinyl imitation Doc Martins in front of a Farrell; they'll see through the fake leather in a minute and you'll be Stinkfoot to the whole school before lunchtime. They'll follow you down the hall yelling, squish, squish, p.u., and the other kids will laugh. Don't let Chrissie Farrell catch you stuffing your bra in the locker room or you'll have boys bumping up against you in the hallways begging to blow their noses down your blouse. And especially, don't try to get back at any of them, especially Lizzie, whose compositions won awards and contained coded references to the doings of people who annoyed her, impenetrable to the adults but clearly recognizable, and hilarious, to all the kids. It was the way the Farrells were, and it had always worked for Lizzie. Boys wanted to date her, girls wanted to be her chosen best friend, and so what if nobody really liked her—if it was all about status, and challenge, and fear? That was the world, as far as Lizzie was concerned. Nobody had ever liked her, particularly, and she'd never liked anyone, and she didn't believe anyone else's experience was any different whatever they claimed.

Until Anton. This is the other part, besides the possibility of abuse, that the counselor can't let go of. Why is he the exception, the only one she let in? Lizzie has lots of reasons, but the counselor doesn't seem to think that any of them are the right one. Lizzie believes they're all true.

For one thing, Anton was beautiful, and strong. Even wasted, he was like a panther up on the scaffolding, painting and cleaning and doing whatever other day work he could get to support them, so Lizzie wouldn't have to sell it. And he loved her, even after her looks went. Why? There's a question the counselor should be looking into, a mystery to sink her teeth into, but she never brings it up, and when Lizzie wonders out loud about it the counselor starts ticking off her good points, as if to join Lizzie in her puzzlement would threaten the self-esteem all these people seem to believe is the foundation of right thinking.

Did Lizzie love Anton? Probably not, if by love you mean what she feels for Louis, the sense that he is the most important person in the world and she would lay down her life for him. Lizzie has never felt this way about anyone, and this feeling is the reason she is going through the bullshit of the twelve-step groups, staying clean, keeping her counseling appointments, and not just because they'll take Louis away if she falls back. She wants to do better. She wants to find out how she's supposed to be, so that he will fit in and have friends and be happy.

It wasn't like that with Anton. At first she didn't even like him. She liked having sex with him, who wouldn't, but she wondered what he was trying to pull, hanging around her all the time. She just enjoyed the sex and waited for him to try to set her up with his friends, or to use her in some elaborate hustle. After a while, she got that he only wanted to be around her, and she started picking on him. It wasn't any fun, though, because he just took it. Not in a wimpy way, because he was scared of her, but like it didn't matter. She would tell him he was getting fat, and he'd laugh and say, "Yeah, better cut down on those burritos." She'd point out his grammar mistakes and he'd thank her, saying how lucky he was to hook up with a smart woman. It was like she'd been declawed.

And then, the night she got the bad stuff and had to go to the ER, and he didn't leave her to fend for herself the way every single person she'd ever known would have; as she would have done to him; he stayed through the whole ordeal of insulting admissions people (no, no insurance, no Medicaid, yes, a drug reaction, here is what she took), and hung around even afterwards, expecting the cops to arrive, but needing to find out how she was, if she wanted anything. After that, she only wanted to be with him. She missed him when he went to work. She had never missed anyone in her life, not even her father when he kicked off. She would reach for Anton in the night, and panic if he wasn't there—if he'd gone to the bathroom, or gotten up to put on the coffee.

She still reaches for him. She swipes money from her mother's purse, like in high school, only now she uses it to refill her Metrocard so she can travel out to the home in Queens, and to buy the toothpaste and aftershave he likes.

Even so, she would not change her whole personality for him, the way she's trying to do for Louis. When he comes out of this, he may not be happy with the new Lizzie. Maybe he loved her just because she was so mean and didn't care about anything. This is a risk she is willing to take, for Louis.

But she can't change herself at home, or at least she can't change the way they look at her. Her mother never misses an opportunity to remind her of how badly she's screwed up. And as far as the neighbors are concerned, she is a mean vicious crack whore who deserves any bit of bad luck she gets. When she doesn't answer back, they think she's high, or that her brain is fried like in the drug ads. Nobody can take in that she's a new person, a decent, responsible mom, worthy to join a playgroup.

So Lizzie has been branching out, using some of her mother's money to travel to playgrounds all over Brooklyn, just to see who's there and how she and Louis might fit in. The counselor says she is impressed with Lizzie's "resourcefulness," but Lizzie is exhausted.

At first it was fun, practicing her new, pleasant personality. Lizzie felt like an actress, just like when she was pickpocketing in Bloomingdale's—the one in the know, putting one over on the mark. She liked spying on the other mothers, memorizing their most successful conversational gambits ("What a sweetie! How old?" "Great T-shirt—Baby Gap?") and then trying out her lines on a new audience.

Unlike at Bloomingdale's, though, this crowd isn't eating out of her hand. Probably it's the teeth, she thinks, plus Louis's color. In Carroll Gardens he could almost pass for Italian, but the moms there all have hairdos and designer diaper bags and have known each other since their own playground days. Forget Greenpoint; they take one look at Louis's nappy hair and call their kids in for lunch. They fit in well enough on the Lower East Side, but Lizzie doesn't want Louis making friends with kids whose mothers look like her.

Brooklyn Heights was a long shot; a desperation stop after a morning of disappointment in Park Slope. The Slope had a reputation for diversity and openness, so she had had hopes of connecting there. And there were other brown kids, playing with white and Asian children, and they were okay with Louis, but all the moms looked so healthy, with shiny hair and Birkenstocks, and everyone was polite but no one would let her in. And at two, you can't have friends unless your mom says so. So, after the lay of the land became clear, Lizzie packed them up and took the 2 train to Borough Hall, then walked over to Pierrepont Playground, not really expecting anything, and look what happened. An invitation.

What did Lizzie think would happen once she got to Cassandra's? She can hear the counselor phrasing the open-ended, superficially nonjudgmental question that, when decoded, would mean, "Well, what did you *think* would happen?"

The fact is, even though Lizzie knows it's over—her looks, her charm (such as it was), her ability to seduce or intimidate people into giving her what she wanted—she doesn't believe it. Deep in her gut she still believes she can walk into a room and take over. So, yes, she thought she could pull this off. Or rather, without thinking, she believed she could.

This is over, too, now. Not that it ever started. The others, Jody and Leslie, had barely spoken to her since she'd arrived. Leslie had asked some nice-girl questions at the beginning—do you live in the neighborhood, will Louis start preschool in the fall—but she obviously didn't know what to make of the answers, and the conversation died. Nobody else made an effort. They talked about people she didn't know, who lived in the neighborhood but were moving to France for three years, and then about a book Lizzie had never heard of. Then the coffee.

The other moms talk around her as she swabs the sofa, ruffling up the velvet but deepening the stain. She sees herself through Cassandra's eyes, a worse blotch than the coffee, which is, after all, home-brewed and so, by definition, clean. For all Cassandra knows, Lizzie is infesting her sofa with all varieties of lice, fleas, and cooties. She feels her face crumple.

"Mommy?" Louis pushes his head under the hand holding the rag.

"Mommy's okay," Lizzie says. "We're going home now."

"No," Louis says. "Playing." He runs back to the train set he has been chugging back and forth on the elaborate track system the au pair has set up.

The conversation halts as the mothers wait to see what will happen. Theo stops chasing Melissa and lurches over to Louis. "Bad boy. Go home now. Bye," he says. Melissa bursts into tears. Jody runs over to Melissa and sweeps her up, glaring at Lizzie.

"Now, Louis."

"No."

"Bad," Theo repeats. He pushes Louis, who falls onto the train track. Louis shrieks. Lizzie jumps up. She can see Louis's hand tighten on the locomotive. She races over just as Louis swings. He clips Theo on the lip. Theo screams, waking Charles, who starts screaming, too. Melissa redoubles her cries.

Theo is bleeding. Cassandra calls to the au pair, who runs out of the room. Lizzie grabs her bag, picks up Louis, and throws him into the stroller. "No, Mommy!" he yells. "No! Playing!"

"Shut up," she says, and Cassandra, who is cradling Theo, says, "Pretty."

A few years ago Lizzie would have eaten Cassandra for breakfast. Today, even if she could think what to say, Lizzie has lost her appetite. She pushes the stroller toward the door, nearly colliding with the au pair, who has returned with an ice pack.

Outside, Lizzie heads for the R train. She bumps the stroller down the stairs, too exhausted even to curse all the able-bodied teenagers hanging around who don't offer to help.

On the platform, Louis is quiet. He likes the trains, likes anything loud and fast. Lizzie looks down at the tracks. It's amazing what you can see down there. Amid the soda cans, candy wrappers, and empty chip bags Lizzie has seen a high heeled silver evening shoe, a dead cat, and a toy metal fire engine, among other curiosities. She notices what looks like a set of house keys as the train pulls in. She wonders whether the train crews come out at night, when nobody is around, to excavate the treasures and bury the dead.

There is a seat near the door, and she heaves herself into it. She pushes the stroller back and forth in front of her feet. Louis falls into his train-trance, eyes unfocused, a blissful half-smile on his slackening face. That's the way to be, Lizzie thinks. Just let it go. It's not going to happen; it's over. She tries to fuzz up her vision like Louis does, to let it all go soft and easy, but she can't help it, she takes in everything, she always has—the businesswoman across the aisle, who is missing an earring, Lizzie wonders if she has noticed, and the old lady doing acrostics in Spanish, and the ads over their heads, for wart removal, hemorrhoid relief, dental reconstruction. The Magic of a Dynamic Smile, she reads. Affordable and Flexible Financing. She pushes her tongue through the gap in front, imagining meeting resistance, a solid, gleaming row. "Magic," she says to Louis. In spite of herself, she twists around to study the subway map posted behind her, noting the green splotches, wondering, trying not to wonder, who goes there to play.

JUDITH TURNER-YAMAMOTO

FROM AWAY

After the dry summer there were only the black-eyed Susans blooming. Sophie knelt at the flowerbed by the rusted metal wall of the boat shed. She opened the newspaper, holding the fluttering pages down with her knees. A brisk wind rippled the surface of the bay, setting the buoys on the lobster traps dancing. The metal sign for Potts Point screeched back and forth above the pier. Clouds the gunmetal gray of the ships built nearby scuttled across the sharp October sky. The wind, Sophie told herself, would not be so bad at the cemetery, away from the water.

She worked quickly, slicing through the woody stems, the pile of flowers in front of her growing. Mondays, Mrs. Chilton liked to shoo her out of the house first thing. Habit, as most things seemed to be with Mrs. Chilton. Sophie imagined her getting her husband off to his boat before daylight, the children off to school, then tying her apron on with a fierce snap, and throwing herself head on into the disorder of a weekend's worth of living.

For Sophie, this Monday had started like all the others. Stuart up before the light, showering. The zip and snap of him dressing in the dark, the brisk closing of his suitcase and garment bag. She lay in bed, her heart hammering with an unnamed anxiety, telling herself this time his leaving was a dream. Then came the starched collar stiff against her neck, the medicinal mint of his mouthwash as he bent to buss her cheek. She stayed there, the covers pulled tight, until the chill of Mrs. Chilton's disapproval seeped in. Sophie somehow found herself here, in the cutting garden.

She struck a match, cupped her hands against the gusts. Smoking was something she'd taken up in Maine. She stopped short of inhaling, but found a cigarette gave her something concrete to do when she was feeling wispy as she did any time she thought of Mrs. Chilton outside the confines of the gray shingle house they shared.

Not that she didn't feel comfortable with her. She did, despite her glaring at Sophie from behind the dust gathering on the mahogany chifforobe or in the no-buff wax building up in the corners of the kitchen. An indifferent housekeeper, Sophie had always relied on help. But no one would clean for you in Maine. Besides, she didn't like the idea of strangers touching Mrs. Chilton's things, moving them around. She wanted the house to stay just as it was.

From away. The locals' description of outsiders came to her, striking her with its fit. Except when she dealt with ghosts, Sophie felt herself operating from a remove. It was this distance that had first put her within reach of the spirits. Before Stuart, she had been a magnet for ghosts. Orphaned, she grew up in her grandmother's old house in Vermont. A string of elders, including a great-grandmother, two maiden aunts, and a distant bachelor cousin had died there. Unlike the children at school who either ignored her or made a point of excluding her, the spirits competed for her attention. They whispered to her in the swishing of the feathery pines outside her window, in the silken urging of the rain. She lay in bed listening to their disembodied desires, longings beyond her child's understanding. Later, as she began to grasp their meaning, the spirits became more insistent, swirling around her, an intimate fog distracting her from her daily business. They left her alone only when she took on their troubles, healed their sadness through her own heart.

She flicked her half-smoked cigarette in the water, wrapped the newspaper around the flowers and began the climb the hill to the car. Soon it would be too cold to smoke outside. She couldn't imagine Mrs. Chilton liking her lighting up in the house. Their differences centered on Sophie's essential fondness for dirt. She even liked the look of it settled on surfaces, its quality of reclaiming things, its indifference to efforts at obliteration. "Cleanliness is next to Godliness," Mrs. Chilton chided her when Sophie tracked mud into the kitchen from the shed where she threw her pottery. When she lined the urns up in the nook, Mrs. Chilton noted the flaws Sophie put in each one, a gap in the glaze, a slight slope to the mouth of a vase. "It's deliberate, to let the life in," Sophie would say out loud each time. She washed her hands at the white enamel sink, smirking to herself as the iron-laden dirt turned the white bar soap and the sink orange. She opened the tap on high, the whine of the old pipes drowning out Mrs. Chilton's dismissive sniffs.

An upsurge of wind caught the small pieces of drawing paper she settled on the passenger seat, sending them swirling through the interior of the car. Sophie dropped the flowers on the floorboard, lunged after the paper.

Funny, she thought, weighting the retrieved sheets with a box of the soft-leaded pencils she used in her work at the graveyard, how making rubbings, and later throwing pots, the constant putting of her hands in dirt, had given her something solid to hold on to. Stuart had done that for her too. "Stalwart Stuart," she'd called him. With his plain, sensible face, his rough solid body, he'd been her surest chance at an ordinary life. His incapacity to understand anything beyond what he could touch, hold, or count had snuffed the spirits out like a candle. Until Mrs. Chilton.

She and Stuart had lived in the house for three months, since July. They'd happened on it early in their annual Maine vacation. Mrs. Chilton had died in the spring and her nephew, Ben Greely, was setting up the estate sale.

"Go on in," he said, struggling to arrange a mismatched collection of porch furniture on the lawn. "You don't need me worrying after you."

Sophie wandered through the rooms, dragging a finger along the scars on the furniture disguised with energetic rubbings of lemon oil. "Annie I, Annie II, Annie III," the names of Mr. Chilton's boats cut from the bow of each one, hung on the wall in the yellow breakfast nook just above a plate printed with the Lord's Prayer and a praying hands plaque.

In the kitchen Sophie spotted a fishbowl filled with sea glass. Amber, cobalt, aquamarine. She ran her hand through the fragments frosted and smoothed by tumbling waves. She pictured Mrs. Chilton waiting for her husband's lobster boat to round Sharp's Island. Scanning the rocky beach, occasionally a glimmer of color would catch Mrs. Chilton's eye, come home in her pocket. Sophie imagined her whisking in the back door, a small quick-moving woman like herself. She'd toss the glass in the bowl that once belonged to one of her children's goldfish, grab her apron—freshly bleached and pressed, it still hung on its hook by the stove—and begin the business of serving up dinner.

"Wouldn't it be wonderful," Sophie said, half to herself as she pressed the starched white dimity of the kitchen curtains between her hands, toyed with the ball fringe, "to come here to our own house each year and just instantly be part of things, to belong?"

More comfortable taking action than imagining, Stuart went right outside and offered Ben Greely an unmatchable price for the house and its contents. A few weeks later, Stuart drove her back to the house, dropped the skeleton key to the front door in her lap. "There," he said, smiling a satisfied smile. "There's your Maine house."

Sophie had let them in, the clunk of the heavy tumblers falling in place. A familiar penetrating cold she hadn't noticed that first day stayed with her as she retraced her steps through the downstairs rooms. Stuart followed along, watching, she knew, for the incline of her head, the intent look that would assure him she was happy.

His pager sounded, the emphatic beeping sending him back to the car and his cell phone. Stuart was so busy, she thought, pulling back the dining room curtain to watch him juggle the phone, scrawl down figures. The house was a gesture, his way of getting close the only way he knew how. She let the curtain drop, joined him outside. She'd turned to look at the dining room window, seeing the expected flutter of the curtain drawn away from the glass. In buying Mrs. Chilton's house Stuart had thrown her back to the very thing he had rescued her from.

She was the one who had decided they should stay on through the winter. She had pictured drifts of snow, an icy shawl enveloping the house. Inside she would bake, the steam slicking the windows, and then, in spring, the purple and yellow heads of crocuses would disrupt the perfect even calm of white. But the house at Potts Point proved as easy for Stuart to leave as the one in Greenwich. In August while he lay in supplies of salt and snow shovels and made arrangements for their road to be plowed so he could keep on with his unrelenting business travel, she'd begun to grasp the coming winter's endlessness.

Sophie pulled into the church parking lot. "Be careful what you wish for." There was Mrs. Chilton again, expressing herself in homilies, prying in her thoughts even here, away from the house. Speaking to her as she had that first night she and Stuart lay together in the four-poster bed. "Home is where the heart is," Mrs. Chilton said just as Stuart kissed her goodnight in his distracted way, turned his back to her. Sophie knew Mrs. Chilton's voice at once, the tone as tight as the stitches in the framed samplers throughout the house expressing similar maxims. All night she lay awake, her restlessness exacerbated by the unfamiliar sound of waves tossing outside her window, certain Mrs. Chilton would not be able to hold her tongue. But Mrs. Chilton had been silent, a perverse petulance Sophie now knew well.

What did Mrs. Chilton want? She reached in her pocket for a cigarette, fumbling with the matches. Other spirits spoke to her about their own troubles, but Mrs. Chilton never talked about herself. Last night, just after falling off to sleep, Mrs. Chilton's presence had startled her awake, setting her heart pounding in the cloaked darkness. Although Stuart lay beside her curled into his side of the bed, and the alarm clock ticked on, she could not escape the weighted sensation that things were very wrong. And there had been something else. That odd urge to shake Stuart awake, to demand that he hold her, that he abandon his plans to leave in the morning.

She crossed the road to Bailey's Store. First a cup of coffee, she would take her time. She tossed her cigarette in the bucket of sand by the front door. "Good morning, Howard." Sophie dropped a quarter in the dusty glass by the hot water urn, scooped instant coffee into a Styrofoam cup. Howard emitted a grunt that passed for hello, continued reading his newspaper. She stirred her coffee, dunked the clumps of nondairy creamer that refused to dissolve. The worn pine boards beneath her feet were splotched with spilled coffee and in need of what Mrs. Chilton would call a righteous mopping.

She stepped onto the porch, peered across the road at the graveyard enclosed behind a low stone wall. She saw no spirits, only here and there the trick of sunlight, slanted and broken by headstones. Still she waited, wanting to be sure. She heard Howard's chair complain as he turned to see why she hadn't gone on down the stairs and about her business. Responding to the push of his stare, she poured the last of her coffee on the ground and started for the graveyard.

She lifted the rope latch, opened the peeling wooden gate. The flowers could wait a while longer. She'd do just one rubbing before going on to Mrs. Chilton's grave. She chose a child's stone, the first in a row of several topped with a crudely carved lamb. She concentrated on the scraping of her pencil, the letters emerging from the velvet of the graphite.

She dug the clay for her urns from the banks of the creek just below the graveyard. She pictured tiny tributaries flowing through the graves like veins through a body, leeching minerals of flesh and bone, depositing them in the clay along the creek bed. Smells of lingering emotions came to her in the colors marbling the earth: the musty gray of despair, the sour yellow of unfulfilled ambition, the unexpected sweet red of forsaken love. The urns, bearing the names of these buried here, would be placed on the graves beneath the headstone. She planned to photograph what she imagined would be their slow crumbling return to the earth from which they'd come. This was a work she could be involved in her whole life, one that might finally satisfy her reluctant affinity with the world of spirits.

She tucked the paper in her pocket, blew on her cold fingers. The idea for the project had first occurred to her when she stumbled across Mrs. Chilton's grave. The headstone, simple gray granite, stated only the facts. "Ann Stover Chilton, Born February 7, 1920; Died March 7, 2005." It reminded her of a stock simmered and diligently skimmed until it was rendered utterly bland. Except for the marble urn attached at the base of the stone. Around its circumference were carved bunches of lily of the valley bundled with curling ivy, the same plants that grew by the steps to the screened in porch. The urn stood there, squarely part of Mrs. Chilton's plan.

Armed with the flowers and the gallon jug of water she kept in the car, she took one of the pea gravel paths bisecting the graveyard. She found Ben Greely down on all fours on his aunt's grave, the manic chopping of grass clippers clacking against the headstone. She watched as he patiently went over the new grass just beginning to form a soft, down-like covering.

"Hello, Ben."

He looked up at her, his face creased like a piece of paper that had been folded again and again as if someone's mind kept changing. He inclined his head toward the grass. "You got to be careful. It's been just six months now. You can't cut too close when it's young."

Sophie nodded. "Yes, I imagine so."

"I keep things tidy for her. But Monday's not my usual day."

"It's mine," Sophie offered. "I bring her flowers. From her garden."

His eyes narrowed. She couldn't tell if he suspected her of some ulterior motive, or if the low sun, which had just popped out from behind a cloud, was bothering his pale eyes. "So that's you. Well, I guess that's fine."

Sophie smiled. She imagined Mrs. Chilton being equally as unappreciative despite her prominently placed urn.

He pulled out the faded blooms, peered inside at the last of the water gone milky with the drained life of the flowers. "No way to dump the old water. Guess she didn't think of that. "Have to bring the hose along next time I come, give it a good cleaning."

He moved aside to let Sophie flush the water. She emptied the bottle, turned her face away. The rising brackish smell transported her to her grandmother's parlor. She was nine years old, her turtle, the only pet she was allowed, had died. She saw herself shaking its bowl until all the water sloshed onto her grandmother's crocheted doily, infusing the house with more death, more loneliness.

"Lonely all right." Ben said. "He left her, weeks at the time, him with his boats and all."

Sophie found room for herself in his blunt abbreviated speech. "But the lobster boats, I watch them. They come in each day in the late afternoon."

Ben pulled at a weed caught in the teeth of his grass clipper. "We're not all lobstermen. You might think so, judging from the buoys clogging up the bay. He was a deep-sea fisherman. Then he up and died young on her, lost at sea in a storm."

"But she had her children."

"Nope. Just me around now and then after my mother died."

Ben bent over, inspecting a black-eyed Susan whose petals were lightly tinged with red as if it had for a moment thought of being something besides a yellow flower. "Annie had black eyes. They sparked something awful, like a pair of snapping turtles. I think she was mad at him, right up to the day she died." He looked away, mopping his handkerchief over his eyes. "They say folks come to the graveyard to feel close to them that's gone. Seems like I just feel the loss more."

Sophie patted his hand. "Stop by for tea some time. You might like visiting the house."

"It's the same then."

She nodded. "It's still hers."

She watched Ben walk away, stop to trim an errant blade that caught his eye. Mrs. Chilton angry. And alone. She hadn't thought of that. Her hand brushed the last of the grass clippings away, the clean buoyant smell staying with her. She unfurled the newspaper, teasing free the first of the flowers.

KERRY LANGAN

LIVE YOUR LIFE

David Tetlow had been portraying Dr. David Hammond on "Live Your Life," a daytime soap opera, for thirty years. More than that, he had quite literally become his character. Affecting an authority on medical matters, he called his relatives each year and reminded them to get flu shots. Whenever he boarded an airplane, he carried a copy of *The New England Journal of Medicine*. He watched medical information shows on cable television, gravely nodding his head as a disease was explained, concurring with the prognosis. David was meticulously groomed, the cuticles on his fingernails never visible, the edges of the nails hygienically short. He ate a balanced diet and took brisk walks about Bayfinch, his hometown in upstate New York, an hour's drive from the soap's Manhattan studio.

His education had not included medical school, college, or even much elementary science to speak of. He graduated from Sycamore High School in Toledo where he had dabbled in the drama club, playing the role of the doctor in "Our Town." But the theater teacher, Miss Sissons, thought he had a classic profile, chiseled Gregory Peckish features, and a voice that could fill Sycamore High's auditorium. It was the only encouragement he'd gotten from any teacher, and he headed for New York a few days after graduation. He had trouble getting auditions, and hid his nerves by acting overly confident at the few he went to. He did voice ads on the radio for several years before finally landing a role on "Live Your Life," at the time a fledgling soap. Playing Dr. Hammond gave him, he felt, hard-earned respect. He didn't realize how hungry he was for it after years of rejection until he put a stethoscope around his neck for the first time, feeling the metal tubes solid and official against his skin. When people asked him where he studied, he assumed they meant medical rather than drama school, and answered evasively "Ohio." He scoffed younger actors arriving in New York with drama degrees from Yale and other prestigious institutions. All that money spent for what? There was nothing to acting. You simply became the character. He and Dr. David Hammond had been one and the same since he was twenty-nine, more than half his life.

When he first joined the soap's cast, his character had just graduated from medical school and was an intern at Loveland Hospital. He was quite the catch in those days, every nurse throwing herself at David Hammond *and* David Tetlow. In real life, he married Lucy, a fellow actress who left him when she got a part in *Hair* on Broadway. On the show, David married Jenna, a sweet-faced nurse with lips as thick as bricks; she was thought to be too bland a character, however, despite the lips, so the writers made her a mercy killer, stabbing patients with lethal injections during the night shift. Doctor David divorced her and married the angelic Alicia, the social worker with Raphaelesque hair and altruistic eyes. David didn't like that phase of the show; Alicia upstaged him with all of her benevolence and self-sacrifice. Luckily, she died during childbirth, and he became the grieving, stoical parent raising a daughter who bore such a resemblance to her mother, it was almost painful for Dr. Hammond to look at her. In fact, David developed a wince of which he was inordinately proud; it came to be known as the "Hammond wince" and was even written into the script occasionally as a direction.

In the course of thirty years, Dr. Hammond had been married four times, had nine extramarital affairs, had three children, had been held hostage twice, had switched a pair of babies at birth, had been accused of murder and had his good name cleared, had performed plastic surgery (even though he was a general practitioner) on a mobster, and had suffered three gunshot wounds on separate occasions. David Tetlow's life was not nearly as colorful, but he strove to make it as similar as possible, exchanging spouses and lovers with nearly the same frequency. He divorced one wife because she had slept with her gynecologist, something he absolutely couldn't forgive, and two others because they, like the charitable Alicia, had upstaged him. Eleanor and Grace were well-intended women, but he had felt that all eyes were on them, when they should have been on him. Eleanor starred on a rival soap, "The Power of Passion," known as "PP" in the trade, and Grace was a housewife with a gift for gardening. She made the most stubborn plants bloom with a verdant zealousness, and Bayfinch residents called the house constantly seeking her advice on a gamut of horticultural problems. David had observed Grace examining plants, touching their leaves, kneading their soil, and it had been too much; she had the life-saving skills of a physician and there was room for only one doctor in the house. Presently, he was married to Caroline, a divorcee with two children in college. Ten years younger than David, she was very charming, and dressed and acted with the flair of a doctor's wife. He approved of her, but this marriage too seemed ill-fated since her son, Greg, was considering majoring in pre-med.

For the past year or so, Dr. David Hammond's role on the show had been drastically cut. For several months, David was unconcerned. He thought they couldn't survive without him. Yes, younger actors perhaps gave the show its sex, its drama, but he fancied himself the *soul* of the show. He was the main patriarchal figure of Loveland, the soap's fictional town, and his picture was still featured prominently in the opening credits. More than that, at midpoint in the show, in between commercials, it was his voice who announced, "Live to Love will be right back." That, more than anything, convinced him that his future was secure.

One day, however, while he was watching the show in his dressing room, he heard a different voice at the commercial break, a woman's voice, English, saucy, with a come hither timbre. It belonged to Kathryn Heckles, the woman who played the newly arrived health club owner. This rankled David more than he could admit to himself because the woman had made outright cracks about his obsession with his character. Most of the cast referred to him as "Doc," a friendly, respectful address, but Kathryn, who exhibited herself in a rainbow of spandex outfits on and off the show, greeted him with, "What's up, Doc?," shouting this into his stethoscope in an uncannily correct Bugs Bunny. She was in her mid-twenties, an aspiring stage actress; she made it clear that her work on the soap was just a brief stint before Broadway called. When she voiced this in rehearsal once, David had thought he charmed her with his response: "My dear," he bellowed, summoning his own stage training on volume and inflection from high school, "we all thought that at one time and. . .here we are!" He waved his hand with a flourish to take in the set. Kathryn had extended her own arm, mimicking him, and said in her wisecracking voice, "No. . . there *you* are!"

Most disturbing was her influence with the head writers. Margaret and Bill were notorious for turning down suggestions flat. They viewed the cast as jealous, vain robots who could be trained to recite a few sentences each show without stammering. Any more than that was gravy. More than a few actors had quit over disagreements with them, but Bill and Margaret had the backing of the executive producer and loved telling an indignant actor where to go. Kathryn, however, was not put off by their reputation and went to them freely, even in her first weeks on the set. David watched her attempts at camaraderie with them with a simmering smile, hoping he'd be present when they really shut her down, told her to stop whining and memorize her lines, or go back to England and get a bit part in a BBC drama. When David saw the three of them having lunch together at the commissary, however, even overhearing Bill ask Kathryn's opinion on a recent re-write, he swallowed a radish whole and decided it was time to take action.

But what was he worried about, after all? He had worked with Margaret nearly the entire time he'd been on the show, and Bill for the last ten years. He simply had to confront them, he told himself. And he did. On the telephone. At night. He called Margaret at home and told her he was overdue for a major story line.

"Overdue?" she said bluntly, irritated at being interrupted at home for such a common complaint. Margaret's personal life was something of a mystery; there were rumors of younger men, aspiring soap actors. As he held the phone to his ear now, David thought he heard bullfighting music in the background.

"Yes," he said quickly. "I haven't had more than a couple minutes air time in two years, when I- "

"Had that seizure," Margaret finished. "Well, what can I say, Dave? Doctors used to be everything on soaps, but people are sick of them now."

Had he heard her correctly? Sick of doctors? "Don't be insane, Margaret; we're the most important of occupations. I suppose you think aerobics instructors are important? That they make a valuable contribution to society?"

Margaret laughed her characteristic, "Ah haa-a!", enjoying having caught David in an openly jealous moment. "Well, since you put it that way, Dave," she said, "doctors and aerobics instructors do have a couple things in common; I mean, they both get the blood pumping, am I right?"

"Rubbish." David felt particularly learned at the moment, disdainful of such ignorance. He had a high card he knew he could play only once. He had played it many times as a young man, but he knew better than to wave it wildly about now. But this was such a moment. "I will demand to be released from my contract if I am not given fifteen minutes air time in a single episode by next month."

He let his statement hang over the wire, waiting for Margaret's astonished breath. He did hear something, but it sounded more like a man's voice calling out, "Ole! Ole!" Margaret partially covered the receiver and hollered, "I *told you* to leave that tablecloth alone!" She spoke into the phone, "I'll talk with Bill," and hung up.

David rejected the first script, a ludicrous story about his joining Kathryn's spa and having a heart attack while doing step aerobics. The scene would culminate with Kathryn performing CPR on him while people in exercise clothes would stand around screaming "Save him! Save him!"

"I'm the doctor, I'm the one who saves people!" he railed at Margaret and Bill, irritated that they were eager to profile Kathryn at his expense. "And besides," he continued, "I would never do step aerobics in a million years."

The second script was worse, much worse. He and Kathryn were to meet at a cocktail party, leave together and go back to her house, make mad, passionate love until he had a heart attack. Kathryn wouldn't perform CPR, but she would lift him and carry him to her car in an audacious display of female strength.

"No one would believe I'd be interested in that woman!" David said, throwing the script on Bill's desk. "She has no class. She's just a loud-mouthed bully."

Bill looked up, giving Margaret an obvious *I told you so* look, but then said, "Dave, the older man, younger woman thing is very hot right now. We think you and Kathryn could be the stars of the trend."

"Then why are you so damn determined that I have a heart attack! We can't very well be hot if I'm about to expire, now can we!" David stood between the two writers and witnessed the guilty shadow eclipsing Bill's face. Margaret normally had a poker face, but he noticed the twitch on the left side of her mouth.

"All right," David said, waving a finger at both of them. "I know what's going on here!" He drew himself up and spoke to the imaginary back row, charging his voice so that Margaret covered her ears. "You're trying to get me to quit the show! You can't fire me before my contract is up, so you're trying to humiliate me into leaving. Well, forget it! Give me a heart attack, throw me together with that loathsome woman, I don't care! Write some cockamamie story about her being my sex therapist. . ."

He stopped shouting because he noticed Margaret was starting to jot notes.

"You can never get rid of me until I say so!"

He strode out of their office as if he were exiting a stage and went to his dressing room, pouring glasses of bourbon until it was time to go home. Once there, he didn't tell Caroline what happened. They had a routine where she would rub his neck and his shoulders as he sat reading the paper and she would say, "Rough day, darling?" and he would respond with details of Lois Medford's recurrence of amnesia, and little Charlie's broken arm. If he wasn't in the show that day, he made something up.

They sat on the patio and drank gin and tonics. Looking at her, David admitted to himself that she was not his prettiest wife; her nose was too high and narrow and her chin was creased too severely, bending in and out as she chewed her food. When she spoke, only her bottom teeth showed, lovely teeth, straight and white, but nonetheless, just the bottoms. But Caroline knew her lines; she deferred to him, she entertained well, throwing the most elegant dinner parties in Bayfinch. If she were a bit loose with money, it was worth it to see her looking so consistently well-groomed in designer apparel. Really, if her son would just drop the pre-med major, she had potential to be the one David would stay with. The events at the studio that day made him see her in a very fond light. She was so gracious, and receptive to all his remarks, even when he complained that her hair color needed a touch-up. They retired early that evening, making love with an energy that surprised both of them. Why, there's nothing wrong with my heart, David told himself victoriously.

When he arrived on the set the next day, Sally, one of the production assistants, reminded him that he wasn't needed that day. This was often the case. Most actors were called at home well in advance, but David came in regardless. A set needed a doctor, he reasoned, so the crew thought nothing of waiting until he arrived each day to tell him.

In his dressing room, he contemplated his future. He had three years left in his contract, and then he would be sixty-two, a respectable retirement age. In a way, he welcomed the thought of not having to come here each day, not having to work so hard at convincing people he was a doctor. It would be much easier, David thought, to be a retired doctor. He and Caroline would travel and entertain at home, attending their children's graduations and weddings, their grandchildren's christenings. So many events at which he'd be the admired and respected retired doctor. Yes, it was a role he would welcome, but only when he decided to take it.

At one-o'clock he turned on the large-screen television in his dressing room. David didn't bother reading scripts unless he had lines, but he hadn't missed a show since the day his daughter was born twenty-three years ago. During the opening credits, he admired his face on the screen; the photo had been taken ten years ago, but he thought it was still a good likeness.

The opening scene took place at the health spa. Kathryn was directing an exercise class, standing on a little stage in a neon yellow one-piece body-suit, her red hair clipped up on her head into a tight assembly of curls. She was bouncing about the platform, calling out to the members of the class. "Push it! Move it!" she yelled, grunting as she kicked her feet out behind her.

"Oh, move it yourself, lady," David said to the screen. He was irked that Kathryn was the lead story in today's episode. She began doing a ridiculous exercise, thrusting her pelvis forward while she waved her arms over her head. David started laughing, thinking that Kathryn looked like she was doing a poor imitation of a Hawaiian dance. Remembering the day she had imitated him, he stood and began doing the exercise in an exaggerated fashion, shaking his hips from side to side, punching his arms up in the air.

"Push it, move it," he repeated, mocking her instructions. He caught sight of himself in the mirror and stopped moving. For a moment, he looked like an aging man struggling to catch his breath, and he composed himself, sweeping a forelock back from his face. He was just about to sit down when he felt a pinching in his chest, like a clothespin clamping down just left of his breastbone, but then it was gone, released, and he wondered if he had imagined it. He got a glass of water and sat in front of the set, assuring himself that it must have been just the start of a pulled muscle.

The second scene began at Salvatore's, the restaurant secretly owned by the illegitimate heir to the Kelliff family fortune. David had trouble remembering all the particulars of the Kelliff family; they'd been rich, then poor, then rich again so many times over the last fifteen years, he couldn't keep up. The camera panned the diners who were dressed in extravagant clothes, and David was alarmed to see nearly the entire cast there. This was unusual. The whole cast was normally only brought together for big events, a wedding or a murder trial. Why, I could easily be sitting at one of those tables, he thought. There was Millicent, his present wife, sipping coffee with his stepson. David was outraged. He planned to go to Bill and Margaret directly after the show and complain. The camera stopped moving and focused on a table of women, Kathryn the focus of the shot although he barely recognized her because she was wearing a white linen suit instead of a leotard in some obnoxious color. The women at the table were leaning in around her. At first David thought they were studying her dessert, not real, he guessed, from the sheen of the frosting, but then Kathryn said, "You heard what I said—he's a fake!"

A woman with a blue pillbox hat said, "Kathryn, you're mistaken. Why, he removed my daughter's gall bladder last year, and she's absolutely fine."

"It's just a miracle she's all right," Kathryn said, "because word is all over town that Dr. Hammond faked his medical credentials and God knows what else." Kathryn looked out across the room and continued to speak. "Poor Millicent. She doesn't have a clue. She thinks she's married to a legitimate doctor."

David toppled sideways out of his chair, his left shoulder colliding with the floor with such force, he wondered if he dislocated his collar bone. But his eyes never left the camera, now showing Millicent who was daintily wiping the corners of her mouth with her napkin.

"Millicent!" David called. "Help me!" He couldn't even remember what the woman's real name was; they had only recently married and he always called his wives by their characters' names. The camera came in close on Kathryn's face. David noticed that she lowered her chin, making her eyes and lips appear bigger.

"He got some medical training in Korea, but he never went to med school. He's been passing himself off as a doctor for years, pulling the wool over your eyes." Kathryn looked meaningfully at each of her luncheon companions, reprimanding them for their blind trust.

David sputtered, trying to find his voice. He raised himself to his feet and picked up a newspaper, hurling it at the TV as he screamed, "Liar! Slanderer! I'll sue the leotard right off your back, lady!"

Another woman at the table clutched her water glass, shaking it melodramatically so that some of the water spilled onto the table. She began to weep pathetically, her eyebrows becoming one although no tears actually fell down her face. "When my second baby died in delivery," she sobbed, "they blamed it on a lack of oxygen. Now I know," she said, trembling, "I know. . . DR. HAMMOND KILLED MY BABY!"

Everyone stopped eating and looked at the woman who by this time was out of control, standing up and shrieking until she was all but delirious.

"Everyone!" she shouted. "Listen to me!"

Forks and knives were dropped and the restaurant became deadly quiet. The woman trembled as she held onto the back of her chair. David didn't recognize her; she must have been an extra. "We've been had! We've been used," she said. "We've been lied to!" she yelled, her voice growing louder with each word. "Dr. David Hammond isn't really a doctor! He's been lying to us for years. He's nothing but a TWO-BIT FAKE!"

The woman continued screaming until she collapsed. Kathryn was at her side immediately, ordering a waiter to get an ambulance while she made sure no one crowded the woman. She leaned her head over the woman's chest and cupped her hand around the woman's wrist. The woman was carried out of the restaurant on a stretcher while stunned, hushed onlookers affected a collective look of terror.

David was befuddled. "But, but. . . I don't even know that woman! What baby is she talking about? I never killed her baby. Why, she's mad, she's insane." He could clear it up, all of it, he told himself. He would simply tell Bill and Margaret that it was all false, every word. How could it be true when he'd never seen the woman before? And since when did extras get to make such pronouncements?

He walked to the set and pressed the power button off. His feet seemed to sink into the carpet, and it was an effort to move. They've done it, he thought, and he felt the pinching sensation in his chest return. They've come up with the one thing they knew would make me leave. He sat before his mirror and looked at himself, at his face that for years looked back at him with such confidence, with such unquestioned faith. Now his expression seemed that of a petty thief, a shoplifter who loitered about the five and dime. He put his hand over his chest, as if he were about to recite the Pledge of Allegiance, and held it there until the pain stopped. He picked up his Grammy, the only trophy he had ever won. He received it in 1978, the year he was on camera for sixty-three shows in a row. That year, he had convinced a patient not to jump from a tenth story window, and diagnosed his own wife with yellow fever. He packed the trophy along with a few other things and left the set, walking out the back door to avoid the cluster of autograph seekers who usually hovered by the front door.

At home, he found Caroline's note on the kitchen table.

"Darling," it read, "Back by seven. Light dinner on the patio?"

She hadn't seen the show. It didn't surprise him; Caroline normally lunched from noon until two with the other doctors' wives, and later watched the show on tape. He wondered what her reaction would be to an early, disgraceful retirement. He'd have to hide out until people forgot about Dr. David Hammond, maybe try to get a part on another show, a better show, a show where they respected doctors.

The phone rang and he ignored it. He listened to the message, an eager young man's voice telling him about a TV series based on the blockbuster novel, "Undercover," about an older doctor forced into the witness protection program after testifying against another doctor who sold drugs to the Mafia. Was he available? The network thought he'd be perfect. The man started to give the phone number.

David fished through his pockets for a pen. After he found one, he looked about the room for a piece of paper, repeating in his mind the first few numbers already given, and then the complete number as he searched, frantically now, for a scrap on which to write. Forgetting that he could simply replay the message, he wrote the number on the wall. Hopping excitedly from foot to foot, he jogged in place until his breath became thin. He didn't call the man, a casting agent for ABC, back; he would wait at least a day and then explain about his contract, demanding enough money so that he could flaunt the figure about the soap's set. His own agent hadn't called him in years, and David wondered if he should let him handle the deal or find someone new.

He sat down on the bed, re-thinking the day's events. Of course, he thought, I had to go undercover; denouncing me at the lunch was just a set-up for my disappearance. Everyone will learn the truth soon enough. "Like a phoenix rising from the ashes!" he shouted as he stood. Opening his closet, he flung jackets, slacks, sweaters onto the bed until he got to the heavier items at the back, winter clothes put away, wrapped carefully in long plastic bags. He removed his beige trench coat from the bag and found his black fedora. He put them on in front of the mirror, tying the belt on the coat tightly, lowering the hat so his right eye disappeared beneath the brim. He thought he looked like Humphrey Bogart in "The Maltese Falcon," except he wasn't a detective, he reminded himself, he was a doctor, an undercover doctor. Still, the resemblance was so striking, he couldn't resist saying "Schweet-heart," through locked teeth over and over again to the glass, until he forgot he was staring into a mirror; he was simply looking at himself.

CHRISTOPHER WILLARD

COMPENSATION

. . .   *"Do you think he suffered," she asked. She being the new secretary.*

"The worst but no worse," he replied. "Only suffered, in the most colloquial manner, a heart attack."

"Poor Mr. Fraschis," she said. "It was the new technology that got him."

Myron transferred his stare from Fraschis to the young woman.

He was Myron—who was known for whistling Tommy Dorsey, Brylcreeming his eyebrows, wearing inherited three dollar cologne, filling his cup with liquid the color of his beard. The woman was Myra—nervously brushing hands against her pleated grey skirt. And there, hunched, face flattened to the Xerox, with his wild eye, spumescent saliva, and distorted lips emerging as copies, was old George Fraschis—in multiple.

"Yo, seventy-five, Poppy," the Puerto Rican kid behind the counter demanded.

Myron reached but the kid retained the waxen cup.

"Seventy-five old man," he repeated.

"I heard you the first time," Myron grunted.

He remembered the day he started at McAllister. Coffee free for the taking. Later, after they fired the woman who managed the percolator, it was the lobby shop—twenty cents, a bagel included—fifty. Fifteen years later immigrants took over and upped the price to two Washingtons for coffee alone. He knew. He'd kept the index cards. Now this, at this stinking deli, nearly a buck for the black stuff.

"Flimflam. *Shande*," he mumbled.

. . .   *That was how he met Myra, not officially of course but unofficially and grotesquely.*

A few days after Mr. Fraschis has been deposited at Cedar Lawn, Myra swayed the same grey skirt and round heavy hips in the direction of Myron's desk.

"Donations," she chirped.

He regarded the bulging manila envelope. "You think he went up or down."

"It's for his poor wife," she answered.

"Nobody says too bad about George," he said.

She paused then stepped back to survey the young man. "Do you always wear such ugly ties?"

He looked at her in the same manner, letting his eyes climb from her Oxfords, up her black stockinged leg to eventually settle upon her youthful face. "How about we go for a drink one of these days or are you one of those egg heads?"

She tittered and covered her mouth with her free hand.

"No, I don't think so Mr. Esterson."

She placed the envelope on his desk and penned her extension on his phone pad.

"This isn't so you can call me," she said. "So next time maybe you won't be so crass."

"So maybe you'll walk by my desk more often," he said.

She laughed again, this time not covering her mouth. "Maybe I won't either."

"Don't wait too long. I'm going up," he said.

Myron shook away the memory. He extracted eight dimes from a change purse and ticked them across the worn laminate counter.

"Five cents change," he ordered.

"Five cents change," mocked the kid in a thick Puerto Rican accent.

"Five cents change," Myron repeated.

"Five cents change," the kid repeated.

"This is homicide," Myron said grabbing the coffee.

. . .   *Myra informed him in a damply lit Brooklyn restaurant that she too had Hungarian Jewish ancestry.*

He put down the menu. "Five bucks for a whole pizza pie."

She stirred the ice in her soda and gave him the overview of her education, "Bates, 19th Century English lit. But studied Jókai Mór, Endre Ady."

"And Ferenc?" He asked?

"The two Ferencs," she said. "And summers in Yiddish classes on the lower East side."

A beer later Myron blurted out, "You're a hamisch you know."

Myra excused herself and rushed to the bathroom.

The next Saturday Myra pulled him to the Morgan Library where she pointed out Charlotte Brontë's tiny pearlescent riding gloves. In front of a Claude Lorrain ink wash fantasy she said dreamily, "I remember walking naked-kneed through ferns at my grandmother's house east of Debrecen. We threw stones into Romania."

"I too visited Hungary as a child," he lied. His parents were from the old country but he'd never traveled beyond New England. Still, her remembrance glistened.

A month of giggling goodnights concluded with Myra acquiescing. "I agree to your proposition Mr. Esterson, but I'll allow you only to kiss my cheek."

"Myra and Myron, My My," her father joked at the wedding reception. It took two tries for Myron to crush the glass at sheva brachos.

First came Avigail, meaning the father rejoices, followed by Shalva. Then came a succession of blessed Februarys, blended Springs, promotions, purchases, the four bedroom in Scarsdale, a boy, Lazar.

Myron stood remembering. He'd chronicled every event on his cards.

"I want to make one thing perfectly clear." He stopped himself. A businessman glanced expectantly and Myron averted his gaze. The men behind the counter shrugged and joked in Spanish.

Myron jerked around and mistakenly shoved his thigh into the chipped brown edge of the nearest table, jolting a woman's tea across the sleeve of her sweatshirt.

"Yeah, yeah," he said.

"Really no, no problem," the woman replied. Myron quickly categorized her as yet another immigrant. Probably Middle Eastern, judging from her black scarf, although he knew it was now called something else.

He shuffled to a greasy table against the back wall where he extracted his index cards. Upon a particular one he wrote down the day's information. "Two thousand, two hundred seventy seven steps exactly from the wooden jamb on 11th Street to the tiled floor of this sordid 14th Street deli." Myron had counted every one, every day. The shysters would make it one more step if they could. They'd slit your pocket with a box cutter to get your money, to suck out your identity. This was his point. The immigrants came and infiltrated what was decent and natural. They distorted it beyond order.

He settled into the stained vinyl seat. If they could charge this much for a coffee he could coddle it as long as he liked.

. . .   *Thirty-seven years, five days a week, not a one without the English knot and oblong tie clip. He commanded the helm and directed the prow toward literary perfection. Myron erected mammoth spires of words that towered into thinner air. He separated himself from the sludge of common language. He received a brass placard engraved in fluid Garamond that said, "Editor-in-Chief." His private dreams were public endeavors.*

Myron pulled the snub nose pencil from his inside pocket.

They poisoned the water cooler and then they poisoned the well. Do what they would, his legacy would remain.

The Middle Eastern woman began to show up daily, always with the scarf. Twice Myron had begun to speak, considering the slightest guiltless apology, but twice he had continued walking to the back of the room where he could see her profile reflected in a mirror where a flock of painted birds were reduced to 'v's.' He watched her scribble on her newspaper, often long after the steam had stopped rising from her cup.

One morning he returned to the counter, bold, intrepid, a pretense built upon a packet of sugar. From that vantage point, slightly behind her, he determined she was completing the crossword and he strained his old eyes to judge her ability but the kids loudly taunted that he had a new lady and she looked back, caught his stare, and efficiently cupped her large hand over the puzzle.

The New York Times crosswords had been his domain, inked letters, capitals only, error free, completed before the Scarsdale express reached the rusting metal sign announcing 96th Street. Each finished puzzle was then wedged between the red cushioned seat and the train wall as a reminder to the next passenger that there existed those for whom legal tender consisted of knowledge and perfection.

Myron returned to his table and considered. The puzzles grew progressively harder throughout the week and no doubt her ability to tackle the crossword, on Thursday as a matter of point, indicated naturalization.

He fished his tattered pack of index cards from his jacket and slid off the thin rubber band. Years of fingering and thumbing had stained them with oil and dirt but he could still unearth each milestone as it had been dated, coded, penciled, filed, arranged, rearranged, ordered. Now prying back the plastic on the lid of his cup Myron said aloud, "Here is one thing." He read, "She never did learn to fold her napkin properly," a sentence he'd once written with a precisionist script comprised of perfect circles and looping 't's.'

The Oath of a Freeman, Cambridge 1638, first printed document in Colonial America. How many people still knew that? He knew it when original Volkswagen Beetles prowled the avenues, when people praised him for this knowledge. It was required. He knew Hemingway's old man was Gregorio Fuentes who finally stopped at age 104. He knew the sea was older and still moving.

. . . Myron rebuked his younger colleagues who attempted to turn weekly meetings into platforms where barbaric travesties like 'narrative deconstruction'' and the 'acquiescence of pluralism' required response. Worse, the newer editors heralded fiction that undid fiction. He didn't need their Baudrillards and Ecos and Foucaults. Magna Cum Laude at Stoneybrook, Harvard graduate. Myron's credentials were framed under glass, untouchable. "One learns quality by criticizing," he chastised, "and through criticism comes a depth of understanding."

They whispered. They talked. They just didn't understand.

Myron sent a memo to the staff of McAllister outlining his technique. He wrote, 'Take a page, any page except the first or last of a chapter. Delete all the words. Leave only the punctuation.' He chose page 54 from Hemingway and Faulkner and contrasted their skeletons.

Hemingway

????? ? ""·"" ...... ""·"""·""·"·"·" """·"·"·""·"·"·""·"·"?"·"·" "??"·"·"·"·",,,.

Faulkner

-,,,,,:·,,:,,.).,:

    Myron explained Hemingway's economizing of words required an excess of punctuation while Faulkner's extended thoughts hovered within limited pauses. In staff meetings he presented the skeletons that his interns spent hours compiling.

    "This is order," he explained.

    Myron surveyed the flat back of the woman's sweatshirt, COLUMBIA. An SUV idled at the red light and the thick stomp of cranked bass shook the smoky tinted windows and vibrated Myron's stomach. Ridiculous. Benny G replaced by Ice T. Arthur Miller was only half right. In the long run it wasn't the Communists but the static of life that invaded life.

    "To quote," he said aloud. He stopped to sip the hot acidic coffee. "To quote ... a republic of mediocrity ...." Ingersoll and a few others still resonated.

    . . .   *The rug they yanked out from under him was presented to line his coffin. "Always a big laugh when a yellow bud is reduced to a twisted filemot leaf," he told them.*

    Myron reset his clock radio so he could arrive at the deli before the Middle Eastern woman. He watched the way her lower lip sagged when she mouthed the order for tea and the manner in which the hazy light accentuated the purple breves of fatigue below her eyes. Always the same time, always the same tea. A foolish consistency he noted considering Emerson.

    . . .   *Abraham Sokolich too. The same Abraham Sokolich who'd come over to eat Memorial Day steaks and sip real Dreher beer on their Scarsdale patio. How could he stand before a judge in the Westchester County court of law and point out Myron's mismatched socks? His client, he said referring to Myra, bore the brunt of a disheveled mind and unlovable character.*

She once singed his youthful beard trying to press it flat. In Butler's field she glowed while he pushed his favorite girl, silver swing chain links shaking, red hair sheets to the wind. 'Don't garden with bare feet,' she once said.

Oh, but Myron understood he still had enough compos mentis to know when he was being railroaded.

He'd stood up and yelled, "Are they all forgotten Februarys?"

Beside her sat Avigail, fingering a glistening plastic purse he'd never seen.

The Middle Eastern woman wrapped the tea bag around her thick fingers to squeeze out the sepia. He leaned, trying to get a better look, and the chair legs skidded on the slick black and white tiles. Myron slapped his coffee sideways and tumbled to the grubby floor, his index cards scattering willy-nilly. The Puerto Rican kids hooted and pointed and cuffed each other's necks with the backs of their hands.

The woman rose and walked over, simply extending her open palm.

"Let me alone," he snapped as he rubbed his hand over the radiating pain that shot down from his left hip.

She plucked napkins from the metal holder and pressed them to the liquid. Myron pried himself to his knees and began to retrieve his index cards. When he finally stood he realized the woman had purchased him a new coffee. Myron stared angrily. Such impetuosity by this woman, such presumption.

... *"Alone, homeless, immigrant." Cutting words, yelled by Myra after the settlement.*

Now they imprisoned him with their impartiality.

He was not yet prone, not yet admitting the earth. He had survived these six and a half years since their judgments. He would show them. On his grave would be written "Solidify the foundation."

The woman retrieved her newspaper, which she laid on the table before Myron. The square boxes of the puzzle contained no letters, but were filled with colored inks, anthraquinone red and cerulean blue ink ordered into a perfect pattern reminiscent of a Persian Kelim carpet.

On this and many more mornings she explained how she came from Chalus, near the edge of the Caspian. She told how in Iran her name meant 'peaceful individual' and how she'd fled a husband whose disposition was the opposite.

They walked together, as they had many mornings, steps he didn't bother to count because she was proximal.

Myron decided that if anyone ever asked he'd tell them he met Mona at the deli after he had fallen.

They arrived at Grand Central terminal and Myron thrust his arm introducing her to the emerald heaven and its unshimmering stars. He inhaled strongly, holding in his lungs the of scent of electricity and of lotus tree oil. Mona displayed her fleshy neck and focused on Aldebaran, the eye of the bull, watcher over the East. Myron took a second deeper breath and exhaled it loudly. His stale air rose quickly, swirling upwards toward the celestial vault where dots of light mapped out heroes and paper grids transformed to prayer rugs.

V
SPIRIT TURNS

MARY KAY RUMMEL

ENOUGH

From the outside it looked like a ghost house. A perfect Halloween setting. It was deeper than it was high with windows marching toward the back. Looking more like the hotel for railroad men that I used to see near the Great Northern Yards in St. Paul than a convent, it had stood on that corner in south Chicago for more than a hundred years. There were three creaking wooden floors, chapel and dining room on first, community room, and older nuns' rooms on second, and four rooms for the younger nuns on third. My room was beneath a gabled roof. Around me on the third floor in 1966 there was much talk of love.

One fall afternoon Sister Elizabeth, who was two years older than I came bouncing up the creaking wooden stairs. She stopped at the doorway to her room that was next to mine. Her blue eyes sparkled and her face that I had always thought so beautiful was brighter than usual.

"I know I'm in love," she said, "with Brother David." They had been leading a youth group together.

"What will you do?" I asked.

"Leave, I think, at the end of the school year. Get married."

"I'm amazed that you're so clear about it. Is it easy for you?"

"Oh yes, I'm really happy. I know it's what I want."

Sister Gwendolyn had the bedroom on the other side of me. She taught religion in the high school and was very kind. Her closest friend was another nun, Sister Patrice, who visited sometimes. On one of those visits Patrice met Sister Renee, who was near my age, twenty-six, and very strong, I thought. Renee seemed to know how everything should be, had all answers when all I had were questions. They fell in love and Gwen lost her closest friend. Patrice and Renee spent every weekend together. "I think they will leave together some day," Gwen predicted, looking very depressed. "I'm okay with it. I guess it's supposed to be." But I knew she was unhappy.

I lay on the narrow bed in my small green room at night wondering what was wrong with me. Loving my students didn't seem to be enough. I wanted to be in love like Sister Elizabeth. Since I was seven and had fallen in love with my second grade teacher, I had wanted to be a nun. It had seemed to be the best thing I could do with my life. Now I wanted sex too but I couldn't admit it. The summer before, my friend Christina had told me about discovering masturbation, how she did it every day and how it had helped her decide to go home. She felt she couldn't take a vow of chastity and masturbate every day. "What was it like?" I asked, having no idea, and even after she told me I didn't want to try it.

I was lonely in that house and there was so much hostility. This assignment must be some kind of test, I thought, but I would never pass it. I arrived at the end of August, before school started, and met Sister Seraphina who would be my Superior during the following year. She was old, soft, rounded, and reminded me of my grandmother, but her blue eyes were small and cold. "What does she want from me?" was my first thought on meeting her. Her expectations hovered in the air and behind her clipped words as she gave me housework assignments.

"You need to get the refectory ready for meals every day and clean it thoroughly Saturday."

"But I'm teaching early," I said. "How can I get it ready for noon?"

"You'll have to figure that out, won't you?"

That evening after dinner I prepared the refectory for breakfast, setting out the bowls and silverware. I checked the sugar bowls and the salt and pepper shakers, individual ones that sat in front of each place. At least I don't have to cook, I told myself. During morning recess I ran home from school to set the table and make sure everyone had what they needed for lunch. After school, I did the same for dinner. It was a good thing that the school was just across the street. On weekends I would clean the whole room and refill the salt and peppershakers. Because I hated cleaning the thought filled me with despair. By October I learned that the house was sharply divided between old and young. There was a war raging between generations here just as in the outside world. With the university only a few miles down the road, change was erupting in the world around us.

Repeatedly I heard a complaint ringing like the bell that called us to prayer, "Those young ones...." " "Those young ones...." " and I was the youngest. Sister Clothilde was the loudest complainer. She was an obese piano teacher, something of an outcast among the other older nuns. Her black eyes flashed with emotion above flushed round cheeks, and she seemed so vulnerable. Even small things she did, like sneaking an orange from the kitchen every night, annoyed her sisters. I would catch the Superior's eyes looking at her in dislike, so I supported her in spite of the criticism and spying.

I volunteered to try out one of the styles being considered for a new habit. Until then, the nuns were wearing what their predecessors had worn hundreds of years ago, long before the French revolution, a peasant woman's outfit from France in the middle ages. The one I chose to wear was a blue suit with skirt well below the knee and a truncated veil. My short bangs hung beneath the veil. Letting my bangs show was my greatest offense in the house. The other nuns who were trying out new habits pulled theirs back under their veils.

Every noon hour I sat at the table eating my meat loaf and mashed potatoes, then feeling heavy and sleepy, I'd have to run back across the street to teach school. Two nuns sat across from me every day, one who had been my high school principal. We had called her "Old Ironsides." Her jowled face was squashed into a wimple tight around her head. Her eyes were small as a crow's. Sister Felicitous, who sat next to her, had a face that resembled Richard Nixon's. Everyday as I tried to chew my noon dinner, Ironsides leered at me and talked to her friend about the evils of men, of sex and my connection with both.

"I know why you young nuns wear those little veils," she'd say. "I know why you let your bangs show. You're trying to attract men." Over the green beans she droned day after day as I tried to chew my food. After those meals I ran back to the school in relief. It was my salvation that year; I was so glad to have those fourth graders and their parents in my life. My students were writing poems and performing plays and growing every day. This seemed good work to me. One November day as I wrapped my wool shawl around me to run across the street, I stopped and just looked back into the dining room. Maybe Ironsides was right. Wouldn't living with a man be better than living with them? Can't I be a good teacher without being a nun, I wondered, and scared myself with the answer—Oh yes.

Because there was beginning to be more freedom in the order we could attend parish events. The parents were like the people I had grown up among, hardworking, poor and very religious. Ken was a parent who came up to school all the time. His wife had died and he had two children. I enjoyed his hanging around me, found myself being flirtatious, then would tell myself—Stop it you're a nun.

One Saturday I was working in my classroom and took my jacket off. He stopped at the door to talk and I could see that he kept looking at my breasts. I had been invisible around men for so long that just this small bit of attention made me confused and guilty. This never happened when I wore the long habit and big veil, I thought, remembering how as a novice I stopped in the dime store where I had worked through high school, saw the manager whom I had dated and no one looked twice—no one saw me. I truly had been invisible. Maybe this new visibility was what upset Ironsides.

Each winter night I went into the community room to talk and read the paper. Sister Seraphina frowned at me from her place across the long wooden table, but she would not talk to me. That winter I took a film course with some friends from another convent. Bergman's films mirrored my own feelings. *Through a Glass Darkly* was my favorite. Once as I turned the pages of the book review section Seraphina said, "All you care about are movies and books. You are not spiritual enough." That was all she said.

Life got heavier and heavier, Bergman heavy. I made a friend of the first grade teacher, Sister Clarisse, who was middle-aged, caught between the warring generations in the house. At night we walked the city blocks when it wasn't too cold or dark. At the end of the street loomed a brown brick building that was the home and hospice of the Little Sisters of the Poor. At Christmastime we visited the nuns who lived there. Clarisse and I talked with one young nun and came away shaken at how medieval her life was. She took us to her tiny cell, room for just a single bed, and told us of her life. She never left the grounds of that damp sunless building for any reason. Only the older nuns were allowed to go out begging in the community for the needs of their dying patients. They never talked, either, unless it was necessary to speak to patients. Sister Emmanuel told us how they had gotten special permission to speak to us that night. She seemed so young, her eyes large in a thin face and her head weighed down by a long double veil. She had a beautiful smile and, in spite of the weight of her habit and her grim surroundings, was energetic. Like a saint, I kept thinking.

"The work is so selfless, every day with no breaks," Clarisse said later. "I couldn't do it."

"When I was young I thought I could do whatever was required to be holy," I said. "But not anymore. Her life seems horrible to me. Much worse than ours. At least we get out of the madhouse."

The neighborhood reflected my feelings as winter stalled around us even as the sun began to set later. The trees were bare against a grey sky and the city blocks ugly in that time before any green begins. Small houses clustered neatly around stone churches. On every block a church served a different ethnic community much like the churches had on West Seventh as I grew up. One April night as the trees were getting that fuzzy, coming alive look, Clarisse and I began to talk about leaving.

"I'm really comfortable in this neighborhood," I said. "I think it's because my own neighborhood was like this. It was close to the river too—the Mississippi." The river was only a few blocks away but we avoided it because of the long dark stretches where there were railroad yards, piles of lumber, and the only lights were from the brewery that looked like a Scottish castle.

"I didn't have a neighborhood," she said, "just the farm. I miss it so much. I could have gotten married before I entered the convent. The man owned a farm near my parents. I should have married him, but now it's too late."

"No, it's not. Why don't you leave?"

"I can't. I'm just too old to take the step. And afraid."

Some nights she cried. "This place is terrible but they're all like that. You're young. You should leave now."

Once a week we had confessions at the convent with a priest from a nearby parish. He seemed understanding and I thought I could talk to him.

"Meet with me," he said, "we'll talk more," so I walked over to his parish house one day after school.

"I'm confused," I said. "I don't know what's right. I think I want to get married, have children. I hate the community I'm in."

"I understand that," he leaned toward me. "I'll help. We'll talk it through little by little."

When I got up to leave, he hugged me. I backed away, dizzied by it. I hadn't touched a man for more than eight years.

I had to decide. In August I was scheduled to make final vows so back and forth, back and forth I went. In school I directed a play with the eighth grade students. They gave me roses the night of the performance and the parents clapped. They could not know they and their children were the thin threads that held me to this life—that human contact and the things I had dreamt of doing.

One summer, working in an anti-poverty project, I visited homes and taught children in community programs. I liked working with people who weren't priests and nuns. We were all in it together. With them my life felt bigger than it did in my little community who were feeding on each other day and night in south Chicago.

"Those young ones," Clothilde said one morning, "watch movies and then don't get up for prayer in the morning."

We watched the news on the small TV in the basement. Images of war and protesting students began to appear. Change was being demanded, and I was unable to make a decision.

"God, please tell me what you want me to do. I want to do the right thing," I prayed thinking of saints like young Therese of Lisieux who found God in everyday things but was tortured by the other nuns in her Carmelite community. They made her kneel for whole days on stone without moving, accusing her of pride. They took away her food even though she was the cook. When she got TB they never let her remain in bed until she finally died. She suffered much more than I ever did. I was ashamed of my feelings, but I kept saying to myself, this life is not enough. My bowl is empty. The lines from a poem that I had written in college kept going through my head.

My father's grandparents
my mother's parents
my own parents grew old
sure there would never be enough.

I wondered if dissatisfaction was in my genes, an Irish emptiness. Weren't we always short of money, clothes, even food?

My answer came with the spring. I woke up one May morning and knew what I would do. I walked through the house knowing I was leaving, knowing I had no place there, but I felt like a deserter in school as I tore through my desk looking for the application forms for the summer program for teachers at the University of Minnesota that had come in the mail in September and that I had kept.

The parents had a dinner for me at the end of the year. They knew I was leaving to go somewhere and gave me a watch. I loved this place, this neighborhood; this was where I wanted to work. How could I tell them, "You are not enough?"

"Come and stay at my house," Ken, the single father, suggested when word got out. "You could help me with the children." I knew there was another, unspoken part to this. He wanted more from me and it scared me.

I cringed at the thought of having no other option but to work for an older man, ironing, cooking. That's something from another time, I thought, when there was no place for women who left the convent. How terrible it must have been. I had a life ahead of me; I was going to graduate school. I went back to my college to see the nuns who had been my teachers, to tell them I was sorry for disappointing them.

Finally, I had to tell Sister Seraphina, the superior who had glowered at me every evening for a year.

"I want to tell you that I have decided not to take final vows," I stammered, nervous.

"Good," she looked pleased. "I wasn't going to recommend you anyway."

"Why?" I asked, looking at her in complete disbelief.

"Because I told you that you're not spiritual enough, and you don't clean well. The salt and pepper shakers weren't kept filled. The plates on the tables were always crooked, and the older nuns complained. You don't work hard at it."

"But my teaching...."

"Yes, you're wonderful teacher and work hard at that but it's not enough."

"Not enough." She sounded like an echo of myself and finally I was discovering why she was so angry.

"You never talked to me," she continued even though I wanted her to stop. "You never came to me with your problems. You're not a good community member."

Would the other superiors have paid attention to her veto of my final vows? I would never know, and I didn't really care. Part of me felt bad for all the lost years, but part of me was singing—I'm so glad to be getting out of this insane asylum.

Elizabeth left the day school ended. She was full of brightness. "I'm going to be so happy. David is leaving the Christian Brothers next week, and we will go on from there."

When I started to cry she hugged me. "You've got so much to look forward to. Sex is great!"

Gwen was in tears. She was staying for life, she decided, and that dark, wooden third floor was going to be so empty. Except for Renee, but she and Gwen had not been able to talk since Renee and Patrice had become lovers.

"I'll miss you," I said, "and Clarisse too, but I'm so glad to be leaving here. Whatever happens next is bound to be better."

My friend, Barbara, drove me to the provincial house the next day. "They'll give you two hundred dollars. We'll go shopping as soon as you sign the papers. Then I'll give you a driving lesson."

I met with the provincial superior and signed my leaving papers, cried a little and, for the last time, walked out a convent door. That very moment I felt a fullness and lightness, as if my body was stuffed with clouds.

A week later, still filled with freedom, I sat on the edge of a battered black suitcase in the wide hall of the Great Northern depot ready to board the train to Minneapolis. The platform where I waited opened into a new world. Beneath my long black coat and shorter black dress my whole body tingled with excitement. I had gone to college as a nun, taught school as a nun, for eight years walked the narrow paths from convent to school and had earned no money. I'd spent eight years hungry for a miracle, waiting for illumination, the bright promise. There had been beauty in that idea, but I never wanted to be that hungry again. I no longer wanted to be a saint. Still more nun than not, I was on my own for the first time in my life. There was no one to watch me, no one I had to please, neither God, nor those who spoke for him and that was enough.

I am looking forward to this review session, knowing that it will provide me somewhat an opportunity to look at my life in perspective & have visions to my-self accomplishing this task while living & then shift into the fruit of it & then should be happier. In any case it should be interesting.

DEVON WARD-THOMMES

BECOMING THE PELICAN

During my second fall semester in college, the sorority house where I lived hosted one of the largest date functions on campus, Assassins. Each couple was given the names of another couple—these were their victims. The goal was to find your victims in the dark, and when you did, they were "killed" and called out of the game; the last remaining couple was the winner. I don't remember now what the prize was for winning, but I'm sure it came with lots of popularity and respect. My roommates and I spent months preparing for it—all through September and October we talked about who we'd invite, what the best hiding places were, how to know your victims in the pitch black darkness. One of my best sorority friends, a Korean girl named Sun, designed the t-shirt—black with white silhouettes of three skinny, big-breasted girls in mini-skirts and platforms holding guns like Charlie's Angels framing the word ASSASSINS on the back. We were *so pumped for this shindig.*

We decorated the dining hall with streamers and made "better than sex" cake—a dangerous concoction of vanilla ice cream, peanut butter, crumbled Oreos, and M&Ms all smothered with chocolate sauce—for our dates after the event; I certainly wouldn't eat the stuff. What I remember of the actual night is fuzzy, out of focus like a bad photograph. My date was Andy Miguel, my beautiful Filipino boyfriend, star quarterback, secretary of Phi Delta Theta fraternity, student body president. We wore our black shirts with pride, and painted our cheeks with stripes of greasy black paint like football players. Everyone wore black bandanas, strips of cloth tied around their arms, anything to make them look badass. Then we turned off all the lights and the chaos commenced.

There were screams and heavy breathing and pounding footsteps down the hallways. I grasped Andy's hand—my palms were sweaty—people were groping and gasping and screaming. We hid under one of the bunk beds in the dormitory for a while, tried to distinguish feet running by, the sounds of people banging around in the dark. We ventured out and ran through some rooms, and then hid in the costume closet, but that was all. Soon, we heard some loud wailing, all the lights came on, and the game was called off.

The dining hall's fluorescent lights were blinding. People sat around on chairs, wiping sweaty foreheads and smearing their make-up. At least two or three girls were crying—someone had a bloody lip, another girl had banged her forehead into the corner of a wall, the popular soccer player, Karen Lewis, had sprained her ankle. Stacey mopped Liz's bloody forehead, Megan blamed her boyfriend for her broken glasses, and they argued until he left, yelling angry words behind him. I don't remember where Andy was. I sat in the corner, heart beating fast, watching the streamers sway and drift around all the angry, red-faced people. Most of college was like this.

At nineteen, I still believed the truth was that not eating lunch, running a marathon, and joining the crew team would bring lasting happiness, the truth of who I really was. If I just worked hard enough then all that pain would bring looser clothes, a flat stomach, pure, unadulterated satisfaction in hard work paid off. I'd learned that beauty equaled happiness. Thin, graceful, tan, toned beauty—the people I wanted to be inhabited the pages of *Seventeen*. Some were even in my calculus class. My peers who seemed happy all weighed less than 130 pounds; they had long, shiny, straight hair and big smiles and popular boyfriends. I thought if I could just control my frizzy curls and have one of those hard-ass stomachs, I would be well, and able to relax, and feel fully alive. At nineteen, this is what I believed.

But I did know a few true things, underneath all the layers of spandex: I had the sneaky feeling that there was more to life than what I could see and hear and touch and taste. I suspected that God probably existed among all of us stumblers. And that almost everyone was struggling to wake up, to be loved, and not feel so afraid all the time. That's what all the clothes, make-up, elliptical trainers, and string bikinis were all about. I knew that I wasn't alone in the dark—I could hear others fumbling around just as awkwardly as I was. The trouble was that nobody knew where the light switch was. Nobody even seemed to care.

By the time I joined the varsity lightweight crew team during the spring of my freshman year, I'd developed a curious and wildly ecumenical faith stitched from scraps I'd gathered in reading and participating in various wisdom traditions—Native American, Taoist, feminist, Buddhist, even Catholic, in those sweet, slow days cherry-picking with my ex-Catholic priest father, who taught me to meditate and believe that we are all sons and daughters of God, whoever that was. According to him, she was most likely female.

My closest friends were my competitors—my best friend Annie Chesnut who turned anorexic our last year of high school, all the girls skinnier than me who rowed on the lightweight team, the sorority sisters who hoarded bagels and granola bars and never came to house meals, my popular, manipulative boyfriend. What I didn't know was that my strictest competitor (and my best teacher) would turn out to be the person I hated most—me and my body.

Before every crew regatta, we'd all had to weigh in, each girl peeling her jersey over her head and stepping on the scale. Sonja, our team captain, weighed 132, two pounds over the lightweight cut-off. So she ate only rice cakes the day before each weigh-in, and then spent hours dressed in five layers of clothing, sweating off the pounds on a stationary bike in the boathouse. One time, she was just a sliver over—130.4 pounds—so we'd all watched as another teammate took Sonja's long cashew-colored hair in her left fist and a pair of scissors in her right, and sliced off the beautiful swishing bundle. It turned out her hair weighed a measly .1 pounds. She'd still not made weight, so she'd fasted all day in order to be allowed to row in the morning.

Although I'd started college 15 pounds over the cut-off, by that spring I weighed 122. I had learned to multi-task: I took my reading homework to the gym. I spent afternoons there sweating on the stair climber, trying to feed both parts of me—the curious student asking big questions about spirituality and the dissatisfied sorority girl who obsessed about exercise. I must have seen some incongruity in this, reading about Jung and his collective unconscious while participating in the sad body image soup that was almost tangible in the steamy air, my fellow sorority sisters pedaling beside me, nose-deep in their *Shape* magazines.

Poetry often helped. When I read Mary Oliver's "Wild Geese" or anything by Rumi, quick bursts of sunlight streamed through my darkness. At those times I knew that if you had the eyes to see, there was beauty everywhere

in nature, even when it rained spittle rain like God was sneezing, or when
sewer stench rising from the river mixed with the sharp odor of wild onions.
I could even see beauty in my girlfriends with large, round bottoms. I was
just glad I didn't look like them. Even though I knew some truth somewhere
in my body, it wasn't what I wanted to believe. I didn't want to listen to
wisdom; I just wanted to have a fast ergometer score, and to be thin.

This time was not so long ago—I was nineteen seven years ago, a
sophomore in college at a small school in Salem, Oregon, where the students
were more conservative than the faculty, and ninety percent of social events
happened at Greek houses. I was a new member of Alpha Chi Omega, the
jock sorority, I was the girlfriend of the hottest boy in school, and I went
to Tuesday night Christian worship services during which young men with
soulful eyes strummed guitars with gusto and fervent girls sang loudly, palms
open, hands held up to heaven. My friends were the ones who looked like
they had the most fun—the ones who wore disco clothes to school and danced
with abandon and laughed a lot. They weren't the ones drinking themselves
sick every weekend. They were mostly part of Campus Ambassadors, a large,
evangelical Christian youth group.

For a few weeks during the fall, I met with three Campus Ambassador
girls on Wednesday nights at 9:00 pm, down by the millstream. We'd stand
in a circle, hold hands, pray together, and tell each other our deepest secrets.
Beth Sweeney talked about how she was slowly beginning to eat again after a
year of being too skinny and too sick. She still wanted to be thin. She knew
it was a problem, but she was doing her best to be healthy. She was taking
a dance class, doing yoga and singing in a women's choir. She asked God
for help a lot. I stole glances at her in the moonlight, her bony fingers and
painted toes lying atop foam flip-flops. I understood the voice telling her that
she would never be good if she were not thin. The same harsh voice echoed in
my ears, but I never told her that. I talked about school and crew and Andy,
and kept stealing glances at Beth's waist. I envied that waist.

Beth was one of my only Christian friends with an eating disorder.
Campus Ambassador parties always included lots of food, which everyone ate
with gusto. My best Christian friend Tracey started a club called Monday-
Nice-Day. Every Monday night, we gathered in a campus kitchen and baked
treats—brownies, lemon bars, coconut macaroons, peanut butter bars—and
handed them out to kids around campus, who, unlike us, were studying hard.
I nibbled these treats, licked the spoon when we were done, but always felt

guilty afterwards. According to those Christian girls, God was full of grace. He spoke any time anywhere but could be heard most clearly on windswept beaches and wet forests, through morning fog and burning sunrises, places far away from asphalt and cars. Christ wanted to be my savior, God wanted to accept me into heaven. But this promise was not unconditional. I had to believe that people were originally sinful, that Christ had died for my sin, and that only He, and no other god, could lead me to heaven. At the service, following lyrics projected onto the overhead screen, I prayed to Jesus to speak to me. I thought my heart was open, but no message ever came. Most Tuesday nights after worship I ended up crying in my dorm room, frustrated that I didn't fit into this nice group of people. I just couldn't stop asking questions. What about all the other people in the world, the Hindus, the Muslims, the Buddhists, the Jews? Didn't they have as much right to the truth as anybody?

For Christmas that year, my parents took me to Puerto Vallarta, where we visited Posada Roger, the hotel where they had stayed 25 years ago on their honeymoon. From there, we traveled north up the coast to a small fishing village called Sayulita, famous for its long-haired surfers and ex-pat artists dwelling in clay-tiled bungalows scattered over the seaside hills. Sayulita was a great place for rituals and celebrations—it was nearly as exotic as India, including the dying animals and polluted streams that smelled of defecation. Dudes with rotting dreadlocks smoked hashish on cement porches, naked babes lounged on the beach, and feral cats dug in the garbage. There were festivals almost every night—New Year's fireworks, fire-breathers and gypsies in the town square selling hoop earrings and jingle-jangle bracelets. Women in sarongs sipped martinis in the bars next to greasy men, children played with kittens along the cobblestones and corn fields, artists set up easels on the hilly roads, and surfers congregated in beach-side restaurants to gorge themselves on fried fish and flan. There was the village church, full of candlelight and poinsettias and beatific, bleeding Christs, there were orgies and mangy dogs and belly-dancers and people in small bits of exotic clothing redolent of spirit and dreams—not to mention tacos grilling in the heat and left-out watermelon, so much juicy life oozing out around the edges. It was enough to make me nauseous.

I got up every morning at 7:00 a.m. for my hour-long run. My parents noticed when I returned red-faced and sweaty and did not want to go downstairs for the abundant breakfast of salted and limed papaya, banana, watermelon, pastries from the corner bakery, perspiring flutes of orange juice. They noticed when I left three quarters of all my meals on the table, the sticky flan attracting flies, and when I studied my profile carefully in the mirror before tying on a wrap-around skit and sliding a sweatshirt over my head for the beach. I did most of this quietly, and they watched quietly, until my stomachaches got worse. Every time I ate, my belly erupted into furious gurgles and grumbles, louder than my rare complaints.

At first we thought it was just *turista*, Montezuma's revenge. But my parents had seen me through a grueling year of lightweight crew racing; they knew about Sonja's impromptu haircut. The world is so full of pain, and it's contagious around people you love. I think my mother suffered more than I as she watched me run and pant and pick at my food. She had always been my confidante. But I didn't want to talk to her about my body; I was listening to that voice residing in a deep, intimate place too tender to expose. But we also loved to read together, so when her attempts to talk about things ended in more silence, she gave me a book for Christmas.

On the cover, rows of aspens stood out against a yellow background, the forest floor thick with their leaves. The title, *When Things Fall Apart: Heart Advice for Difficult Times*, surprised me. Was my mother saying I was falling apart? Did she think I needed heart advice for difficult times? When I first opened the package, my mother must have seen my distress at being given such a book; she said her secretary had recommended it, that she wanted to read it after me, that it wasn't really as self-helpish as it seemed. The picture on the back intrigued me—an American Buddhist nun dressed in maroon and yellow, shorn hair fuzzy around her head. "Pema Chödrön is the resident teacher at Gampo Abbey, Cape Breton, Nova Scotia, the first Tibetan monastery in North America established for Westerners," I read, curiosity piqued. One morning in Sayulita, I packed the book in my backpack and after my ritual profile-examination in the full-length mirror, headed to the beach.

I spread out my towel, whipped off my sweatshirt, and flopped down on my tummy lickety-split, so nobody would see my round white belly. I lay there for awhile, watching all the tan, skinny girls around me brush sand from their oiled thighs and wave at their boyfriends, wet and salty in the pelican-strewn surf. Then I took the book from my bag, careful to keep the title hidden from view, and started to read. I don't remember if I really hoped this book would help me, but I do remember how I was soon mesmerized, agape. Pema Chödrön didn't seem to say anything I didn't already know about fear and truth and the present moment, but it was the first time I'd heard this information given in such a kind, funny, wise, human voice. She spoke from that same dark, tender place where my neurotic voice resounded, but her message was gentle. It said: Relax. Be kind to yourself. You don't need to do anything else, you're already awake, precious, whole, and good. I thought: of course, yeah, I knew that. But now I could really believe this truth, this truth that spilled out in the quiet relationship between writer and reader.

As I read about calm abiding meditation, that profound practice of watching the breath, I noticed my belly pushing against my ribs, the sand beneath me every time I inhaled. My body responded viscerally to this wisdom, I felt each cell settle and stretch, feeling itself as if for the first time. People say about experiences like this that "the veil lifted," but for me, it was as if I'd been clutching the edge of a cliff and I'd just let go into space. But it wasn't a scary free-fall; it was a loosening into innate freedom, space that had been there all along. Pema Chödrön wrote about discovering what is brilliant and confused in our own hearts, about what is bitter and sweet, and how when we discover ourselves, we discover the universe. And I felt as though my lungs had just doubled their capacity for breath, for inspiration.

I read all afternoon, belly down on my towel, toes curling in the sand. There was only me, the book, the sun warming the earth; sunglasses on the sweaty bridge of my nose, the smell of sunscreen, the *shush* of pages turning, the occasional shift of light or limb. The wrinkly flower of my heart was opening in slow motion. I felt I was universes away from those women sprawled on their towels a little ways off.

Pema Chödrön said meditation is a good idea. So I did it. I began meditating every morning, right before going out on my run. I would sit cross-legged on the brick patio of Tía Adriana's Bed and Breakfast, palm fronds striping shadows across my legs, and I'd listen to my breath, feeling my stomach push in and out, just like Pema said to do. When my mind got all tangled and distracted, I tried to relax with whatever arose. I said "thinking" in my mind, and tried to come back to the breath. I felt air scrape against the inside of my nostrils, my dried-out lips slightly open with the tongue touching the roof of my mouth. My parents observed me without saying much; I think they were relieved, maybe bemused by my sudden change of habit. Sometimes I sat with my running shoes on, afraid I would not go running if I was not completely prepared beforehand, like somehow my meditation would calm me down enough to see the truth I did not want to see. I was afraid that if I saw truth I would accept myself for how I was at that moment, which would mean eating a chocolate bar instead of running, and then just getting fatter and more miserable again.

One day I went running in the afternoon. In the golden light, I ran past watery-eyed cows and dull-eyed men hanging out at the local bull-fighting ring. I ended up at the beach. I felt sick to my stomach, sick of how it stuck out against my tank top if I did not hold it in, sick of the garbage and dirty dogs and rotting fish all over this god-forsaken paradise. I went down to the water and sat on some big boulders and watched large black pelicans fishing. They were humongous, more like pterodactyls than birds, wings stretched reptilian against the sky, and then boom! They'd jack-knife and plummet toward the waves, beaks wide and scissor-like. God knows what I'd do if one of those things came at me like that. After scooping up their catch, they'd settle on the waves, scuttling their feathers back into place, like everything was hunky dory. No cause for concern, no big deal, I'm fine, everything's just fine. Not like I just took the biggest hara-kiri bullet-trajectory path out of the air from twenty feet up and just landed with a PLOOSH in the waves, mouth full of fish. No, no big deal.

I cried big, heaving sobs, snot running down with sweat and tears into my cleavage as I watched those birds dance. And then when I was done crying, God was everywhere. I breathed God in the wind, tasted divine salt on my lips, looked down to see God's hands resting on God's skinny legs, blotchy and red from running. God pounded out rhythms in my chest, and when I looked down at the sandy shells at my feet, there God was staring back at me, from eyeballs protruding on long antennas on a frightened, side-stepping crab. I collected as many of the purple and orange half-shells as I could and made my way back to Tía Adriana's, white teary flakes still sticking to my cheeks.

That was the day I pecked a hole out of my dark eggshell and saw the world full of birds and fishes, the parts of God that would guide my spiritual path. This was the day I knew the ingredients that would serve me—wind, water, love, color, prayer, meditation, community. I knew that resurrection of the heart was possible.

I started praying, not the usual old prayer of "God, send me a sign" or "God, may I be thinner," but new ones—like just feeling the scrape of my breath or the stretch of my hamstring and delighting in sensation. The divine was everywhere whether we called it God or Goddess or Buddha nature, poor old Buddha nature, just waiting for me to notice and say hello. Pema Chödrön said, "What makes self-kindness such a different approach is that we are not trying to solve a problem. We are not striving to make pain go away or to become a better person. In fact, we are giving up control altogether and letting concepts and ideals fall apart," and I finally understood that this was no platitude. People were going to come into my life. Many of them would leave. Most of the people, even my family and close friends, would roll their eyes and laugh nervously when I mentioned meditating or anything Buddhist. My sorority friends would stop calling when I moved out the next semester.

My parents weren't there when I got back to the bed and breakfast, so I went into our room, spread out a towel, and did 200 sit-ups and 60 push-ups, half on my knees. It would be two more years before I took vows of refuge and officially became a Buddhist student, three years before I went on pilgrimage to India and began 100,000 prostrations in the traditional preliminary practices of Tibetan Buddhism. Seven years after that day with God and the pelicans on the beach, I sat down to write this story. But I still remember sitting up from that dirty towel, stretching my quads and calves, and then walking out onto the veranda to watch the sun go down beneath a hazy veil. I felt euphoric and exhausted, as if I'd just plummeted right out of that dark sky, eyes wide and black wings spread, and hit the water with a crash.

ACKNOWLEDGEMENTS

Stefan Kiesbye's "Water Park" was published in *Unsquared*, an anthology by 826 Michigan and the Neutral Zone.

Kerry Langan's "Live Your Life" was originally published in *Other Voices*.

Katharyn Howd Machan's "Forgotten" appeared in *River Oak Review* and "Jacket" in *RiverSedge*.

Frank Salvidio's "English 379 Revisited" was originally published online by *Winning Writers*.

Nicholas Samaras published "After the Children Have Gone to Bed" in *Luna* and "The Culture of Moving" in *World Literature Today* (University of Oklahoma).

Alexandrina Sergio's "Baby of My Bones" was published in *Listen* under the name of Annie Cunningham.

Heather Tosteson's "Maids" was published in *New Virginia Review*.

AUTHORS

Edward Beatty received an MA in literature from the University of Wisconsin and then taught literature, composition, and philosophy at Sauk Valley Community College for thirty-two years. He retired ten years ago and since then has had poems appear in a number of journals, such as *Fulcrum, Prairie Schooner, Natural Bridge, Georgetown Review, Cider Press Review, Rhino, The Cream City Review, River Oak Review*, and *Poetry International*.

Wendy Brown-Báez is the author of *Ceremonies of the Spirit*, love poems sensual and celestial published by Plain View Press. She has published in dozens of literary journals, including Wising Up Press' issue *Illness & Grace, Terror & Transformation*, and *The Litchfield Review, The Awakenings Review, The Chrysalis Reader, Sin Fronteras, Minnetonka Review, Mississippi Crow, Mizna*, and on-line *Lunarosity* and *Flask and Pen*.

Shireen Campbell has a Ph.D. in Modern Literature from Tulane University and teaches at Davidson College in Davidson, NC. Her publications include writing scholarship in professional journals and textbooks, and a creative nonfiction piece, "The Wait," appeared in *Momwriterslitmag.com*.

Emilio DeGrazia has authored two novels, *Billy Brazil* (1991) and *A Canticle for Bread and Stones* (1996), and two award-winning short story collections, *Seventeen Grams of Soul* (Minnesota Book Award, 1995) and *Enemy Country* (Writer's Choice Award, 1984). His most recent book is a collection of essays entitled *Burying the Tree. Walking on Air*, a second collection, will appear in 2009. He lives in Winona, Minnesota.

Meredith Devney received her MFA from Emerson College in 2006. Her work has most recently been published in *Sawbuck, The Cherry Blossom Review*, and *Coe Review*. She currently teaches high school English full time and is an adjunct instructor at Marshall University.

David Harris Ebenbach's first book of short stories, *Between Camelots* (University of Pittsburgh Press), won the Drue Heinz Literature Prize and the GLCA New Writer's Award. His short fiction has appeared in *Connecticut Review, Greensboro Review*, and *Crazyhorse*; poetry in *Phoebe, Mudfish*, and *JAMA*; and non-fiction in *Writing Fiction* (Bloomsbury, USA). He has a Ph.D. in Psychology (University of Wisconsin-Madison) and an M.F.A. (Vermont College), and teaches Creative Writing at Earlham.

Joan Fondell has published poetry in *Beyond Lament: Poets of the World Bearing Witness to the Holocaust* and non-fiction in *Generating Business With Value: From Inside the Minds: The Art & Science of Legal Recruiting* and co-authored *Best Resumes For Attorneys*. She holds a J.D. from Loyola Law School in Los Angeles and a B.A. in English from U.C.L.A. She is Vice-President of Russo & Fondell, Inc..

Emilie George is an Albanian-American, retired French teacher, a singer/songwriter who performs international folk songs. Three albums recorded for Folkways are now available in the Smithsonian Catalog. Recent CD with Stefan George, "My Father's Mansion: Hands Around the World with International Songs." Poetry published in: *The Sow's Ear, Lifeboat: A Journal of Memoir, American Recorder, Meridian Anthology of Contemporary Poetry*, and *Love After 70*.

Lynn Hesse is a retired cop turned anti-war activist, who must write and dance to be happy. She gardens and sews when she needs to hold a product in her hands and satisfy her working class ethic. Her grandchildren like going on adventures with grandma and her husband, Dean, a photographer. She dedicates her first published short story in memory of her mother, the source for many of her tales.

Eboni Hogan is a spoken word poet, actress, playwright and teaching artist who has performed in over 16 U.S. cities and internationally in West Africa. She is the 2008 Urbana Grand Slam champion and a member of the 2007 Nuyorican Slam Team. She currently resides in a bat-cave in Brooklyn where she regularly steals internet access from her neighbor Brad.

Yolande House works at the University of New Brunswick in Fredericton, New Brunswick, Canada, and holds a Master's in history from Queen's University. She writes memoir and poetry, organizes local writing workshops and events, and searches for bizarre ads in old newspapers. Her work has been published in the poetry magazine *Breadcrumb Scabs*. She is working on her childhood memoir, which will detail the full story of *Learning to Leave*.

Stefan Kiesbye is the author of the novel *Next Door Lived A Girl* (Low Fidelity Press) and the upcoming story collection *The Devil's Moor* (Dzanc Books). His work has appeared in *Hobart*, *The St. Petersburg Review*, and the anthology *The Art of Friction*. He lives in Los Angeles with his wife Sanaz.

Kerry Langan's short fiction has been published in more than three dozen print and online literary journals during the last fifteen years. Her stories have been published in the United States, Canada and Hong Kong. Her non-fiction has appeared in *Working Mother*.

Phyllis A. Langton, Ph.D., Professor Emerita Sociology, George Washington University, is now writing and publishing creative non-fiction. Three chapters of her memoir in progress, *Life at the Kitchen Table: Promises I Made my Husband*, have been published in *Wising Up* anthologies, including her essay, "Waiting," published in *Love After 70*. This essay is from her memoir in progress, *Sweet Abandon*.

Katharyn Howd Machan was born in Woodbury, Connecticut, in 1952. Her poems have appeared in numerous magazines, anthologies, and textbooks, and in 30 collections, most recently *Belly Words: Poems of Dance* (Split Oak Press, 2009) and *When She's Asked to Think of Colors* (Palettes & Quills Press, 2009). A professor in the Department of Writing at Ithaca College, in 2002 she was named Tompkins County's first Poet Laureate.

Maria Nazos has work published or forthcoming in *The New York Quarterly, The New Plains Review, Main Street Rag, The Dead Mule School of Southern Literature,* and various other places. She lives and writes at the edge of the world, in Provincetown, Massachusetts.

Susan O'Doherty is the author of *Getting Unstuck without Coming Unglued* (Seal, 2007). Her work has appeared in numerous journals and anthologies, including *Eureka Literary Magazine, Northwest Review, Apalachee Review, Mama, Ph.D., Sex for America, The New Writer's Handbook,* and *About What Was Lost.* Her advice column for writers, "The Doctor Is In," is featured every Friday on the publishing blog *Buzz, Balls & Hype.*

Deidra K. Razzaque is a passionate advocate for marginalized youth and intercultural education. She has been writing since before she learned her ABCs, and has been published in the anthology *Kiss Me Goodnight,* on women who lost their mothers as children. For years Deidra has thrived in the warm forests of Costa Rica. Now she is experimenting with seasons in Vermont, where she lives with her husband and daughter.

Carlos Reyes is a widely published poet and translator. Poetry: *At the Edge of the Western Wave* (2004), *A Suitcase Full of Crows* (1995), *Nightmarks* (1990), *The Shingle Weaver's Journal* (1980). Translations: *Poemas de la Isla / Island Poems* by Josefina de la Torre, *Obra poética completa / Complete Poetic Works* by Jorge Carrera Andrade. For 27 years a poet-in-the schools in Oregon, Washington and Nevada. Awards: The Fortner Award, Oregon Arts Foundation (Poetry), Heinrich Boll Fellowship, Fundación Valparaíso, Yaddo Fellow. *A Suitcase Full of Crows* (1995) Bluestem Prize.

Cassandra Robison is a graduate of the State University of New York, Fredonia, (B.A., English); the University of Arizona (M.Ed., English); and Walden University (Ph.D., Education). Her poems have been published in various online and print literary magazines. She is the founding editor of *Magnolia: A Florida Journal of Literary and Fine Arts Imprints.* Her book of poems, *Leaving the Pony,* is forthcoming from Finishing Line Press (August 2009).

Mary Kay Rummel's newest poetry book is *Love in the End* (Bright Hill Press, 2008.) Her other books of poetry are *The Illuminations* (Cherry Grove Collections, 2006), *Green Journey Red Bird* (Loonfeather Press), *The Long Journey Into North* and *This Body She's Entered* (New Rivers Press.) She often performs her poetry with musicians. She is professor emerita at the University of Minnesota and teaches at California State University, Channel Islands.

Frank Salvidio is a poet and translator whose poems have won various awards and been reprinted in other publications. A retired English professor, he is the author of *Between Troy & Florence* (original poems and translations), as well as translations of Sappho of Lesbos (*Sappho Says)* and Dante: both the *Vita Nuova* and, most recently, the *Inferno.*

Nicholas Samaras won The Yale Series of Younger Poets Award for his first book, *Hands of the Saddlemaker.* Currently, he is near-completion for two new manuscripts of poetry. He lives in West Nyack, New York and teaches in Westchester County at the Charles Xavier School for Gifted Youngsters.

Alexandrina Sergio's poems have appeared or are forthcoming in *Long River Run, Caduceus, Connecticut River Review, Encore, Wisdom of Our Mothers* (Familia Books), *Love After 70,* and in a collected volume soon to be published by Antrim House. Her work has been performed by a professional stage company. Awards include first place, 2007 Connecticut Senior Poetry Contest, and second place, 2008 NFSPS Dorman John Grace Contest.

Anna Steegmann, born in Germany, has lived in New York City since 1980. A former psychotherapist, she now makes writing her priority. She writes in English and German. Her work has been published by *W.W. Norton, The New York Times, guernicamag.com, sic, 138journal.com, Promethean, The Wising Up Press, Epiphany, Ezra, Absinthe, Dimension[2,]* and several German magazines. She teaches Writing at the International Summer Academy Venice, Italy and at City College of New York.

Sylvie Terespolski's writings have included magazine articles that have appeared in *Insights, Main Line Magazine, The English Journal,* op-eds in the *Philadelphia Inquirer,* and short stories published in *Love After 70* and *Reconstructionist.* She has works in perpetual progress that include three plays and a novel currently titled *The Jew and the Pope.*

Don Thackrey spent his formative years on a Nebraska farm as part of an extraordinary family, the source of much of his verse. He now lives with his wife in Dexter, Michigan, where he is retired from teaching and administering at the University of Michigan. He is the author of a book on Emily Dickinson, and his verse has appeared in a number of journals and anthologies.

Natalie Haney Tilghman is a graduate student in the low-residency M.F.A. in Creative Writing program at Pacific Lutheran University. Her work has appeared or is forthcoming in Main Street Rag short fiction anthology (Spring 2009), *Main Street Rag Magazine*, and *Gapers Block*, a Chicago webzine. Natalie received honorable mention in the 2008 Dorothy Sargent Rosenberg Poetry Prize contest. She lives in Chicago with her husband, Rich, and two Chihuahuas.

Judith Turner-Yamamoto has received VCCA and Fundación Valparaíso residencies, the Thomas Wolfe Fiction Prize, the Governor's Screenwriting Award, and Virginia Individual Artist Fellowships. Stories and poetry have appeared in *The Mississippi Review, The American Literary Review, The Village Rambler, Parting Gifts, Gravity Dancers* and *Best New Poets 2005*. An art historian, she writes criticism and features for *Travel & Leisure, Elle, USAir, Art & Antiques, Southern Accents,* and *The Boston Globe Magazine.*

Devon Ward-Thommes has published in *Spirituality and Health, buddhadharma, elephant journal,* and *Cézanne's Carrot.* She completed an M.F.A. in Creative Nonfiction Writing at George Mason University in May, 2008. Afterwards, she moved to Colorado to serve as Program Manager at Tara Mandala, a Buddhist retreat center. Eventually, she plans to teach and write in India and France, and live in Oregon as a creative writing and yoga instructor.

Christopher Willard is the author of the novels *Sundre* and *Garbage Head.* Shorter fiction has appeared in numerous publications including *Ranfurly Review, Broken Pencil, Ukula, Sobriquet, Ars Medica,* and in *The Broken Pencil Anthology* to be released this fall. He currently lives and teaches in Calgary, Alberta.

miste = lose

en tillid = confidence, trust

tælle talte, talt = count

. enten = either

undertiden = sometimes

ut vrivlsomt = without doubt

optræder = appear

fløj = wing

alligevel = still

ingenlunde = not at all

ligevægt = balance

nedrustningen = disarmament

tilsyneladende = seemingly

opfattelse = concept, possibility

kravet = demand

ofskaffelse = prohibition

muligheden = possibility

opretholde = upholding

Netop = just

EDITORS/PUBLISHERS

HEATHER TOSTESON is the author of *Visible Signs* and *Hearts as Big as Fists* and, most recently, *God Speaks My Language, Can You?* She has received a Nation/Discovery prize for her poetry and fellowships for poetry, fiction, and photography from MacDowell, Yaddo, VCCA, and Hambidge and has published poetry, fiction, and essays in numerous literary magazines. She holds a M.F.A. in Creative Writing (UNC-Greensboro) and Ph.D. in English and Creative Writing (Ohio University). She is founder and co-director of Universal Table and Wising Up Press.

CHARLES BROCKETT, having worked from an early age in a small book bindery co-owned by his father, is enjoying his second career as a book publisher and co-director of Universal Table. He has written two well received books on Central America and numerous social science journal articles. A political science professor, he is a recipient of several Fulbright and National Endowment for the Humanities awards. His Ph.D. is from UNC-Chapel Hill. He lives in Atlanta.

See our booklist and calls for submissions for new anthologies
www.universaltable.org
wisingup@universaltable.org

www.ingramcontent.com/pod-product-compliance
Lightning Source LLC
Chambersburg PA
CBHW030347020726
47493CB00003B/728